Authors note

I started reading at the age of fifteen and never thought I would become a bookworm. I admired every author with each book I read that captured me. I found it amazing how someone's mind can be so creative, which took me to another place and time and lived through their stories. To achieve such a goal was startling.

The smell of a new book, and the thicker the better, always excited me, and could not wait to get home to start reading.

In my wildest dreams, I could never imagine achieving such a goal, to be able to create a new world for someone else to live through my imagination - to create characters, personalities, love, and so on — what - me - never!

Well, here I am — publishing my first novel and achieved my wildest expectations in creating another place and time with characters that I, myself, came to love and admire, as they came alive in my mind. I am very excited to share my stories with you.

As you read and get to know my characters, I hope you come to love them as I have, and continue with the three-part series that grows with passion, heartache, mysteries, and just plainly how someone copes through loss and change in the next chapters to come.

Michelle

TAKEN

Three-Part Series
Part one

MICHELLE WALTERS

FOR MY SON

PAUL WALTERS

You have an amazing sense of humor toward life that
always makes me cry with laughter
Love you always and forever
In this world and the next
You are my rock — I'm very proud
and blessed to have you in my life.
I love you . . .

ONE

Thord loved the open sea. The freedom he felt and the tang of the ocean air always brought excitement to him and his trusted fellow travelers. They were on one of their trading voyages and were nearing France; they ignored this port for a long time. Many years ago, his father and another tribe joined forces, had raided these lands, left, and have never returned since. Thord decided it was time for a revisit, with a friendlier outcome — hopefully.

He was standing on the prow of his boat, taking pleasure in the wind blowing through his wavy flaxen hair that reached his shoulders. He was a hunky young Viking, strong and fierce, tall and extremely well-built with a golden tan, comfortable in his skin. His father was the chief, well respected and feared by other Viking tribes.

Thord was proud to be a Viking and would be next-in-line as chief when his father grows weary in age to step down. His lineage went back generations through his father's bloodline.

He was content to wait and still learn under his father's ruling, adamant about making him proud.

For many centuries, the Vikings were known for their raiding and pirating — known to be fierce warriors. Though recently, now in the eleventh century, the years of pillaging have passed for most tribes, they started trading more and love to explore the open seas and new lands. They became known to be excellent merchants amongst most trade markets, which they have visited so far. At first, they only traded wool. Their island was scattered with sheep and was skillful in the trade — one of their many professions. Their island was called the Faeroe Island—Sheep Island. Everything was made out of fleece. Now they traded various products.

In most markets, the locals pussyfooted when the Vikings came to trade, except for most women, whom upon seeing Thord for the first time, would gaze dreamily at him and would flirt a little. He was ignorant of their stares and was always cautious. However, he was chivalrous all the same — always well-mannered during trading.

At the crack of dawn, they docked at one of the many shores of France. They declined to stop at the local tavern as they often did at other ports. Instead, they gathered information about all the markets' and their locations, hired a few horses, and took straightaway to the road. It was a long trip inland; Thord and his men were anxious to observe the trade markets. He hoped they were welcomed to trade with the locals.

Usually, when traveling en route toward markets, people would keep their distance, avoid eye contact and whisper amongst themselves. Strangers were still terrified of encountering a Viking on the road. However, the markets had a different atmosphere.

Thord expected to encounter many of the locals on their path. However, they stumbled upon none — this was not normal! People were always traveling back and forth. He knew this from the many other lands they had visited. This terrain could not be different from the rest!

Hours passed before closing upon the first small town. According to the innkeeper's directions, they had a few to pass before reaching their destination.

Upon approaching the town, Thord had a strange feeling about this place. He always listened to his gut as it had saved them many times. He had a knack for foreseeing trouble, urging him to warn his men to be watchful.

Where was everyone? The town looked abandoned! Only a few houses had clouds of black, grey smoke escaping from their chimneys. It seemed that they were all locked up tight, not even a window was open or a curtain drawn — all was quiet. A few domestic animals and chickens were freely roaming the streets, undisturbed.

The weather was fine out, so there was no explaining their fear of not being outside. Thord was already uneasy, and this made him even more suspicious. *Could this be a trap? Did news really travel so fast that Vikings were en route to the Castle?* Though they came on friendly terms, he was not sure they knew why they docked on French soil.

Obeying his gut feeling, he backed up his horse and shouted, "At arms, men!"

His men at once drew their swords and slowly started to retreat into the forest from whence they came. Olaf, always too eager for battle, jumped off his steed, ready for action. Thord loved Olaf as a brother, they were very close since youths, but this was not the time to fight when they had no idea what awaited them.

"Olaf! Get back on your horse and retreat!"

"You sure? Since when do we retreat or run from a fight?" He was keeping his stance and looking at all angles for any imminent attack.

Thord answered, "We are not retreating per se. I'm not sure what is going on here. Let's move to a safer location and discuss this on safer ground. We can review our situation and go from there."

"Yeah, yeah," Olaf half mumbled with disappointment. He mounted his stallion, turned about and followed his future chief.

They took shelter further along the riverbank. Thord sent one of his men back to town for recognizance to ascertain what was happening and report back as soon as possible. While waiting for his return, Thord took his horse to drink water and left him to graze on the soft green grass growing abundantly along the banks.

He sat down on the ground, leaning against a massive rock, and looked at the men who always traveled with him — the fiercest of them all. Only one woman fought with them, and she outwitted the best. She was tall with a neat bob that was often tied back when they traveled. Her name was Helga, meaning 'hero.'

Thord's best friend and brother in arms was Olaf; he was a short, round man but not fat. Big-boned with huge muscles, he was a hard man from the outside — a fierce warrior, but a softy on the inside to those who got to know him. Since they were young, the stocky Viking had been by his side, and he had always protected Thord. Not that he needed it of late; he could fight his own battles.

If his gut were right about this place, they would have to leave and trade with more familiar ports. Returning home was not an option as they recently departed, and this was their first stop. Their island was situated off the coast on its own, away from everyone. It was well protected, away from unwanted guests, and usually, strangers weren't welcomed. They did not share land as other Vikings did with the locals nearby. They have been living peacefully for centuries. Stories are often told of the events that occurred on their island — history that made him even more proud to be part of that clan.

Still waiting for his rider to return and getting impatient, Thord wondered if he should ride out to see what was keeping him. He was so deep in thought he was unaware of his horse approaching until the beast made a snorting sound and tossed his head back. When Thord turned to see what spooked it, he heard a moan from behind the rock he was leaning against. Mystified, he stood up to investigate. Drawing his sword, he slowly peered around the boulder. A person laid there concealed and was wrapped in a blanket. Given the placement and the luggage nearby, Thord knew someone left the individual here, but why?

It made him more curious about what was happening in these parts, and so far, his gut did not like it. Looking at the bundle, he noticed a blond curl hanging out. Using his sword, he slowly moved the top part of the blanket aside to inspect the face. She was beautiful, yet, also pale and looked dreadfully sick! He was baffled and wondered who in their right mind would leave such a creature here unattended and in her condition?

Absorbed as he was in his musings, Thord did not hear the man return from town. Olaf intently listened to his report, which frightened everyone. They saddled their horses and were eager to leave this place. Realizing their leader was not among them, Olaf saw him staring at something, looking perplexed, so he went over to see what was so interesting and to inform him that they should leave straight away.

"Thord, my brother!" Olaf called out while walking toward him.

For the first time since finding the girl, Thord looked up. Olaf stood staring at the creature as well, "Wow! What have we here? She's a beauty, a bit pale, but still a beauty. Is she alive?"

"Yes," was his only reply. Thord was wondering how to handle this. Should he leave her or take her with them?

Olaf spoke again, "Bad news, Thord, Bjorn came back. He knocked on a few doors until someone answered. This town, and further up the mainland, is infested with measles. By the looks of it, so is she." They both looked at her.

Thord turned and looked at his men already mounted – anxious to leave. He was about to turn but froze on the spot.

"Thord?" Olaf wondered why he was hesitating.

Thord spoke, "Tell the men to leave and get the ship ready to set sail. I'm going to wait a while longer to see if anyone comes to claim her. You and Helga can stay behind." That was an order. Olaf obeyed and left without argument. He issued the commands; the men did not wait for a second longer and rode off with speed, leaving a dust cloud behind them.

TWO

Jessie started packing before dawn. It was still dark outside; she quickly filled a bag with clothes she thought the young girl might need, which was not much as they would return someday soon. Not far from their home was a river that ran for miles through the countryside and a path for travelers that led out of town, which they had to be on shortly.

They needed to go to a secure place since her home was no longer safe. All the household staff was sent home weeks ago. The poor girl was alone; Jessie was the only one left to protect and keep her alive until the epidemic passed. It was the only alternative she could think of, to leave this place as quickly as possible.

Eventually, they stepped out into the slightly chilly air. A light breeze whispered through the trees. The sun began to rise, and the rays streamed through the branches as the day promised to get warmer. The air's scent was fresh and sweet as the flowers began to bloom, and the symphony of birdsong was loud in the tall trees. They were unaware of the beauty and nature around them as both women had other things on their minds. The twigs and dead leaves crunched under their footsteps as Jessie helped the girl walk on the pathway.

The girl was too weak; she had a burning fever and lacked energy for their outing. She had to concentrate not to fall and focused on each step she took. Without Jessie's support, she would have fallen. Neither of them spoke as they left their warm beds behind.

Even though the girl was dressed warmly, she was shivering. She knew she was sick but was naive as to how badly. She was disoriented and had many questions; had no idea what was happening or why she was out walking with Jessie. *Why were they leaving her home and a warm bed in the first place? Where was Jessie taking her?* She longed to stay in bed as the coldness crept into her bones. *Was she dying? Why were they alone, and where were her parents? Was the sun rising or setting?* Memories came and went. She then realized she was too tired to question Jessie's actions. All the girl wanted to do was lay down and sleep. She was ready to pass out from exhaustion.

"Jessie, I am tired!" the girl complained.

"We're almost there, my dove. A few more steps, and then you can rest."

Jessie was relieved to find no one on the road. Not that she had expected to run into anyone. Everyone was locked up and too afraid to leave the safety of their homes. Many had left months ago; whether they would return was still to be seen. A small number of residents who had stayed behind were raiding houses. As a result, a few nights ago, their stables were raided.

All their horses were taken for those who needed to escape. Thankfully, they left Jessie's old steed and one carriage behind, which was too heavy for her poor horse to pull on its own.

For that reason, they could no longer stay in the house unaided. Jessie knew they would be raided again, and this time, they would enter the house with force, whether they respected the tenants or not. The girl was wealthy, which made them even more vulnerable to attacks. They were defenseless against an angry mob of villagers; the girl was too sick and incapable of standing her ground to protect her home. It did not matter that the house belonged to her. The mob will kill if need be to claim the treasures she had to survive and feed their own. Jessie was scared for the girl's life, as well as her own.

They had walked for half an hour when Jessie noticed the enormous rock alongside the riverbank, the one she was searching for. The girl would be safe there until she returned – or so she believed. Jessie felt guilty leaving her unguarded, but she had no choice in the matter.

Jessie never owned a saddle. All she had was a small leather pouch that hung over each side of her horse. The pockets were always filled with herbs for medication. She had thought of taking the girl with her, but sharing a mare was difficult, though not for the lack of trying. The girl needed her strength to help, and Jessie could not embrace her securely along with the luggage she packed.

While she helped the young girl walk, her steed was carrying the baggage and obediently following them. She did not want to leave him behind. There was a strong likelihood of him being taken. Someone desperate enough who wanted to leave would not think the horse was too old for a long journey and would surely ride it to death.

She would leave the luggage behind, so her journey back to her own home would be more comfortable and faster. She would repack it with her belongings when she returned. Her destination so far was unsure. All she knew was to keep the girl safe and do her best to heal her.

The girl was shaking and unhappy with the outing. She wanted to protest and complain, as she was confused and scared. It felt as though she was losing her mind. She sighed with relief when they eventually stopped.

Jessie took the thick blanket from the horse, covered the girl, and gently laid her on the ground. She thought Jessie was overdoing it and could not move how she wrapped the blanket snuggly around her. The girl had no strength even if she tried, but did not complain much. She was thankful for the warmth; the shivering was too much, and she was shattered.

Jessie spoke, "You're safe now and can rest for a while. I will be back as soon as I can."

The girl had an ear infection. Jessie stuffed her ears with cotton before leaving the house so the cool morning breeze could not enter. She could vaguely hear what Jessie was saying but understood that she was leaving her behind. She voiced her dismay and begged Jessie to stay – she was scared!

Jessie could see how troubled the girl was and tried to reassure her, "It won't be for long; I'll be back as soon as I can."

She made sure the girl was wrapped snuggly once more and was as comfortable as possible on the ground. The rock was big enough to hide a stallion. She backed up towards the road to see if it was safe from prying eyes and was satisfied. Jessie returned to the massive rock and stood there watching the road and her surroundings. She still felt uneasy leaving the girl; however, she had no other choice. It was the only safe place she could think of to hide her until she returned, and the only road to travel on if they wanted to escape the plague. The opposite direction was further inland, toward the castle, where the epidemic first started.

The sick girl could feel Jessie's presence and tried to plead one more time. She could only protest and could not wrestle out of her situation. She was too weak to get up or even move. The walk had tired her out.

"Please don't leave me, Jessie!"

"I will never leave you. I promise I will return for you!" Jessie's heart was breaking. It was eating her from the inside to leave her alone. However, it wouldn't be for long, or so she kept telling herself!

She was wasting precious time standing around. She bent to kiss the girl on her forehead and felt the warmth from her fever on her lips. When Jessie spoke, her lips were still warm from the girl's high temperature. The last words she heard was Jessie asking her not to move.

"I won't take long; just rest and pray, do not move. Promise me you will not move!"

Even if I wanted to, I could not, she thought and answered, "I promise!" Her voice was weak and sounded sleepy.

The girl tried her best to keep her eyes open and her wits about her, but she failed.

Jessie heard the girl give a light sigh before she slumbered away. She hoped and prayed she would stay napping until she returned. Jessie kissed her one last time, walked over to where her mare was grazing, took the luggage off, and placed it by the girl's feet.

She was anxious to leave for her home to pack some necessary items, including herbs for the girl's fever and a small cart that her horse could tow. Jessie climbed on her mount and rode as fast as she could. She was already making a mental list of what to pack and do when she got there; time was of the essence. She was restless and knew there was no time for loitering. It would have to be an in and out job, and needed to return as soon as possible.

The girl felt exhausted and fell in and out of consciousness. In-between her consciousness, she wondered where Jessie was. She tried to remember how long it had been since she last saw her. She knew she was close to the river, the familiar sound of the ripples was loud and soothing, but she did not know where.

The river was long and ran for many miles; she could be anywhere.

She tried to open her eyes to see her surroundings and if anyone was about, but to no avail. Her eyes felt too heavy, and she was too weak even to try. Even so, part of her head was covered with the blanket, enough room to breathe. To try to move the flap was hopeless!

Where was Jessie, and why was she taking so long? Why did she leave me alone? The girl wanted to call out, yet her throat was dry and only a whisper came out, leaving her feeling thirsty from the effort. She was in distress.

She had the shivers, every part of her body was in agony, and the need to scratch was piercing. *Why must I be so sick? Why did this have to happen to me?* She was certain life was slipping away; she lost everything dear to her and felt like giving up! Her heart was broken — everyone was leaving her. What did she have to live for?

The young girl heard a noise and tried hard to make out what it was. Was it horses — people? Yes! They sounded muffled, which means they must still be far away — or were they? It seemed like they were getting closer but was still barely audible, almost like an echo.

They stopped close to where she lay. From what she could make out, it was men's voices, and there were many of them. She could not recognize a familiar voice among them, nor understand what they were saying. She then realized they were not from her village or homeland and began to wonder whether she was exposed. Not that she could move; she tried to stay even more still and passed out again.

As she went in and out of consciousness, she felt the sun on her face and squinted. The sun was too bright to see who removed the top part of the blanket, but she could hear two male voices whispering. She could not understand as they spoke in their native tongue — a language she had never heard before.

The girl tried to tell them to leave her alone. She wanted to say she was expecting someone to come for her, but all that came out was a moan. She was a little relieved when her head was covered again; the sun was too bright and was burning her eyes. She heard one of them walk away and guessed that the other one stood close by — she passed out once again.

THREE

After Thord's men left, he leaned against the rock and waited while Olaf explained the situation to Helga.

The tall Viking was very upset and voiced her anger, "What are we doing, anyway? Risking our health for whom — for what? I don't like this!" She started to pace up and down.

Thord saw the distress in his fellow men; they did not like the idea of a deadly disease spreading. He came to a decision. He knew if he left the sick girl behind, his conscience would haunt him. It felt right to take her with them and try to help her. He stood up once again and ordered Helga to settle the girl on her mare. His Aunt Popi would know what to do. She was the best medicine woman he knew.

At this point, the girl woke up when Helga roughly handled her, half dragged her on the ground, and threw her over a horse like a sack of potatoes, scared that she might be contagious, likely to be spread by contact. Thord shouted at Helga for being a fool. Not that he could blame her for being scared. No matter her state, you don't handle a woman that way; thus, he dealt with the girl himself.

Thord's loud bark chilled the girl to her core. She felt hopeless in her condition and couldn't stop them or shout for help. Her fever was worsening, and she passed out yet again. It felt like hours when she eventually woke up. 'Can someone feel even more exhausted from sleeping?' That's how she felt; she was worn out. She felt sick to her stomach. It felt like she was floating on air and being rocked. It felt soothing and sickening all at once. She slept through everything, but not for the lack of trying to stay awake — she could not!

When they arrived back at their island, Olaf, Thord, and the sick girl took a dinghy, sailed to the other side of the beach, and went ashore. A small cottage stood alone and abandoned on the beach that was used for lookouts in the olden days. It was well away from his people and the village.

Olaf opened the door for them, and Thord sent him straight away to call on Popi and ask her to come quickly. Her house was inland, and he had to walk on foot.

The girl's senses were more alert when she became conscious again and felt no presence nearby. She was on a soft bed and still shivering. Remembering the men that took her — she was in distress, not knowing where she was or what they had in mind by kidnapping her. If they took her to harm her, they couldn't do any worse than how she was feeling. The sickness broke her spirit and did not want to fight anymore — she wished it was all over!

She fought hard to remember something while passing out all the time. A man carried her at some point – she was startled at the thought; he held her as a mother would carry a baby, with no weight problem.

She froze when she heard a noise. Someone was there! But who? Must be one of the thugs. More blankets were placed over her; she was thankful for the extra warmth and even more confused with the kindness.

A fire kindled for the room started to get warmer, and the smell of smoke was strong. She heard him leave and was relieved, but not long, he returned. His footsteps came closer toward her, and she froze, not knowing what to expect.

She got a fright when a cold, wet rag was placed on her forehead. He must have noticed the sweat was pouring down her face and gone out to wet a rag to comfort her stress. The person did not speak once; she was too tired to wonder about her captives and the situation she was in, so she slept further.

By the time Olaf reached Popi's house, he was exhausted and was thankful to relax while she got ready. Returning to the beach, they both traveled on horseback, which made the trip quicker. When they eventually arrived, Thord was delighted to see his aunt. He was thankful to be out of the cottage and for the girl to be taken off his hands.

"Thord, my dear child, what is going on?" Popi had been shocked to see Olaf at her door and not on their voyage. She thought the worst and was relieved to hear he was fine. Olaf explained about the girl, and she packed a few herbs before they headed out.

Thord explained, "She's inside; I think she has a fever as well. She had luggage, but we were in a hurry to get here and forgot it on the ship. I will bring it when we return from our trade voyage."

Popi went inside to examine the young girl. She pulled the covers back and noticed her neat and clean garments — she was dreadfully pale! It was not going to be a short duration!

She looked around to see what was in the cottage. It had been unoccupied for too long; there was nothing to boil herbs or cook in. She made a mental note of what herbs to bring and kitchen accessories. When stepping out of the cottage, ready to leave and start her mission, she realized Thord was still there. Olaf was waiting for him in the small boat.

He walked with her to the horses and spoke, "Do me another favor, please aunt, and send a message to my father to inform him of this news. We are still sailing and will return in a few weeks. Hopefully, none of my men caught this ailment. We will have to wait and see if any get sick."

Popi looked worried, "If any fall ill, you come straight home to me and I'll fix it. Do you hear me! Don't wait it out and think it might go away. I'm not sure what is wrong with her, but she looks in an awful state."

"I shall return if any fall ill, I promise." He kissed her on the cheek and left.

"Safe voyage and good health to you all," Popi called out.

They were off to their ship — if they had waited a while longer on the other island, they would have encountered her claimer, who was not far off.

The girl was getting worse and could feel herself sinking away. The urge to fight and stay awake in her surroundings, since been taken, took a toll on her. In her physical state, she could hear voices. This time, however, she heard a woman's voice. She thought and hoped it was Jessie; she must have found help to carry her. She felt disoriented but believed she was in another place close by her home or safely in Jessie's cottage. She felt a sense of despondency in her heart and could no longer take the suffering. Thus, she gave up and went into a deep sleep, not knowing how significantly her life was about to change.

When Popi returned to the cottage after being home, she had all she needed for a few days. She would have to travel back and forth for fresh stock. Before she left her home, she sent one of her children to the chief with the news of this new development on the island. She had to inform her husband that she wouldn't be back for a while as well. As always, Var understood and was supportive of her calling.

Popi placed a pot of water on the fire to boil certain herbs for a drinking medication. While waiting for the water to boil, she threw other herbs in a mortar and used a pestle to grind them to a paste for an ointment for all the marks on the young one's body — it was overrun with spots.

When everything was ready, she gave the girl her full attention. Instead of undressing the girl properly, she decided to cut the dress off instead. Popi had to first wipe her down before taking the salve and covering every mark she could find on the poor child. She would have to do this often. Thus, she left her naked under the covers to make it easier to do her job. Hopefully, if all goes well, Popi would have to find other garments for the girl to wear, something more comfortable, and their clothes will have to do for now until her luggage returns with Thord.

FOUR

The girl sank deep into her bedding as the fever burned inside her, drenching the covers with sweat. She was in and out of consciousness for days. Time was passing — weeks, months; she had no idea how long she had been sick or if she would ever recover. Her entire body ached, and her temperature was elevated. She could not open her eyes because a rag covered them. Still feeling weak, she decided not to fight.

The girl concentrated on the sounds around her like a blind person. She heard wood crackling in the hearth and could smell the smoke. There was another delicate scent, but she could not place it. She tried to sense a presence in the room but was unsuccessful. She heard water swashing outside — the river never sounded so rough before! There must be a storm happening outside, and was thankful that the cottage was warm and still standing.

She was sweating badly and could not take it any longer! Her body was stiff and throbbing; she could hardly move, moaning as she tried to throw the covers off. She soon felt a cool cloth on her head. She could hear a woman speaking — or was she singing. She sounded strange! The woman tried to give her something to drink. She didn't know whether it was water or medication. Her throat was itchy and swollen; she could hardly swallow the liquid, what she managed to take in, tasted sweet and slightly bitter. The woman kept feeding her the liquid; there was a soothing relief after a few swallows.

She could hear the wind howling outside and hit against the cottage. For some reason, it calmed her, so she slept further.

Upon waking again, unsure how long it had been since the last, she got a whiff of something gratifying for her empty stomach. The girl's carer was cooking, and it smelled delicious. She moaned once more, then heard a chair move, and a few seconds later, she felt a spoon in her mouth. When she swallowed, it was the same liquid as before. She was disappointed and could hear her stomach rumbling. Before long, the spoon came again. Expecting the same bittersweet taste, she felt a warmer, thicker liquid go down her throat instead. The soup was perfect and she wanted more. Although she could only get a few spoons down, the soup was satisfying.

The cloth was removed from her eyes, and she forced them open, everything was a blur, but she tried her best to focus to see who was with her. What she saw frightened her — she did not know the woman who was helping her! Her eyes were also terribly itchy — she lifted her hand to rub them when the other woman lightly slapped her hand away.

The woman started to rub a cool ointment over her eyes again, followed by another cold, wet cloth, which helped relieve the tension. Once again, her world was in darkness. Not long, the strange woman also added a few drops of liquid in each ear and stuffed a small piece of cotton fabric to keep the liquid in place.

The girl could smell the aroma of all kinds of herbs used to make medication, but how did she know that? She was confused! She knew she was always fascinated with the herb mixtures for whatever illness a person had and their healing technique. Was she a healer? Confusion blocking all thoughts — she slept soundly.

The next day, when she woke, the girl realized there was no cloth covering her eyes. To her relief, she could open them a little. It burned; however, because she had been blind and sick for so long, she wanted to have a peek at her surroundings.

She was in a one-roomed cottage, partially small with an extra bed made of wood and straw, covered with thick fur and blankets, including hers. There was a small table with two chairs placed close to the hearth. The fire kept the cottage warm. The girl has never seen such a place before, or the woman sitting and sewing close by — or she can't remember! She assumed that perhaps it was convenient for her guardian to leave her with this woman while she went out on business. The aroma of food was tickling her nose, and it smelled good. Her stomach reminded her that it was empty.

Popi, the woman sewing, realized the girl was staring and gave her a friendly smile. The girl smiled in return, and then a frown creased her forehead, concentrating hard to remember if she knew her. She was confused, as her memory seemed blank. Maybe it was too soon after being conscious again. Nevertheless, she still wanted answers.

The older woman saw the confused expression on her face. She was just thankful the girl was awake after all this time and alive. She stood up and walked toward the girl. Popi was a talkative person, so while the girl was unconscious for the past two moons, she often told her stories and such. Without thinking, it felt normal for Popi to continue in her native tongue,

"Ah! It's nice to see you with the living again, love."

The girl looked confused. Her throat was dry and scratchy, so when she spoke, it came out in a whisper, and in French, *"Who are you and where am I?"* she thought it was best to get straight to the point instead of acting as if they were acquaintances.

Popi then realized her mistake and tried another so that they could understand each other. The girl looked well-educated and should have been taught more than one language. Since trading began, English was learned on the island. Most could speak it well. Popi tried again and hoped they could communicate adequately this time.

"Do you understand me now?"

"Yes," she whispered.

"So sorry, love. I forgot for a second that you don't talk my tongue. You must be hungry. I will help you to be seated properly and will bring you a bowl of my famous stew. My name is Popi, and what may yours be?" She asked while she helped the girl to be seated properly to be fed.

The girl sounded confident at first. "My name is... My name is..." She thought if she perhaps said it slower, it would come to her. "My – name – is..." With confusion and fear, the girl stared wide-eyed at the big strange woman in front of her. "I don't know!" she answered with an alarm in her voice.

Popi was relieved that they could communicate, although this memory loss was another matter altogether. She sat next to her on the bed.

"Oh my, you must have lost your memory! Can you remember anything that happened to you or where you come from?"

What is wrong with me? Have I lost my mind? The girl thought before answering, "Do I know you? Do *you* know who I am?" Her throat was still sore, but she had to ask.

"Sorry, dear. Your fever was bad. You fought it well at the end, but not so well in the beginning. It was as though you had given up on life itself and had no interest in fighting or the will to live. It all turned out fine, and I'm so happy to be talking to you. That is, except for your memory. You were extremely sick! You had so many infections; your body must have switched off at some point and restarted. That's how I see it or think that's what happened. Something must have then triggered in your brain that blocked everything out." Then, Popi remembered the name the girl kept calling in her sleep in the beginning.

"Who is Jessie?"

"Jessie?"

"Yes, dear, you kept calling for her in your sleep."

"Jessie is... Jessie is my... I don't know who Jessie is. Strange, how can I remember her name, but not the person?"

"I don't know, *Lillé*." Giving her a nickname felt right. "We had it once before. This person had a hard blow to his head and could not remember who he was. After a few days, we decided to hit him on the head almost as hard as before, and he started to remember. You, of course, are a different case! We can't go hitting you on the head!" Popi laughed at the thought.

"Hopefully, it will come back to you in time. That usually happens when you are in familiar surroundings. I'm afraid it will take some time before all your memories return. I think small things will trigger certain memories for you. The only solution is to wait and be patient. You might remember Jessie because she was probably the last person you saw and was on your mind before you sank into a state of unconsciousness. Just guessing, yet, it sounds reasonable." Popi wasn't sure if she should tell the girl where she was and why it would be difficult to remember. *One blow at a time*, she thought, and this one was enough for today. She stood up to dish some food in for the girl.

Popi was a rotund woman and had a friendly face. She returned first with the medication and then brought the stew and fed her.

After a few serves, the girl shook her head with the spoon close to her mouth and said, "I'm full, thank you!"

The old woman smiled, "That's understandable, you lost a lot of weight and your stomach has shrunk. It will take some time, but we'll put the meat back on your bones in no time! Get your strength back so you can be up and about. How are you feeling?"

The girl gave a lazy smile before answering, "My body still aches a bit; the fever seems to be gone, and my eyes burn when I open them." She felt exhausted too, just by sitting up and eating. She did not want the woman fussing too much, so she did not mention this to her.

"Your temperature is back to normal, thank the heavens. Your body aches because you have been lying in bed for so long. You will get some exercise soon. Yes, I see your eyes are bloodshot. The only solution is to rest them for now, so sleep again, *Lillé*, and when you wake, we can eat more and speak further."

The girl liked the name Popi was calling her. With her eyes closed and close to drifting off, she asked one last question, "What does, *Lillé* mean?"

"It means, 'little one.'"

The young girl smiled lazily. She felt content, and soon, she was sound asleep.

Popi did not want to tell her how close to death she was when arriving. It took her a long time to try to put liquid down the girl's throat while she was out. She had to bathe and cover

28

each spot on her body at day's end until they faded. The fever had given her nightmares in the beginning.

At times, she became so quiet that Popi was worried and had to see if she was still breathing. The old woman used all her skills to bring this poor child back to health. The girl still had a way to go before she would be her healthy self again. So far, it all turned out well.

The girl woke up early the next morning and needed to relieve herself. Her eyes felt much better and could open them without any pain. She noticed that Popi was not around, and she didn't know where the lavatory was, or Popi for that matter. She decided to try to get up by herself.

She lifted herself and swung her legs off the bed. The girl felt confident that she was strong enough to handle such a small yet essential mission. She was still weak and felt dizzy before her feet reached the floor. When she tried to stand, that's when Popi came in singing and was shocked to see her climbing out of bed.

"By all the gods, my child! Where do you think you're going?" she asked, feeling stressed for the child's health. "It's too soon for you to be out of bed!" Popi ran to her side to help her.

"I need to go to the lavatory!" The girl felt embarrassed to share such a personal matter and attempted to handle it unaided. She felt ridiculous and hopeless all at the same time.

Popi smiled, "Ah! Nature calls. You will need help for now until you can go by yourself. First, put this on because it's cold here in the mornings."

While Popi was helping her to stand, the girl felt something heavy under her garments. She tried to feel what it was, and it kept trying to fall off. She decided to stay quiet, not sure what the older woman dressed her in. Popi covered her with a woolen cloak and helped her to the door.

When the girl stepped out, she was shocked and took a step back. She was in awe; she had never seen the ocean before, or that is what she believed. What was weird was that their cottage was the only one in sight, and there weren't any people but them on this beach, or perhaps on this entire island.

"Where am I?" she asked and felt dizzy, looking at Popi with scared eyes. It was early in the morning, and the scene was out of a painting. There were a few white clouds in the perfect blue sky, and the sun was still rising. The sea was bluish-green and white foam was lashing onto the dry sand — it was all breath-taking! Her emotions were mixed with amazement and fear.

Popi held onto the girl for fear that she might faint. She knew it was time to explain to the young girl where she was. Though not now, she will wait a little longer or when the time is right. She felt sorry for the young girl to be in this odd place, and hers was strange. Trying to soothe her, she said, "Let's first get you to your business; then we can speak further inside where it's warm."

When Popi left her to do her business in private, the girl lifted her garment and found a rag of some kind wrapped around her privates, as you would dress a baby in a nappy. She realized what it meant and felt truly embarrassed, knowing what Popi had to do to keep her clean when she had no self-restraint on her bladder while being unconscious. Thank the heavens it was still clean. She loosened the knots on the sides and let it drop to the floor. She never wanted to see the rag again.

When she stepped out, Popi noticed the girl was red in the face and saw the fabric she had folded in her arms.

"Oh dear, I forgot all about that!" Popi took it from her. The medication she gave her was strong. The poor child had no control and not knowing what she did while sleeping, which was sorely needed.

"No need to be too embarrassed, dear. It's a natural thing that happens when one is bedridden, as in your case. It's normal, my child. There is no need to worry. Let's forget all about this and never discuss it again. Come, dear, let's get inside."

Once inside, Popi helped her back into bed and gave her a hot bowl of soup with a small chunk of fresh bread. The girl was hungry and started eating. Her mind was racing with questions and had no idea where to begin — she would start when she cleared her bowl.

Popi thought she could try to cheer the young lady up; she looked so fragile and sorrowful. So, while the girl ate, Popi cleaned up and chatted away, "When you are feeling better and your memory returns, we can arrange for you to go home to your parents. They must be missing you and very worried! I know I would be if one of my kids went missing. Though I have no idea how young Thord came to find you or thought of bringing you here, then again, just looking at you, I can understand."

Popi burst out laughing and blabbed away, not noticing the girls' expression when mentioning her parents; she went on speaking, "On that matter, we will need to ask Thord about that one day when he has the time for us. He always seems busy and only arrived two days ago after a long trading voyage, which, I must add, was successful."

The girl sat staring at the empty bowl in her hands, not saying a word. The scene outside was forgotten for now. Her memory was blank! She felt awful. She never even thought of parents — her parents. *Where are they? Who could they be?* She could not understand. As much as she tried, she could not remember them. Yet, just thinking of parents brought a sense of grief. *Does she have parents that are worried and looking for her, or not at all?* She began to worry all over again; she was truly on her own. *Who was this woman, and where had this Thord person taken her? This woman took her in and saved her life.*

She had a feeling she could trust Popi. She's always smiling, kind, and caring toward her. She had to get her strength back, find out where and who she was, and try to get back home — wherever that may be. Or not. *Was there someone waiting for her or even looking for her? Was this Jessie woman important in her life? Where was her home? Who was she, and whom does she belong to?* These were all vital questions.

Popi wondered why the girl was so quiet. When she turned to see if the girl's bowl was empty, she noticed that something was amiss.

"What's wrong, love? You look dreadfully pale. I know it's not my cooking. Everything I cook is always clean and fresh."

The girl looked forlorn and had a distressed look in her eyes. Popi wondered whether she had said something wrong.

The girl spoke up and shared her anxious thoughts, "I don't or can't remember my parents." She tried to smile through the sorrow, "I can't remember anything about my life. I can't remember who I am!"

"Oh, dear! One thing we know is that you spoke French in the beginning, so we know you come from France. However, that is all I can tell you! We'll get to the bottom of all this in no time. I assure you that you will find all your answers sooner than you think. Be positive and try not to stress too much, or you'll force your memories further away. You should try to relax and let it return as naturally as a baby starts to take its first steps. Memories will come back slowly, one at a time. We have to remain patient. I promise I will not send you anywhere until all your memories have returned. You should rest for now; you are still weak and need plenty of rest and fresh air. We can talk more at lunch."

The girl said nothing further and obeyed the older woman's orders. Feeling weak once again, she lay down and slept until Popi woke her for lunch.

When they finished eating, Popi asked her, "You seem to be at a young age. I think you might be the same age as my youngest daughter. Can you maybe remember how old you are, dear?" Popi wondered.

"I don't know!"

"That's all right." Popi was trying her best to lighten up the situation with a nonchalant conversation. The girl should try to accept the path she is on now, to make her life easier for herself until she remembers. She decided that while the girl was in her care, she would make her feel safe and at home.

While fixing an old skirt of hers and humming a song, she sensed the girl staring. When she looked up, the girl looked away. Popi smiled and went on sewing. She guessed the girl wanted to ask something and wondered why she hesitated. When the older woman looked up again, she caught the girl staring once more, and her cheeks were slowly turning red. Popi tried her best not to laugh. She smiled broadly at the girl and asked, "Yes, love?"

"No, it's nothing." She stared at the fire. She did not want to be rude by asking. Thus, she kept her thoughts to herself. The way Popi dressed and spoke was weird. Popi was definitely different, and even though she couldn't remember where she came from or who she was, it was just a feeling that felt right. *If she knew Popi, then she would have understood her language — memory loss or not — not so?'* She was frowning a lot, concentrating on this subject.

Popi wondered if this was the right time to tell the girl where she was and about her people. *One blow at a time,* she thought. She did not want to stress her out so soon, or it could help her come to terms with her situation. They still had a while before they could leave, which meant the girl had time to accept the circumstances she was in now. Her clothing that Popi had to cut off, in the beginning, was made of fine fabric, which meant she came from a high-class home and was raised by decent folks.

Popi meant to explain all this much earlier, but the girl's memory loss stopped her. She was still not sure what to do, or if the girl could handle it or not! She knew she had to tell her at some point, so why not the present? She had a feeling that it would all work out in the end. The girl seemed brave for her age. She must be wondering about all this anyway.

She looked at the girl and went on sewing when she asked, "Would you like to know where you are, dear?"

The girl smiled and answered, "Yes, please." She tried to sit up straighter to pay attention.

Popi explained, "Well, *Lillé!* You can say we are from two different worlds. We are called many names; Vik's, Vikings, explorers, warriors, pirates, and so on. This island is called the

Faeroe Islands, which means the Sheep Islands, because we trade mostly with wool and herd many sheep. We trade with several other items as well, but that is our main source of trade."

The girl listened intently and was fascinated, to be honest, a little frightened and thrilled at the same time. *A different world! Wow!* Strange... she remembered something. The Viking name triggered a memory. *How can that be!*

Popi stopped speaking and saw that the girl was frowning again.

"What's the matter, dear?"

"I don't know! I think the name Viking triggered a memory; I believe with my father!"

"Oh?" Now Popi looked intrigued. "Do share."

The girl was staring into nothing as the scene played through her mind.

"What I can remember, is that my father used to tell me stories about the Vikings. I loved listening to him — he was a good storyteller. It sometimes felt as though I lived in the story. He eventually stopped telling them, then started with other fairy tales. He said that it was time for new ones. Sadly, that's all I have of the memory."

"Can you remember your father now?"

"No, just that he told many stories and how much I loved to listen to him. I still can't remember his face or who he is." The girl looked pleased with herself and her new memory and started to relax more. She looked at the old woman and smiled,

"Please continue with your story." She was feeling hopeful at last.

"Ah... Yes... So where was I? We preferably don't accept outsiders on our island. We prefer to stick to our own kind. Don't worry! You are an exception, and times are changing everywhere. The chief's son brought you here. His father rules these islands. Just as you have a king that rules, so do we. The only difference is the name. Ours is called the chieftain.

"His name is Chief Thorarin; he is feared and respected by all. He is a fair ruler. Don't you be afraid now, little one; he's hard on the outside and soft on the inside — like most of us Vikings. At first, we look scary; however, it's not true with all Vikings. Don't dare tell anyone!" Popi smiled, "The chieftain has to be feared to keep his position and respect. We are warriors by blood. You will meet him, and I believe you will come to like him. His eldest son—"

The girl noticed a slight pause from Popi when she said 'eldest son,' then went on speaking,

"—Thord, that's who brought you here, is expected to rule just like his father, the chief. Never show weakness in front of your people, and always be ready for battle. Finally, yet importantly, your people come first. We have been living like this for centuries, and we are content on this island. I hope you come to love it here as well. Everyone is curious about you, in a good way, dear." Popi could see that the girl was anxious, "The rest you will find out for yourself."

The girl did not know where she was or what was waiting or expected of her and wondered whether she would ever see her homeland and parents again.

"You look worried, dear! You mustn't be. All will be well. Just give it some time; you'll see."

All the girl could do was smile at the kind woman. She would figure out what to do when the time came.

Popi said, "That's enough talk for today. You look exhausted. I will wake you when supper is ready. Now, straight to sleep again! Tomorrow you will have a bath."

The girl passed out as soon as she put her head down. Popi stared at this young child; she was becoming fond of her and felt she needed protection. The girl looked so fragile, not like her people. You could break a coconut over their heads and they would laugh at you. She was not worried about the chief and his son, except Thord's sister might be difficult, but that would be a problem for later. The more weight the girl gained, the better. Popi noticed she was easily embarrassed and couldn't hide it.

FIVE

Early the following day, Popi started heating water over the fire and poured it into a wooden tub. She added a sweet, fragrant liquid to wash the dirt off one's skin, and it helped to soothe the body as well.

Feeling comfortable with the old lady, the girl took off her linen nightdress and climbed naked into the tub. She still had a few marks on her from the measles, resulting from scratching too much initially, which would eventually fade in time.

She couldn't remember when she last had a bath. She felt content relaxing in the warm water while Popi went about to wash her hair. The young girl felt a slight headache coming on with a memory that was surfacing.

She could see herself bathing in a river that was close to her home. Her mother sat on the riverbank dangling her feet in the water, just passing the time with conversation. It was a hot evening, she convinced her mother into joining her, and once in, they had so much fun that they lost track of time. Her father eventually came out to see what was keeping them. He found them both laughing and splashing water at each other. When he called out, they squealed, giggled, and rushed to get out.

Popi was right. Her thoughts will return on their own time or when triggered by specific effects like the bath has done.

The older woman could see the girl was lost in thought and did not want to disturb her. She must be thinking of something nice, for she was smiling. Popi was pleased to see a genuine smile. Since waking up from her illness, she always looked sad and lost. She let the girl be while washing her hair.

She was a pretty girl with long curly blond hair and ivory skin. She noticed the girl's hair was colored white for some reason, and her natural hair color was growing out. It looked like a dark red, and wondered why or who would do this?

The girl tilted her head back and looked up at Popi from the tub. She smiled broadly and shared the memory she just had.

Popi was pleased and did not expect any memories to return so soon. She said it was a wonderful memory of her parents and asked, "Do you now remember who your parents are?"

"I'm not sure. I see their faces now, but I can't remember who they are or what kind of parents they were. How can that be, Popi? Is this normal?"

"I don't know, dear? I wish I could answer all your questions and give you peace of mind. I am just happy you are getting any memories so early. We should be positive. I know for sure you will get better."

The girl would not force her memories to return and will abide to be patient. She started to trust the old woman and was fond of her.

Popi thought of a way to cheer her up and asked her to explain how her parents looked.

"Well," she thought, "My mom has long dark auburn hair and still looks young. She's beautiful and has a lovely smile; she looks like a kind and caring person. I wish I knew what kind of person she was instead of just guessing with one memory. My father," she looked back at her memory. "He has light russet hair, cut short, and is well built. He looks a little older than her and good on the eyes; big, broad smile and a little tomfoolery personality. He has a naughty jokey side to him."

"Well, that's a pretty good description with just the face to go by, don't you think? I think by the sounds of it, you might be remembering your father more than your mother."

The girl smiled fondly, "Now, it's your turn, Popi. I would love to hear about you."

Popi smiled and said, "I don't know where to begin," After rinsing the girl's hair, she sat down and began to explain with pride in her voice, "Let's see, I have three kids; two girls and one boy. The oldest one, Astrid, just got married, and hopefully, they will soon give me a grandchild. She still comes to the house most days to help with certain things. The love of my life, Var, works in the fields, growing crops — farm life. Depending on the weather, he works in a workshop with wood or iron on his off days. I run the house and cattle farm with the help of my other kids, Sigrid and Cnut."

The girl interrupted Popi, "Sorry, I feel awful taking up all your time and keeping you from them. They must miss you!"

Popi reassured her that they could handle the house and the farm by themselves. They were raised to do such things.

She went on to explain, "You are my priority right now. I would like to see you well and up and about; you have become important to me as well, *Lillé.*" The more time Popi spent with her, the more she started to care. Call it a mother's instinct.

The girl was deeply touched by her words and still curious and asked another question. So many thoughts were going through her mind.

"Thank you, Popi; I've grown fond of you as well!" There was a pause. "Popi, please tell me how I came to be here and how long I've been sick?"

"Well, you've been sick for almost two months."

She was shocked, "Two months! Wow, that's a long time!" The girl could not believe it took so long to get well.

"Well, yes, you see, I'm a healer on my island. I'm called a medicine woman by my tribe." Popi smiled, "It's in my blood to heal the sick. I take that very seriously, and my family understands."

The girl looked surprised; she never expected her to be a healer as well. Why did she say '*as well*'? Was she a healer, or did she know someone that was one?

Thinking back to when she fed her medication, she never considered how Popi got it. It was obvious – how fascinating!'

"Are you remembering something again?" Popi saw the girl frowning.

"I'm not sure, but I think I was training to be a healer."

"Now that is fascinating," Popi said.

"Perhaps my mother was a healer and was teaching me the trade?" The girl was not sure. "Maybe...?"

Popi spoke, "I don't know, love. The garments you were wearing say you are a Lady. Perhaps your father married a healer; we won't know until you start remembering again. It's just a guessing game at this point. Anyhow, how you came to be here, you need to ask Thord. He was the one who brought you and asked me to look after you. It was too dangerous to take you close to the village, in case it spread amongst our tribe."

"But weren't you afraid for yourself?"

"The measles gave you many infections. You were well in the fever for it to spread. It will only spread if it's fresh, but a person can never be sure. I know the healing trade too well and would know what to do to handle myself."

Popi went on talking about her family and made the girl laugh at times.

When she was finished soaking in the tub, Popi put a chair outside for the girl to dry her hair in the sun while she made them something to eat. Later, when they finished eating, Popi started to comb the girls' hair.

Popi had beautiful hair and seemed she has a lot of pride in it, brushing it daily on occasions — it must be a Viking thing. She would soon find out who these people were. The girl was lost in thought and unconsciously staring strangely at the older woman.

Popi started laughing as if reading her mind and said, "You will learn our ways, little one, and you'll pull that sweet face of yours a lot."

She noticed the girl looked sleepy and continued, "We'll take a walk on the beach later if you feel up to it. You need to get some exercise." While the girl was resting, Popi decided to have a bath and warmed extra water to pour into the tub.

The girl woke, listening to the waves crashing outside. The sound was becoming familiar and soothing. Whenever she went to the lavatory, she could not help to stop and stare at the scenery.

"It's so beautiful here," she thought aloud. She was becoming attached to this place in her short duration after being out of bed and well. The thought of leaving was depressing.

Once inside, Popi gestured that she eats at the table. She made more of her famous stew. They both enjoyed the food and each other's company. She was happy to see the girl was getting her appetite back. When Popi finished cleaning up, the weather was warmer outside, and they went for a walk on the beach.

The girl looked up at the mountains surrounding them. There was a forest close by as well. Thinking of her attire, she said, "I hope no one sees me. I'm not properly dressed!"

"Don't worry about that. No one comes here; this is a private beach and is secluded. Tomorrow morning, I must leave for a few hours. I need to get more food supplies, and the chief expects an update on your health as well. I will have to send one of my kids with a message.

"I will also give my daughters your dress size. They will make you an outfit for traveling and then some for when you meet the chief. I want to make sure you are well before you leave; therefore, you will be staying at my house first for a few days before going off to the main house. How does that sound?"

"I would like that very much! I can't wait to meet your family, and to be honest, also a bit nervous. I don't think I'm ready to face the chief yet, and it scares me just thinking about it! But why the chief's house? Why can't I stay with you?"

Popi reassured her that there was nothing to be scared about meeting the chief. It's meeting her family that she should be afraid of, and they both laughed.

"It's just a precaution for you to be in the main house, nothing to worry about now. You still have time to adjust before then. Let's enjoy the time and get your strength back first."

The sea was a gorgeous color — it was like nothing she had ever seen before. The girl loved every moment and wished they could stay forever. Leaving and facing the people in the village was frightening. It was peaceful walking on the warm sand sinking under their bare feet, both not saying a word, just enjoying the scenery and the warm sunshine. It was a long walk before turning to return to the hut. She looked at the log cabin against the mountain. It looked like the cottage was seeking protection from the giant mountain, hiding snuggly against it — all was stunning!

The girl stared far out to the ocean and said, "Isn't that a beautiful color, Popi?"

"Yes, dear, I believe it's the same color as your eyes."

"Really?" She never thought about how she looked. It did not even bother her to sneak a peek at her reflection from the water.

Popi laughed at her expression.

The girl responded, "Then I can say I have beautiful eyes."

"That you do, little one, one of many blessings."

The girl blushed.

Popi was dressed warmly in a woolen cloak and left early the next morning after a quick breakfast. She wanted to return before lunchtime. She implored the girl to wait until the sun rises if she decided to go for a walk for fear of catching some other illness.

"Don't you worry too much now; you are very safe here on your own. I'll be back before you know it!" Popi kissed her on the cheek and left.

The girl went for a walk when it got warmer and enjoyed the time alone. The sea was once again a beautiful turquoise color, and the water was extra cold. She decided to stay on the warm sand that felt wonderful. While the wind was gently caressing through her hair, she took a deep breath and inhaled the salty sea air.

The mountain near the hut ran right into the sea, cutting the beach off from the other side. The water was so blue and clear; you could see fishes swimming about. She wondered what was on the other side. In the opposite direction, the beach ran much further down. There was a bend, and again, the beach was cut off short; the water was rushing over cobbles, with many pebbles and shingles lying around, making it impossible to walk over, especially when she was barefoot. She was like a child, picking up shells and trying to build something with the sand. At times, she would just sit and soak up the sun. After a few hours of exploring, she felt tired and went in.

When Popi arrived back at the cottage, she found the girl passed out with a flushed face.

The days went by, and a strong bond grew between the two women. The girl felt she knew Popi's family well by now with the stories she told. You could hear in her tone of voice how much she loved them. The day grew closer for them to leave.

The villagers were curious about the sick girl their young chief brought to their island. The girl was nervous about meeting them, especially the chief, and kept saying she was not ready.

She was a beautiful and innocent young girl. She was picking up weight and looking healthier by the day. Her hair color was becoming more visible too — half scarlet and the other half white. Popi thought of doing something with it before leaving but decided to let it grow out.

She returned with an extra horse for the girl to travel on as well. Popi's girls sent over a linen dress with an extra woolen cloak with a hood dyed red and a brooch, as well as woolen socks and leather shoes for traveling. She was grateful for all the gifts.

SIX

The girl was well mannered and often offered a helping hand with their meals, and every time Popi declined. During these periods, she would sit alone on the beach, waiting to be called to eat. She loved being outside, with the smell of the ocean and the wind blowing through her hair.

She often wondered where the village and people were that Popi kept speaking about. It was hard to believe her at first, and honestly thought they were on a deserted island. That's how quiet and peaceful it was. However, lately, she had noticed small fishing boats far out to sea when going to the outside lavatory in the mornings.

So, there were other people on the island! She thought to herself. Everything still felt so surreal — that it was just the two of them alone on a mysterious island, and she was ready to explore its wonders. She laughed at her silly fantasies.

A few days later, she saw a man on a steed staring at her from atop of the mountain. For how long, she had no idea. Popi said it could have been Thord checking on them. It was almost time for them to leave their little cottage. The girl was scared and nervous to leave her safe haven, but Popi frequently tried to ease her mind by speaking about everyone. She reminded the girl, once again, that she would be staying at her place before the festival and explained a little about their tradition.

"We have three festivals a year, and each lasts for up to two weeks. The first celebration of the year is early in the summer. It's a tradition held by all Vikings; it's called 'Sigrblot,' and it signifies the beginning of the warm season for growing crops. Everyone looks forward to these events. It is entertaining and enjoyable, and I think you will love it!"

Popi looked excited while explaining about the celebrations; however, the girl could not feel the same. She had a feeling that she liked to socialize with people, but this situation was different. The thought of engaging in their traditions of which she knew nothing and with strangers, made her nervous. To top it off, for two weeks! *Was that normal?* Perhaps she was being silly! She was tense with nerves but tried her best not to show it and forced a huge smile.

"It all sounds fascinating! Two weeks — I hope I can handle that!" She ended with a nervous laugh.

"You will be just fine, *Lillé*; you'll see."

They were at the cottage for almost three months, and it was time to leave. After they had breakfast, Popi told her that they were leaving very early the next day. Once everything was cleaned, they started packing some equipment that was not needed for the day.

The weather was hot, and the little cottage was warm inside. The girl desperately wanted to have her first swim in the ocean and tried to talk Popi into joining her. She agreed to a bit of swimming, but Popi hadn't gone swimming in a very long time. She was also not sure if she could anymore.

Rather safe than sorry, she sat close to let the waves wash over her while watching the girl enjoying herself immensely in the water. She, too, did not go too far and stayed close to where Popi was sitting. Popi knew that no matter how much the girl ate, that would be the weight she'd keep. She was so used to the Viking's big-boned bodies that when comparing the girl to them, she was tiny and fragile.

After supper, they had a late bath to wash off the sand, and they both slept like babies that night.

On Popi's last return home for fresh stock, she brought an extra horse for the girl to use. They were organized and finished early, and as planned, after a small breakfast, they soon hit the road with their little belongings.

They trotted down the beach and came to a narrow pathway that was invisible to the eye. Someone who did not know the land, much like the girl, would have never guessed this was an entrance to the village.

The girl stopped to survey the scenery one last time, at the only home she knew, which she would miss. Although she was sick most of the time in the beginning, this was the only place that felt like home.

The forest was wild and thick, with many tall trees and bushes scattered everywhere. The twigs were crunching under the heavily loaded horses. That was the only sound she could hear as the birds flew away in fright with their passing presence. She looked up to the tall trees to stare at the rays of sunlight passing through the branches; a squirrel was sitting on a trunk staring at them. When they made eye contact, it scurried away. She smiled at the peace she was feeling and not pondering over her anxiety about meeting the natives on this strange island.

The path eventually stopped. She wondered how Popi could remember the ins' and outs' in all this denseness. There was no path further on. It felt as if they were going in circles. To her relief, they eventually came to another road — if you could call it that. Not like the roads that were frequently used where she grew up — another memory! It seemed insignificant to remember a path!

"This way, *Lillé*," Popi said as they turned around a vast bushy tree. For the first time, still far off, the girl spotted a house. She had an uncanny feeling of déjà vu.

No words were spoken between the two since leaving the cabin, both in their own thoughts. Mainly because the paths were narrow and Popi was leading — until now.

Popi looked at the girl and saw the surprise in her eyes. She was taking in the scenery and couldn't help saying, "That there, little one, is my home."

The exquisite scenery bespoke of real farm life; it wasn't just the sight that pleased the eyes. The smells and sounds delighted the senses as well. The lush green grass was spread everywhere like a blanket covering the ground, filled with sheep, goats, chickens, and cattle were roaming freely. All lay under a shrine of a crystal-blue sky – a perfect day and scenery never to forget.

Nearing the house, the girl noticed its unusual shape; it looked like an upside-down ship with green moss covering almost all parts. She had another odd déjà vu sensation, which she ignored at once. The forest was behind the house, and in front was a beautiful meadow; you could still smell the salt sea ocean from here, which she loved.

Another memory surfaced – her homeland was mostly brown sand everywhere, and big pools of mud formed in some areas when it rained. It was starting to evolve; big houses and buildings were being erected. They had many trees and some bushes, but not like this – this was stunning – another insignificant memory. She wanted more of her parents and the life she had.

Nevertheless, a memory was a memory. She should be happy to glimpse something – if nothing important yet. They still had a way to go, and her nerves were on edge.

The girl looked at Popi and saw her beaming, happy to be home again. She felt so guilty for having this beautiful woman all to herself. Her family must have missed her and she, them. She was feeling a little tired and was not sure why. Maybe it was unnerving to be finally coming out to the living and amongst strangers. She had to deal with this on her own. Not wanting to worry Popi, she tried to show her excitement.

"It's genuinely beautiful, Popi! I don't think I have ever seen such beauty before." She meant every word and could see Popi was proud of her home. When they reached the house and got their belongings off the horses, the girl realized there was no one to greet them.

"Where is everyone?" she asked with a confused expression.

"The men are in the fields tilling the ground, preparing it for planting season, dear. My daughter, Sigrid, is helping in the village while I was gone. We have two weeks left before the festival. They will be here at suppertime, and then you will meet my family. They are very excited to meet you, so why don't I show you to your room and I'll make something light to eat, and you can rest until then."

At the entrance of this unique home, along the walls hung oil lamps, dried herbs and flowers. Massive wooden beams supported the roof that was sunk deep into the ground. She followed Popi inside. It was not what she expected; it was spacious with a cozy feeling and a homely atmosphere. As Popi told her, life is changing for them, and you could see the changes made to accommodate a new style. A massive table with wooden chairs was close to the entrance.

Adjacent to the walls were a few built-in benches scattered with feathery pillows. The benches were broad, a size of a single bed. It must have been their old sleeping quarters before building the extra rooms. A few places along the walls had shelves containing personal effects. A large fireplace kept it warm, and there were no windows in this area. Close to the hearth were two chairs with soft seating and a furry hide on the floor as a carpet.

Popi took her further along the small passage to the three bedrooms and explained, "You will be sharing a room with Sigrid as Astrid does not live here anymore. However, you will meet her later today; she still comes over a lot. You may put your belongings on the bed. You can pack them away later. The room across from you belongs to Cnut, and the one next to yours at the end is mine. So, I'm close whenever you need me." Popi walked off and left the girl to get used to her surroundings.

The girl thought that if everyone was as friendly as Popi, then everything would be well. However, that never happens; each person is their own self. Popi once told her that everyone knew everyone's business on this island, which meant everyone knew about her and now living with Popi. Suddenly, everything seemed so real and frightening.

The girl put her few belongings on one of the beds and quickly looked around the room. It was small with two single beds and a cupboard for clothing — one side was empty. There was a small fireplace with a woolen carpet on the floor, which made it look welcoming.

She had a quick peek through the window and saw it was facing the other side of the fields. She noticed a vegetable garden nearby, and next to it was another. It looked familiar, like an herb garden. She knew this by spending so much time with Jessie in hers.

"Jessie was the healer!" she said aloud. *Not my mother.* Jessie occasionally taught her a few things. Now, that was a memory to share! Looking at the herb garden brought back a few good memories with Jessie and how close they were. It made her long for her home. She wished nothing had changed and that everyone was together, but that was not so. She was here in this strange place, and the only friend she had – knew – was Popi.

The girl walked back to the entrance area and could hear Popi singing. She followed the sound. Popi was busy making something to eat and gestured for her to sit. The girl stopped dead in her tracks and was amazed at what she saw.

In the kitchen area was a small table with four chairs, and there were many shelves and cupboards everywhere. What made it strange was the room right next to it; it had a massive hole in the middle of the roof – definitely not normal! And in the middle of the room sat an enormous pot she had ever seen. There was another door leading outside.

Popi joined her at the table and put a sandwich down in front of her. She had never seen this before. When Popi picked hers up with her hands and took a bite out of it, the girl copied her.

She liked it a lot and could not help asking, "What is this? I don't think I've ever eaten bread like this before, but more importantly, why is there a big hole in the roof?"

Popi poured them both a mug of skim milk and explained, "There's nothing fancy about the bread; some butter on both slices and meat in-between. It fills the belly, and it's easy to make when you are out all day. The hole in the roof," Popi laughed, "That's for the smoke to go out. Our pot is too big for a fireplace and works well for us. We only use it when we entertain a huge crowd. We don't use it much, though. Not all the houses have one; the chief has one, and there is one in the village's main eating hall. Sometimes we all eat together when the food runs short.

"We are a very close tribe, and we all support one another. We are one big happy family with one father that rules. It suits all of us. When we first moved into this house, we just had the main room in front where we all slept together. Later, when the kids got older and times changed, we decided to build extra rooms and this kitchen area. Although, some people don't like change and still have the old sleeping habits."

When arriving, the girl was mixed with nerves and now delights with all these weird things; she couldn't help but giggle aloud. *These people were really from another world.*

Popi laughed too and was happy to see that the girl felt relaxed. While they continued eating, she shared her memory and what triggered it.

"Well now, who would have guessed that Jessie was the healer? What do you remember about her?"

"Not much, just that she was a healer and that I was fascinated with it. I think I was a frequent visitor at Jessie's and helped her in her garden. That is why your garden triggered the memory. Perhaps she is family. I don't know?"

"Can you see her in your memory like you see your parents' faces but don't know who they are?"

"Sadly, no! Her face is a blur. However, her name is familiar to me."

"It's still a good start, and I'm happy for you."

When they finished eating, Popi told her to rest until supper time. Before the girl went, she thanked Popi for all her time and care she bestowed upon her so far and how much she valued their friendship. Popi thanked the girl for her kind words and hugged her.

She went to her new room, for now, and packed her few belongings. Before passing out on the bed, she had one last peek through the window.

Loud voices woke her. The girl just lay there listening to everyone speaking. She wasn't sure if she had to get up or stay where she was. She wanted to stay and hide; however, decided it was best to get up and meet everyone. Popi would expect that. She was wearing one of the new dresses made of light linen, and it fitted her nicely. She felt comfortable in it.

When she entered the main room, everyone went quiet and just stared at her. The girl blushed slightly at her audience and smiled. Popi turned around in her chair.

"Ah! *Lillé*, you are awake. No sleeping when this bunch walks in the door!" She laughed at her own joke, "Come, come meet everyone." Popi pushed her chair back to stand up and started to introduce her family, "This is my husband, Var, my eldest daughter, Astrid, and the other one is Sigrid. My youngest one is Cnut. Don't mind him; he's being silly." Popi moaned at her youngest son, "Cnut, close your mouth and be polite to our guest!"

Cnut was beside himself with their beautiful guest. He jumped up and told her it was a pleasure to meet her, then pulled a chair out for her to sit on. Everyone roared with laughter as they had never seen Cnut taken with a girl before, and the poor girl blushed again. When Cnut returned to be seated next to his older sister, Astrid slapped him on the head without looking at him. Popi spoke further when everyone had settled.

They were all friendly toward her. The girl could not be introduced because she had no name! No one asked, as if they knew. She was grateful to Popi for not making it even more awkward and tried to enjoy the evening.

Sigrid sat next to her and started a conversation, "That dress fits you nicely; we were worried that mom made a mistake with your size."

"Yes, I want to thank you and your sister for taking the time to make it. The red cloak is my favorite. Thank you!"

A few questions were thrown her way, and the conversation continued for a while before everyone started to complain that they were hungry. They all stood up and washed their hands at a nearby table. Not sure what to do, the girl stood up and followed suit. The water looked slightly milky, and it was warm. There was a cloth to dry your hands as well. This was done every day before meals.

Popi went out to make this a special occasion – the table was set before them; smoked fish, pickled fish, fresh bread, vegetables, and a whole chicken. There was skimmed milk, honey, and mead to drink. They explained what drinks they made on the island and promised that she would taste them all at the festival, including buttermilk, whey and beer. The girl said she would stick to skimmed milk, and Popi added a little honey into it. She enjoyed the treat.

There was much laughter, and the conversation went on with the girl being center stage. She could not believe that all the food had gone at the end of the meal – only bones were left. Everyone picked up the dishes and walked toward the kitchen, where they walked through the back door that led outside. They dropped all the dishes into a big wash-basin.

The two men made a fire in a pile of rocks and sat down while the women cleaned the dishes. The girl wanted to help, but they declined. Var started to tell stories of their history; everyone kept quiet and listened. When he finished, she only then realized that the women had finished cleaning. It was a fascinating evening, and she enjoyed every second of it.

It was getting late; Astrid went home to her husband, and it was time for everyone else to retire. The girl had no idea why she was nervous in the beginning. Popi had a beautiful family. She should have known that anyone associated with Popi must be wonderful. When lying in bed, she went through the evening with Popi's family.

Astrid had a more serious nature than the rest. Maybe she had more of her father's ways than her mother's, but only time would tell. Sigrid was more like Popi, and they instantly became friends. Cnut was jokey and always seemed playful, which somehow infuriated the girls. It must be a sibling thing.

Var was sweet and wasn't sure how to handle her or what to say, but relaxed more by the evening's end. The girl felt welcomed and at home.

She woke early the following day with a door slamming and feet shuffling in the passage and noticed that Sigrid was not in the room. There was a fresh bowl of water and a towel on the sideboard. She climbed out of bed and started to wash up. While drying her face, the door slowly began to open, and she jumped back into bed. It could be one of the men and she wasn't decent.

Sigrid walked in. "I'm sorry! Did I frighten you?"

"No, it's fine. I thought you were someone else."

"Yes, you should watch out for Cnut. He can be a handful at times." Sigrid closed the door behind her while the girl stood up once again.

"How did you sleep last night?"

"Very well, thank you!" She went on with what she was doing before being disturbed.

"My mom told me you can't remember your name. It's a little weird because I don't know what to call you. Maybe we can find you a temporary name for others to call you by?"

The girl started to tidy her bed. "Yes, it's true, but my memories are slowly returning, and a name would be great." They both sat on their beds, facing each other.

"We will work on that later." Sigrid looked excited about something and had a big bundle in her arms.

The girl guessed she was the same age as her and not much taller. Sigrid had beautiful long, dark blond hair, a nice tan from working in the sun most of the day, and her mother's same friendly face. She just knew they were going to be best friends. Her sister, Astrid, was two years older – nineteen – she looked much older; she was slightly taller than Sigrid and well-formed for her age.

Sigrid put the bundle on the bed and said it was the rest of the clothes they made for her. The girl was so embarrassed and amazed; it was almost a whole wardrobe.

"I don't know what to say – this is too much! How do I repay you and your sister? I can't thank you enough." She then stood up, hugged Sigrid, and thanked her.

"It's nothing. It was fun making it. That's what all the women do on this island. We mend, make clothes, shoes, also preserve and cook the meals. We help in the fields when it's time for harvesting. Some women even go to war with the men."

"No! Really?" The girl could not believe this and looked shocked at the news. "But how can they fight, and how can the men allow it?"

Sigrid laughed, "Wait until you see some of these women, then you'll change your mind; they are big and rough, sometimes rougher than most men. I must say, even the women that are built like me or my sister go to war. They are trained well in the art of fighting."

There were many outfits and extra woolen socks, two more pairs of leather shoes. There was another white woolen cloak with a hood attached. It was lovely, now she had two to wear, including the red one. They spoke more about the clothes and discussed which one the girl should wear.

While she dressed, Sigrid had to ask, "So what's up with your hair?"

"What do you mean?" She has not seen her reflection since... she couldn't remember. She had no idea what she even looked like. It did not bother her until now.

"It seems you used to change your hair color, and the color is fading." She thought the girl knew.

She was touching her hair as if to feel the difference. "I don't know! What color is it now, or changing into?" *Why did Popi not tell her?*

Sigrid felt sorry for her; it must be awful not knowing yourself or who you used to be.

"Your hair was colored white by the looks of it, but it would seem you have scarlet hair."

"Oh!" she said, still touching her head. She was feeling self-conscious.

"Don't worry, it's not that bad; you still look pretty. I'll go fetch a mirror for you."

So, she still looked pretty with a two-toned head! Why would someone color her hair? When Sigrid gave her the mirror, she was too scared to look.

"Go ahead; it's not that bad." Sigrid took the mirror and held it in front of the girl to see her reflection.

She was not that bad-looking, or that's what she thought anyway. She had long hair, but that she knew without looking, and the color was fading. The tips of her hair were white, while the rest was a beautiful scarlet. The girl wondered why it was dyed in the first place and preferred her natural color.

She was wondering about something while examining her hair, then Sigrid put the mirror down and said, "That's enough of admiring yourself — are you now satisfied? I told you, you are pretty."

The girl laughed, "No, it's not that. I was wondering if you or your mother could cut it so that I don't get any more questions that I don't have any answers for."

"I can do that!" With excitement, Sigrid ran out to fetch scissors.

Eventually, when they both walked out of the room to greet the day and have their breakfast, the girl felt much better about herself. Her hair was much shorter, close to shoulder length, and it suited her well. Thanks to her new friend, her hair was one color now – her original color. The curls were looser and bounced over her face. She looked more stunning with her natural color.

Popi wondered what they were up to all morning with Sigrid running about all the time.

When they eventually came out to greet the day, she was surprised at the change. When she saw the girl with her full scarlet hair and the innocent smile on her face, Popi's stomach flipped. She had a strange feeling of déjà vu. She could not understand why she felt the way she did. Was it a memory stored away with pain? It could not be!

Popi shook her head, dismissed the feeling at once, and voiced her approval, "You look much better now, dear. Sigrid has done a good job."

"Why did you not tell me about my hair?" the girl wondered.

"I don't know. At first, you had so much going on that it seemed insignificant at the time. I thought it would grow out eventually, and you would not notice. I guess it did not bother me again to tell you or ask. I'm so sorry, *Lillé*. Do you know why it was colored?"

"No, I can't remember. That's why I wanted it off!"

"Well, you look beautiful. Now, both of you eat, and off you go. There's a lot to do today."

The week flew by too quickly for the girl. She went out in the mornings to help Sigrid feed fodder to the goats and chickens. She became close friends with Sigrid, and Cnut was always at their heels. They spent the late afternoons fixing clothes and helping Popi with the food. The girl was not doing a great job with the sewing, which triggered another memory. Her mom made all her dresses, she helped with the design and cutting of the material, but that was it.

Sigrid had to fix all her mistakes, and they were getting nowhere; thus, she was sent to help Popi in the kitchen. They preserved most of their food; they pickled and smoked their fish, meat, or anything to last for long periods – she learned a lot during that week. She was exhausted every night and passed out as soon as her head hit the pillow. The day was nearing for her to move into the main house. It felt like they adopted her, or she adopted them. Either way, she felt at home and wanted to stay.

To no avail, the two girls came up with many names and could not agree on one. Sigrid would sometimes make jokes using her mom's nicknames for the girl, little one, dear, and love. It sounded weird coming out of her mouth, which made them laugh. She was tired of picking names for her new friend and decided to wait patiently for it to return.

The girl was counting the hours when she had to leave Popi's house with regret. She wished she could stay. Popi felt the same toward her, although, knew it would be better and safer for her to stay in the main house if anyone wanted to harm her — not that they would — but rather safe than sorry.

Popi explained this to her one morning. The girl understood and did not want her family in harm's way because of her presence in their home. She started helping Sigrid in the herb garden, pulling out the weeds and watering the vegetables. There was not much work — it was well kept. Not far was a beehive where Sigrid had to work at times. The girl did not follow out of fear.

Sigrid told her that her mom was teaching her to become a medicine woman. It was her job to take over her mother's line of work. The girl was envious and wished she could learn as well. She had always been fascinated with herbs and their healing powers. Sigrid knew most of the herbs and called each by name. The girl also started to remember a few and joined in.

They spent their mornings feeding the animals and heading off to the herb garden with a mental list to pick certain vegetables for supper that evening. Not everyone grew vegetables of the same kind; some were sent out to other families on various days, and different vegetables were sent back in return.

Popi made a farewell dinner for her last night, and they all ate outside. They had two roasted chickens on the fire, raw cabbage and carrots cut into small pieces, with a hint of honey and garlic mixed in. The girl noticed that garlic and honey were used in most of their meals. They must love it! There were fresh loaves of bread with butter and honey on the side if anyone wanted extra. She had some beer for the first time that night and enjoyed it with the food, but the taste was not for her. She would never drink it for fun the way Var did.

She had no idea what was expected of her at the chief's house. During her short visit, the girl became fond of Sigrid; she would miss her new friend and their days spent together. It was like having a sister and wondered if she had any siblings of her own. They spoke until late that night and promised to visit each other all the time.

SEVEN

The time arrived for the girl to move into the main house. After having a hearty breakfast, Popi waited outside with their horses while the girl packed her belongings and ran out to meet her. They trotted slowly towards the village. By now, everyone was curious as to what she looked like.

When they came close to the village's central part, she could see habitable houses scattered all over the place — all shapes and sizes. There was a stream close by with a few women washing clothes, and the children were running around playing. There were stables too, although the horses and cattle were roaming freely all over the place. You could hear metal hitting metal in the workplaces and people shouting openly at each other, and others in the fishing moor. It was so much to take in all at once; she felt giddy with anxiety.

Further to the right was the start of a mountain. She guessed that that was the same mountain she pondered over during her days on the beach by seeing the fishing boats. The shore was at the end of the village, and fishermen were busy going out or returning with their catch for the day. In the thick of the morning mist, she was awestruck at how the village bustled with people and activity. Not far on the left was a steep hill, where a house stood out from all the rest; she guessed it was the chief's house, away from all the commotion in the village.

She took a deep breath of the crisp morning air to calm her pounding heart. Some of the villagers paused in their activities and watched them as they rode toward the house. There was a path leading the way, and because it was a path made for walking, they had to climb off their horses.

The girl was aware of all the glances and wondered what everyone must be thinking of an outsider being on their island — which the young chief must answer because he brought her here. Something she pondered over constantly and would like to know as well.

A few kids ran up to her, greeted her, giggled, and ran off again, which made her laugh — she truly enjoyed the friendly welcome from them. Someone came walking down the path from the main house to greet them in person. The girl was the center of a considerable amount of attention. She felt faint with stage fright.

While Thord approached her, the girl felt disturbed at the sight of him, and her heart almost stopped. His enchanting face was lit with a dazzling smile. She had never seen such a man before and had a strange feeling in the pit of her stomach. He looked godlike, tall with golden blond hair and a short, rough beard. He was exquisitely built with muscles bulging out everywhere — incredibly handsome.

He stared at her for a while, finding her a real beauty. The last time he saw her, she was sick and had white hair, which was now short and scarlet. She looked different, and it suited her well. Her body filled out nicely, and was plump in all the right places.

He held out his hands, and with a charming smile, he said, "I welcome you to our island and in my home."

Thord spoke in a loud enough voice for their audience. It would eventually spread on its own – there was no need to shout his welcome.

He gave no other explanation as to who this young lady was or why she was there. Everyone already knew the girl was near death when she arrived and had no memory of her past life.

The morning air was chilly, which made her cheeks glow, and was thankful because it hid her blush. She was spellbound as they stood holding hands. She thanked him, and to her disappointment, he let go of her hand and never said another word while he turned to lead her indoors.

The spell was broken! Only then did she feel Popi's absence and glanced around – she was missing! *Where had Popi disappeared to? Had she left her alone so soon?*

Once inside, Thord asked her to wait and left her standing alone in the hall. The girl shook with nerves, not knowing what to expect. She had not expected such grandeur and stood looking around, trying to calm down. The house seemed ancient and generally modish. They were indeed pirates to accumulate such treasures. The house was made of stone and appeared warm in tone. Great huge carved wooden doorways surrounded the hall, and a broad stairway reached the upper part of the house.

Admiring what she saw, she never noticed Thord standing next to her or heard him approach. She flinched when he touched her shoulder and was embarrassed for being absentminded. For a man, he was genuinely light on his feet.

"I'm sorry!" she almost stuttered. Having him so close and touching her made her nervous.

Thord smiled and asked her to follow him. While they entered one of the doors in the hall, she became more tense than usual. Relief washed over her when seeing Popi. She welcomed the girl inside and stood next to her for support for the meeting with the chief. She gave the older woman a quizzical look. *How did she get here before her?*

The biggest man she had ever seen stood up to greet her, and self-consciously, she took a step back. Popi could not help but smile and put her arm on the girls' back if she decided to run. The *chief* was an intimidating man. He took the girl's hand and covered it with his.

She looked down, saw how huge his hands were, and felt slightly dizzy. His voice was loud, almost like a roar. When he spoke, she jumped with fright, and a chill ran through her body. Her face grew hot and the heat spread all over, then a zinging sound started in her ears, and blank — she was out! Popi caught her before her head hit the ground. She looked at the girl lying in her arms, then looked up at the chief.

The chief spoke first, "Odin's sweet breath! Popi, I thought you said she was well. She looks awfully pale to me. Is she all right?"

"Thorarin!" Popi scolded him.

He looked startled. "What? You can't blame me for her fainting!" He had a slight smirk on his face.

Popi continued, "You were the first person she saw entering, and you roared like a lion at her! Could you not find a gentler or softer voice at first?"

"What are you talking about, woman? This is my voice!"

"Never mind," She looked at Thord and said, "don't just stand there, carry the girl to the couch!" Popi looked at Kiti. "Kiti, stop laughing and ask someone to bring a bowl of water and mead for everyone!"

Thord picked the girl up; she still felt as light as a feather when last he carried her – she looked so innocent sleeping.

The girl stirred slightly in his arms and came to when he laid her down. His face was close to hers, and all she saw was his smiling lips that were magnets for hers – thoughts she never expected from herself, which made her blush all over again. With fear and confusion, she called out for Popi.

"I'm here, dear; all is well." Popi sat next to her. She gave Chief Thorarin a look that said hush, don't say a word. He smiled and lifted both his hands in surrender.

A bowl of water came with the drinks.

"Thord, be a dear and please pour us the mead."

Popi cooled the girl's head with a damp cloth and told her to drink the mead. The girl obeyed, took a few sips, and started to feel better. The scene unfolded in her mind and flushed with embarrassment.

Popi could not help but smile, "How are you feeling now, my *Lillé?*"

"Much better, thank you," she answered in a whisper. She sat up and looked at the chief. She had a strange feeling of *déjà vu again,* and once again, brushed it aside. He was a huge man; his tall frame bespoke strength and power — a real *Chief* to respect! He had long wavy hair, almost grey all over, and one could still notice a few strands of the natural color he had before; dark blond with some red tints in some places. Though his forefront was intimidating and scary, he had friendly eyes. The girl then remembered what Popi said about them being soft inside and hardcore on the outside.

The girl forced a smile and said, "I'm so sorry for the drama. You must be Chief Thorarin. Popi was kind enough to explain a few things to me when we were on the beach." She was holding Popi's hand for comfort — not realizing how tight she was squeezing. She was trying hard to control herself in her situation.

Thorarin was scared to speak; however, the girl needed to get used to it, seeing that she would be living with them and he couldn't go around not speaking for fear of her fainting. He tried speaking in a lower tone, "Well, I'm sorry to hear about your predicament. I'm sure your memories will come back to you soon enough." He gave a pause, testing his voice. She seemed fine and not fainting.

Popi and the chief's son, Thord, started laughing, and the girl looked confused. Popi patted the girl on the hand and reassured her it was nothing; she would explain later. She was amused at the chief trying to soothe his voice, though to no avail.

Chief Thorarin did not find it funny, gave the two a look, and went on speaking, "Popi has been telling me a lot about your troubles. I believe you were very ill when you arrived. You look healthier by the looks of it – thanks to Popi. Well, for now, you will come to learn a lot on this island and learn that we are very different from your kind."

"Thank you, chieftain," was all she could muster!

Popi spoke with a giggle still in her voice, "She remembers small things. However, I'm afraid it will take longer as she's not in familiar surroundings and we can't send her back, to whom we don't know. She'll remember when certain things trigger a memory." —Popi explained what she meant.

Thord stood listening, and when Popi finished, there was a pause in the room. He knew his sister had no manners or any interest in the new visitor; thus, he introduced her.

"This is my sister, Kiti; she will show you to your room later and appoint a handmaiden for you."

The girl was slightly stunned that they had handmaidens waiting on them, or was it just for Kiti's benefit? She cannot remember whether she had one herself. The girl greeted her, and Kiti just nodded and continued speaking to her father in her native tongue, which seemed ill-mannered! The girl decided to ignore her rudeness. She had other more important things to ponder over.

She noticed that Thord and his sister were very alike. They had the same golden blond hair, but hers was much longer. Her body was slim and delicate, long-limbed, and gorgeous. Her eyes were the same color as Thord's, which held no welcome — not like her brother and father. Kiti wore a linen dress that revealed too much in the girls' eyes. The girl couldn't hear or understand what they were saying and turned to speak to Popi.

The girl whispered, "I thought you left me! You could have forewarned me that you were going ahead. My heart almost stopped, thinking I must face them alone!"

Popi laughed and also spoke in a soft voice, "Sorry, my dear, you looked preoccupied when Thord came to you. I thought you were fine, so I decided to go ahead and speak to the chief before you got here. I never thought you would think I left you.

"However, I am here now and must leave soon. You need to get used to me not being around. Don't worry too much about Kiti. She's not as bad as she seems. She's just like her mother, both controlling and demanding women with a huge heart and love for their people. It will take some time for her to get used to you, you being an outsider and all."

The girl could swear she saw sadness in Popi's eyes when she spoke of Kiti's mother. She realized now was not the time to ask questions. The girl took a sip of her mead and noticed her mug for the first time. It was made from real horns of an animal, and a stand was designed to make it stand up straight. She was fascinated by this new treat.

Kiti left the room without saying a word. The chief gave all his attention to the new arrival in his house. He noticed she was pretty with delicate skin. The girl would occasionally steal a glance at his son. He couldn't blame her as Thord was a handsome young man. However, this could mean trouble if any feelings should brew between them. The chief trusted his son to know the rules and try to keep her at a distance.

He noted that Thord gives no notice to her presence — or was trying not to. Either way, he would still need to speak to him on this matter, just to set things straight.

"So, young lady, I hope your stay on our island has been pleasant so far, and Popi has treated you well? How do you like our island? I don't believe you have seen much with you being sick?" Chief Thorarin asked.

The girl smiled and looked at Popi.

"What I have seen thus far is amazing, and I would love to explore more! Popi has been dear to me and I'm sorry to leave her so soon. She's been incredibly loving and caring. I'm grateful for all she has done. I believe I should give thanks to Thord as well. As I don't know what happened, and from what Popi has told me, he was the one who brought me here?"

The girl wanted to know what happened and was hoping he would catch on and tell her. Thord just smiled and did not respond. Kiti re-entered the room and took her place next to her father. Popi started to explain how it was during the first few weeks on the beach. There were a few laughs; she was an excellent storyteller.

The girl noticed that everyone was very fond of Popi; it was as though she was part of the family. She would need to ask her about this at some point. Popi failed to mention her relations to the chief through her storytelling on the beach, but when could she ask her?

Was she free to roam the island – or forbidden to leave this house? She was too scared to ask any questions as to what the rules were while living with them. Popi stood up and said she had to leave and saw the girl looked petrified to be left alone.

"Thorarin, it's always a pleasure seeing you. I have to take leave; my family is expecting me back soon. *Lillé*, walk me out, and when you get back, Kiti will show you to your room." Popi gave Kiti a look that said 'behave' and gave her a loving smile.

Kiti smiled back and said, "Bye, Aunt Popi. Your next visit should be longer. We don't see you as often as we used to and would like to."

Thord kissed Popi on the cheek and excused himself from the room.

When they were outside, the girl exploded with questions, "Aunt? Why haven't you told me, and what have you not told me? When will I see you again – are you related to her mother – what happened to her mother – and why haven't you told me?"

"Odin's sweet breath, my child! You are asking too many questions all at once. I will see you again and will explain. However, now is not the time! We have a short time to say goodbye and remember to listen and obey the chief at all times. If you have any problems, come see me when you can, I will leave the horse for you. It is yours for now." Popi hugged her.

"So, you mean I can leave here and visit you whenever I want to and explore the island if I wish?"

"Of course, little one, but you have to get used to living in this house. You can visit tomorrow and help as you have been doing so far. Sigrid will fetch you in the early hours. You can't go roaming on your own; it might not be safe yet to do so.

"If you wish to go out, ask Cnut or Sigrid to accompany you. Wait until after the first celebration feast to roam around, where everyone can get to know you. I have explained to you about the first week of summer?"

"Yes, I remember, Popi! Just nerves and all, you must understand."

"Yes, I understand, child. Take the time to learn our ways and how things are done on the island. You never know; maybe you will become one of us!"

Popi regretted saying that – it just slipped off her tongue. Words she could not take back either. Giving the child hope was cruel. She knew the girl would eventually go back to her own kind. When that will be was up to the chief. She did not know what else to say – the child looked hopeful. She kissed her on the cheek, gave a last hug, then turned and walked away. The girl could not see the sadness in Popi's eyes.

She stood for a while, watching Popi climb on her horse and ride off, building up courage before going back in. Kiti stood waiting at the stairs for her, and in a high-pitched voice, said, "You can follow me!"

They walked up to the first landing and went down the corridor past a few doors; Kiti showed no interest in communicating with her. Was it possible that Kiti had taken an intense dislike to her in such a short time? *Why though?* The girl knew that they were not going to be friends anytime soon. It did not bother her — Kiti probably had her reasons. The girl also had her own concerns not to be bothered.

They came to the last door in the passage, which was behind a bend. An enormous door stood in front of her.

In a nonchalant tone, Kiti said, "This will be your room while you live here until you return to your homeland. Don't worry, it might be soon. Lunch will be served in a few hours. A handmaiden will be sent to you after supper or maybe tomorrow." She turned and walked away.

The girl watched as the ice queen left. She then stood alone staring at the closed door. It looked solid, and there was no handle! She decided to push on it and realized it was a swing door. To her surprise, it opened smoothly and quietly. It only had a latch from the inside. After the fascination of the door, she looked at the room, and once again, she was gob-smacked.

The room was stunning, and it had a fireplace. There was a huge bed, and on each side were small tables. There was a chest of drawers for her belongings, and on top was a jug of water and a bowl for washing; two towels were supplied, one small and one big.

It was more than she ever expected. She was blessed with a small balcony, which had a view of the ocean. She could see part of the yard and a small area of the village as well. There were trees and beautiful flowers everywhere.

The girl stood staring and fell in love with the place immediately. She wanted to forget about what happened this morning; all she wanted to do was fall on that soft bed and sleep. She drank too much mead to calm her nerves and decided to rest for a while; lunch was still a long way away. She had nothing better to do anyway.

She first unpacked her new clothes before resting and found another strange bag at the foot of the bed. When she opened it to inspect, she found garments and a few well-made dresses. Not like the Vikings, but more modern, and other items as well. She closed the bag and left it alone, not sure whom it belonged to — she would have to ask. She laid down and very soon fell asleep.

Bells started ringing loudly, and she jumped with fright off the bed. *How long have I been sleeping? Have I missed lunch? They are going to be so upset with me!* The mead she drank must have knocked her out. She ran to the washbasin, washed her face, combed her hair, and put on a different outfit. Thinking she looked all right, she ran to the door and pushed it open only to find Thord about to knock. She stumbled back with fright, not expecting anyone.

"Oh, Thord! Sorry, have I missed lunch? I fell asleep and was woken by the bells ringing, and why are there bells ringing?" she wondered out loud.

Thord gave one of his heart throbbing smiles and answered, "You missed lunch and must be starving by now. The bells ring half an hour before supper. I came to fetch you to show you where we eat, seeing that you don't know your way around the house yet."

She never thought of that or bothered to ask Kiti. She also noticed that they don't change for supper, so why did she? She smiled shyly and thanked him for his kindness. She would have wandered all over the house and opening all sorts of doors, which would have been extremely embarrassing.

Before she closed the door, he noticed her bag was untouched where he placed it and asked, "I'm sorry I have not brought your personal belongings earlier, but I heard you received new outfits and thought you did not need them."

She was confused, "Excuse me. What do you mean?"

"That bag on the floor belongs to you; it was with you when I found you, so I brought it with."

"Oh, um... I had no idea. Thank you!" There was no time to ask the many questions that were flooding her mind. They would have to wait for another time.

She closed the door and followed him. They walked down the stairs to the main hall and entered one of the many doors. This room was more superior to the ones she had seen before. She told herself not to be surprised anymore and just accept it. She will be amazed a lot, but will eventually get used to it soon, as everything was still new to her.

There was a long table in the center of the room and a few others scattered around, with a fireplace burning in one corner, which kept the room warm. At the entrance were two bowls of the same milky-colored water to wash your hands, as was done at Popi's home. It would seem that this was performed all over the village.

One had to wash the day's filth off before entering and eating. One of the servants stood there to assist the people. He also had to make sure the bowls were refilled with clean, warm water when it got too dirty and add the special liquid made for these moments. The liquid gave it that extra help to cleanse the dirt off.

After they both washed and dried their hands, Thord led her to their table. Once she was seated, he walked towards his sister at the other end of the table. The girl was a little disappointed. She had these strange feelings whenever she came close to him. She never had such feelings before; they just seemed to flow through her mind lately, which was very disturbing. She tried to shake it away and looked around at who was present at the table. A robust short man came to sit next to her and greeted her.

"Hi! I'm Olaf. I am pleased to meet you, little lady." He was a strange man. He had thick hair with a thick beard — a short, round man; not fat as his body seemed solid, he also looked incredibly strong. He had a friendly face, and she took a liking to him straight away. She gave him a sweet smile and greeted him back. For Olaf, that was an invitation for conversation.

"You know you are famous on this island — you are the main talk on everyone's lips. I'm pleased to be seated next to you. The last time someone was this famous was when I was born!" He made her laugh — she liked him.

Olaf went on speaking, "Don't worry, you are safe when I'm around." He smiled and started dishing food onto his plate. "You better grab what you can; this bunch doesn't waste time eating, and all we shall eat," he ended with a hearty laugh.

The chief gave their gods a short blessing for the food; everyone picked up their wooden spoons and knocked it three times on the table before digging in.

A lavish meal spread all over the table, fresh bread and lots of meat, potatoes and vegetables. She wanted to laugh watching everyone eat and realized why it was essential to wash your hands before meals — most items were eaten by hand!

The girl took a piece of red meat and some potatoes. Olaf poured her a drink and filled his to the full. The eating began, and the conversation was everywhere at once. She ate very slowly and spoke to a man on her left as well. Olaf spoke most of the time and made her chuckle a lot. She noticed the chief sat at the head of the table. He was still the biggest man in the room. His chair was different from everyone else's.

She smiled and was not surprised that Olaf was not joking about them finishing all the food. During their meal, he offered to share some drinks to taste and complied as not to offend him. He found it funny the way she kept pulling her face with each sip. She soon felt a bit warm inside and decided to stop. To make a fool of herself on her first night would not be appropriate.

With the food all gone, a few stood up to leave. Others were still seated in conversation. Olaf stood up and pulled her chair for her to stand. She thanked him with a pleasing smile, but what was she to do now? She slept almost all day and was wide-awake.

Thord came to her side once more. The two men greeted each other by grabbing each other's shoulders. Still holding the man, Thord asked her, "I hope my friend didn't make a nuisance of himself? Olaf has a way with the ladies." They both roared with laughter. She just smiled.

Olaf said goodnight to his friend, then turned to her and said, "It was good to meet you, and I hope to see you in the village soon." He took the girl's hand and kissed it. She blushed, and both men started laughing again.

Thord led her out, and once in the big hall, he asked her, "Would you like to go for a walk in the gardens? It's fitting to walk after such a large meal. Olaf, on the other hand, drinks further until he can't anymore," and laughed.

The girl was happy, she wasn't ready for bed yet, and a walk would be great.

EIGHT

The girl could not sleep after walking with Thord in the garden. She was standing on her balcony and went over the evening's events with a dreamy look in her eyes.

It was a beautiful night; the moon was full and bright — it lit up the sky to almost daylight. It seemed so close; you could reach out and touch it. The stars were scattered like moondust — flashing and flickering above them. She was in awe at such gorgeous scenery and the person walking next to her — a handsome, stunning man.

Thord treated her with kindness and spoke of his tribe with pride in his voice. She could hear how proud he was to be a Viking. The girl hung on to every word he said. He talked for a while before asking her if any memories had returned.

She explained Jessie to him, knowing her name but not the person, and how certain things triggered a memory. She knew what her parents looked like; however, she couldn't remember them as parents or what kind of people they were. He listened intently and without interrupting. There were a few other people in the garden who greeted them when passing. She only had eyes for the man next to her. The girl worked up the courage to ask him about the day he found her. When she asked, Thord thought about it before answering. He explained where he found her and what happened thereon.

She wondered who left her there and why. It all sounded as though she was thrown away and left for someone else to find. *But that couldn't be,* she thought. She was hidden; therefore, whoever left her there, planned to return, and if that person returned and found her gone, they must still be searching! She thought it was considerate of him, a stranger, to care for a sick person on the road.

It was more than just that for Thord. He always had a fair judgment of people and a sixth sense about any situation – the girl was one of them. He knew that leaving her there was not an option. She would still play an important part in their lives. He couldn't comprehend what part yet, or when it would happen. But when it did, he would know.

The subject was bringing her mood down as she concentrated hard on memories that wouldn't surface. She knew she shouldn't force it. To change the subject, she noticed a beautiful rose garden near the house, which grabbed her attention. The roses were all different colors, and they were starting to bloom.

"Oh my, this is so beautiful!" She walked toward them.

Thord explained, "My mother used to love roses. This was her favorite spot; she used to spend many hours keeping it weed-free. In her memory, we keep it tidy and the way she would approve."

"The roses are gorgeous, and all these colors mixed — I've never seen it before. I think I like roses as well."

Thord stared at her while she spoke and noticed when her expression changed at the end of her sentence. The girl took a step back, seemed dizzy, or about to faint. He was worried and not sure how to handle the situation if anything should happen.

He touched her on her shoulder and asked, "Are you all right? Should I send for Popi?" He sounded concerned.

She slowly looked up and faced him. First with a straight face, then a smile started to appear and grew wider. All at once, frightening Thord, she started laughing out loud, jumped up and hugged him. Not knowing what was happening, he hugged her back and smiled, thinking that she lost her mind. She seemed happy about something.

"Oh, Thord, how wonderful!" She grabbed his hands while speaking, "Remember I told you how certain things trigger a memory?"

"Yes...?"

"Well, the roses have done that. I know what my name is!"

"Well, what is it?" he asked, smiling in return and was happy for her with her discovery.

She let go of his hands and stood proudly, saying, "It's Rosaline Labella Dumont, but my parents called me Rose." She wanted to shout her name out so everyone could hear, and she couldn't wait to share the news with Popi and her family.

"That's a beautiful name." He gave a slight bow, "Pleased to meet you, Rose."

Rose blushed and was thankful for the dark. It only just occurred to her then how she reacted. She straightened herself and took a step back, thinking he must believe that she had gone insane.

"I'm so sorry I jumped you like that. You must think me a fool! You must believe I was not thinking at the time."

It was his time to laugh, "Don't apologize; it's understandable in this situation."

"I wish I could tell Popi somehow; waiting until morning is going to kill me!"

Still laughing and understanding how she must be feeling and how fond she was of Popi, he said, "Well, it is still early, and I believe they are still awake." He was expecting her to be happy with the offer.

"I can't! Popi told me not to leave the house, especially alone. It will have to wait until morning." She Looked disappointed, totally misunderstanding him.

"Silly, Rose, I will take you and bring you back. Come, it won't take long." He led her to the stables to get their horses.

She did not say a word until they were on their way. Thord saying her name for the first time sounded like a song from his lips.

Rose ran straight into Popi's house. She was surprised to see the girl and was worried.

"My dear child, what are you doing here? Did something bad happen — and why do you look so flushed?"

Just then, Thord walked in. "Hello, Aunt Popi."

"What's going on?" she asked, looking concerned.

"I have the greatest news ever!" Rose exclaimed, "I remember my name, and I could not wait until tomorrow to tell you, so Thord offered to bring me. Hope you're not mad!"

Sigrid, hearing the commotion, came out to see what was happening and heard the news.

She was thrilled for her friend, "Oh, how wonderful! So what is it? What's your name?" Sigrid demanded to know.

Popi was smiling this time and let them be. This *was* big news, and she understood why she could not wait. "Don't keep us hanging. Tell us, dear."

"Rosaline, Rose for short. My full names are Rosaline Labella Dumont."

"Well now, isn't that a mouth full and a beautiful name too. It suits you," Popi said, smiling. Vikings had only one name; there was no need for middle or surnames. You were called on your birth name, and that was it.

Thord sat and watched how the girls were overjoyed with her name returning.

Sigrid hugged Rose and said, "Why did we not think of a flower name for you? There are so many beautiful names. You might have remembered sooner!" They all laughed.

They spoke for a while longer, then Thord said they had to leave. On their way back to the main house, Rose thanked him for his time and understanding.

"It was nothing, and I had nothing better to do with my time," he said, giving her that dazzling smile.

When Thord walked her to her door, she wished he would kiss her. She had no idea why she wanted that to happen, but she did. The thought of it made her blush. She was being silly and was confused about her feelings toward this handsome man and everything that had just happened. He smiled at her, a smile that made her knees weak. He then bid her good night and left.

Rose went to her bed to lie down; she was wide awake and wondered how she would sleep after all the excitement of the evening's events. There was nothing to do, and even so, she had to be up early for work.

Not long, there was a knock on her door, and hoped it was him — who else could it be! She jumped to open the door.

To her disappointment, a woman in her early twenties stood staring at her. "Yes, can I help you?"

"Evening, miss. My name is Magdalene. Miss Kiti appointed me to be your handmaiden. The chief asked me to help explain some of their traditions to you as well, especially about the festivals."

Magdalene sounded like them; however, she looked different. "May I come in, miss? We can discuss what you expect my duties to be."

"Oh yes, I'm so sorry, how rude of me, please come in, Magdalene – pleased to meet you as well. My manners ran away from me for a second. My thoughts were elsewhere." Rose opened the door further for her to enter. Magdalene was not used to such politeness and found it pleasing. It was going to be a breeze working for her rather than Kiti.

"So!" Rosaline was not sure what to say to this woman. She was more curious about how she came to this island and how long she had been here.

"Magdalene, to be honest, I'm not sure what to say to you? What have you done for Miss Kiti?"

Everything she asks of me, miss. The usual things; tidy her room, comb her hair in the mornings and at night, and so on."

"It sounds about right; you can keep doing what feels normal for you. Now that we have that behind us, I can't sleep. Would you be so kind as to tell me a little about yourself? Oh, and my name is Rose."

"Pleased, Miss Rose. What would you like to know?" Magdalene was not sure why this young lady wanted to know things about her or what to say. It was unusual, and she was not sure how much she should share.

"Please help me with my hair. I think I have a few knots, and enlighten me with your story. I am only curious, that is all.

Everything is still new to me, and I love hearing stories." Rose gave her a friendly smile.

Magdalene picked up a brush and started to brush the young lady's hair. She thought to get straight to the point. Her life was just serving people, nothing else — nothing interesting; but being a servant, or as the Vikings called them, a thrall, was something else.

"Well, miss, you see me as I am — I'm an open book. My life is not that exciting at all! As far as I can remember, I was born on this island, and my mother has been here since she was as young as you. When I was younger, she explained where we came from and how life was there for her and her people. The Vikings constantly raided their town, and one day, they captured her to work on this island as a slave. We are not the free willing workers, as I can remember my mom telling me. Though, times have changed slightly on this island."

While Magdalene was speaking, she kept her eyes on Rose's hair, concentrating hard on what to say. If she looked up, she would have seen how shocked Rose was with her story so far.

Magdalene went on, "We are called thralls, and we are bound to our master to whom we belong and may never leave. The Viking law does not protect us, miss. Our master has the power of life or death over us. A thrall might also be used as a sacrifice at a funeral to serve in the spirit world. A little good news is that our master, for both hard work and loyalty, might free us.

"I inherited my mother's status as a thrall and started to work at an early age. You must understand how it was for a young child to hear all this and try to accept it. I cried a lot and received many thrashings from my father, who was also a thrall, naturally. We are not permitted to have any relations with a Viking. There's an old man that tells stories of important history of their clans. You should hear the one of the Swedish Chieftain and his thrall woman. They do not give her name, but the story is well known. It's one of many of their favorites." Magdalene was silent for a second and looked at the young lady's hair.

"Your knots are all out, Miss Rose, and may I say you have lovely hair." Magdalene looked up for the first time. Rose's expression was full of anger and disgust. Magdalene was frightened.

"Sorry, miss, you asked and I told you; please don't tell anyone, they will be furious! Times have changed a little since Chief Thorarin's father died. I see my story does not please you!"

Rose was speechless; she could not believe that they would do such things to another human being, to have no care or feelings. Rose saw the frightened look on the woman's face, who was about to turn and run.

Magdalene could kick herself for not thinking how her story could affect an outsider.

"Wait, Magdalene, I never expected your story to turn out like that. I'm so sorry that you must live this way and not have a life or choice of a life of your own. My goodness! Who is your master?"

"I was the chieftain's deceased wife's handmaiden at first. On her death, I was appointed to Miss Kiti. We fall on the next member of the family and obey them. Thralls are looked at differently nowadays. They don't sacrifice people anymore, not on this island, though. I can't complain; I've been treated well so far. I thought some history would interest you as my life is boring."

"I see! Don't you ever wish to leave or was offered to leave?"

"I do, miss, but we *are* happy here. Sometimes, I wonder how life is out there. I would like to see and experience it for myself instead of hearing it from my mother. I would love to see the world and my own kind. To learn new ways, and yes, to be free, do what I want to do, and get paid for my hard labor. We get food, and a roof over our heads, which is most I hear, but please, miss, do not speak of this to anybody," Magdalene begged her.

"I promise, Magdalene. How do your parents feel about leaving?"

"My mother is happy here and will stay even if they offer her freedom. She was not that happy before they captured her and suffered a lot from hunger and the cold. Here she is fed and clothed and is thankful for that alone. My father died two years ago of heart failure."

"Sorry to hear that."

"It's getting late, miss; I will see you tomorrow morning." Magdalene made the bed ready for Rose, ensured there was fresh water in her jug, and bid her goodnight.

Rose sat there stunned at the new information she received about the Vikings. Her walk with Thord was all forgotten. When she asked the woman to speak about herself, she never meant so openly! What did she expect anyway? Rose did ask her to tell what her life was like here. What else could she say? All that information was a blow to the head.

On his way down from bidding Rose a good night, one of his father's men approached him, "Thord, your father would like a word with you before you retire."

"Thank you, Armod. I am on my way."

When he entered, the chief poured them each a drink and motioned Thord to sit down.

"How was your evening walk with the young lady?"

Thord knew where this conversation was going!

"It was a pleasant evening for a walk after such a huge meal. You should have joined us, father. She's a delight to be around. Everyone seems to be laughing more. She remembered her name, it's Rose, actually, Rosaline. She could not wait until morning to share the good news, so I offered to take her to Popi. They were happy with the news. They are all fond of her, not just Popi. It was a happy moment."

What Thord did for her was out of kindness and an innocent gesture on his part. He had no thoughts of interest toward her. Rose is a beautiful young girl, but his people come first. Rules are rules. His father brought him up with Viking rules from a young age; he loves and respects his father too much to break any of them.

"I'm glad she has a name to call on, and it suits her well. Remember that she's an outsider, not a Viking, and will be leaving one day soon. I know, I have eyes in my head, she is attractive, but nothing can come of this. You will be chief one day and must set an example for your people. I know times are changing, but one thing at a time, please, my son." There was sadness in his voice. Old family history — the past is always there to haunt you.

His father was old-fashioned and still tried to live by the old ways as his father had done, but the chief was slowly accepting the new ways as well, as he said, one thing at a time. Thord's grandfather was more brutal in his ruling; times have changed. Thord would *always* obey his father. Everything he had done so far was to please the chieftain. There was a sad family history that no one mentions — still to this day. He did not want to disappoint him. The pain was still festering.

"I know this, father; I'm trying to make her feel welcome, that is all. She is a sweet young girl, and I know my place. I do feel sorry for her memory loss. It can't be easy not remembering who you are or your past. It was truly an innocent gesture on my behalf, nothing to worry about!"

"That is fine, my son. You are all I have and my only heir, and your sister, of course, though, she cannot run my island." He had different aspirations for his daughter. He went on, "A good marriage would do her good, but she's stubborn just like her mother! She wants to hear nothing of marriage."

Thord could not help but laugh. He was very close to his sister and had an earful about her thoughts on the matter; he would never share this with their father. It was not pretty!

Thorarin was pleased with his son. They continued speaking about their next trading mission, where they would be going, and trading supplies. Thorarin decided to go on this voyage with his son. He was pondering on the idea of an early retirement, stepping down so Thord would have to take his place as chief. He believed his son was ready.

NINE

Meanwhile, back at the village of Chinon, Jessie was distraught. She had failed her Lord and Rose; she had broken her promise to them both. Panic-stricken, Jessie rushed around looking for her. While searching, she pondered over the events of the past few days.

Half of the town's people succumbed to the measles, and many left for other places. On his deathbed, Lord Jacq begged Jessie to take his beloved Rose away from the pestilence that invaded their town. He asked that she try her best to save his daughter, and when she's well, to take her to the castle. He was sure the king would care for her and that she would have a safe and happy life with his son, Philippe.

Jessie promised that she would do all she could for Rose and always be there for her whenever needed. Jacq passed away the following morning and was buried next to his wife.

The house was raided not long afterward, and all their horses were stolen. A few days later, she packed some of Rose's belonging and hid her well along the river. She promised to return with a pull-cart and more supplies. Jessie thought Rose was safe where she left her! No one was about, and the roads were tranquil. So, how did she disappear? She was sure she hid Rose well behind the big rock, but when she returned just over an hour later – Rose was gone!

She noticed many horse and shoe prints around the area and stressed for the innocent girl. How stupid she was to leave her alone! No time for regrets or ifs and maybes. No matter how long it takes, she will do her best to find Rose and keep her promise to her father.

Jessie tried to ignore the twinge of guilt she felt for abandoning Rose. Her first destination would have to be toward the castle. Whoever found her must know who she was and must have taken her there – hopefully. She would have to search the house one last time; maybe Rose stood up and walked home by herself, which was unlikely in her state!

Everyone knew who Rose was and was promised to marry the king's second eldest son, Philippe, who recently turned twenty-one. The family had been preparing to visit the king for two weeks and then announce it.

Jacq had not informed his daughter about the betrothal to the prince. He was hoping that once they met again, the two would decide to unite in marriage. They had met on numerous occasions in the past and seemed fond of each other, but Jacq's plans changed when they heard of the illness spreading and decided to wait. Then his wife Sara fell ill, and the disease spread rapidly. He never left his wife's side and became infected too.

Jessie turned the cart around and started toward the castle — not knowing that Rose was far away in the opposite direction out of town.

King Louis's eldest son, Louis II, died. He was the one who brought the virus to the Kingdom.

He went to visit his bride-to-be, and it was there that he became ill. His betrothed passed away, and he returned with a broken heart. Not long afterward, he, too, passed away.

Philippe was to take his place. He never thought this would ever befall him. It was a huge responsibility to run a Kingdom, especially when everyone was dying and leaving. What was he supposed to do? With his father also ill in bed and not knowing the outcome, he was stressed out.

Prince Philippe was an outgoing person and loved to have fun with hardly any responsibilities. But now, much sooner than he anticipated, he would have all this on his plate! His younger brother, Antoine, who was eighteen, was more dependable. When Philippe was outside having fun, Antoine was inside reading and learning. Philippe thought that his younger brother would be a better ruler than he could ever be.

When he mentioned his fears to Antoine, he wholeheartedly disagreed and promised to help Philippe become a good king and be his right-hand-man — if it came to that. Their father was not dead yet.

The priest stayed with the king and cleansed the room, praying for three hours at a time. From his bed, he gave orders for Philippe. The king instructed that all the dead must be buried or burnt outside the castle walls. The Kingdom was vulnerable, and he feared that they might be in a war for their land. His guards were sparsely spread all over the Kingdom.

News arrived that Jacq, his leading general, was deceased by the illness, along with his wife. Thus, a new general had to be appointed.

For now, Philippe would take the lead of that position until a new general could be appointed from the surviving defense force. His first orders were to keep the castle well guarded. While Philippe obeyed his father's orders, his brother went through the Kingdom's finances. The tax income dwindled, and there were food shortages – soon to result in famine.

It took longer than Jessie thought to get to the castle with her old steed. When she arrived a few days later, she heard the castle was closed to all. No one could get in or out. She restlessly waited at the main gate, trying to get in or send a message. The guards would not budge or listen to anything she had to say. Their orders were strict about keeping all outsiders out – no matter what.

Jessie had never been to the castle before; this was her first time, and felt scared and uneasy. All she wanted to do was leave a message to inform the king that Rose was missing – taken! She had no wish or any interest to see or meet the king.

A messenger was ordered to look in at Rose and to determine her health. He had to bring her to the castle if she was well. Philippe knew about the betrothal with Rose. She lost her parents and was alone; he was fond of her and felt very sorry for her loss. She could stay in the castle until they both agreed concerning the date of their marriage.

Upon leaving the palace, Jessie recognized the messenger and thought it was a blessing. She anxiously rushed to him, asking if he saw Lord Jacq's daughter, Rosaline, in the castle.

"No, ma'am, no one saw Lady Rose here. I was told to escort her to the castle. Is she missing?"

Jessie's mind, full of thoughts about where the girl could be, did not answer him straight away. Maybe she was with Anthony, Lord Jacq's assistant in Chinon. He helped collect the monthly taxes and assisted Jacq with the daily problems in their small town. Yet, somehow, she knew Rose was not with him — he secured himself in his house, too scared to leave! When Jacq's household started getting sick, Anthony locked himself in his home and must either be dead or still in hiding.

Jessie decided to spread the news; more eyes looking for Rose would help and maybe find her sooner.

"Could you please inform the King that Rose is missing and was last seen close to her home? We need to put the word out and search for her."

"Will do, ma'am."

Returning to the exact location where she last left Rose, Jessie followed the road they would have taken out of town. Days had passed before she ran into people camping on the road. She asked them if they saw anything suspicious or bandits on their path. They told her about the strange-looking people who passed by about a month ago. The trip to the castle had delayed her. She should have followed her instincts but could not fathom that she was taken — what would anyone want with a sick girl? Hardly any strangers came through their town. She was confused as to whom these strangers were and wondered if they could have taken her.

Jessie cared for their sick and asked for more information about these foreigners.

They must have left as soon as they saw what was going on in these parts. So why did they take Rose then — a sick girl? Jessie stressed for her. She prayed that Rose was safe until she found her again.

Jessie kept following the road and acquired as much information she could from the squatters, whether they'd seen these strange people and which direction they went. She followed all the signs and listened closely to their descriptions of them. Some said you couldn't miss them. They were dressed differently and were huge with long hair and long beards, and some were tall and muscular.

After traveling for a long time, she ended up in a small village close to the shore. Her horse was old and slow. She could not push him and had to rest a lot. He was given to her as a gift when she was only a child. She loved her horse as one would love any pet. He was family and the only link she had to her mother that was so far away. If she lost her steed, she would have to carry and half drag her belongings behind her.

Arriving at a tavern, she ordered a hot meal and asked the innkeeper to tend to her horse. She placed two silver shillings on the table.

"Yes, ma'am, would you be staying for the night as well?"

"No, thank you." Jessie sat down at one of the empty tables and waited for her food. She preferred to sleep outdoors; she was used to it, and it would keep the little money she saved in case of an emergency. She had a lot saved up, but she could not risk a penny not knowing what would happen next. The night was warm, and her small carriage would do just fine.

Being a middle-aged Indian woman, Jessie had spent many nights outside; it was like going home. She preferred it most of the time as it reconnected her to her ancestors. She missed her people and their ways and was sure she would never return to them. Jessie was once very happy with her people until her husband was murdered. They were married young and were very much in love. With her loss, she decided to leave — searching for happiness in this world to ease her pain.

When she was little, her mother taught her everything she knew about medicine. There was a close bond between mother and daughter. When Jessie told her mother she was leaving, she begged her to stay, worrying that the outsiders may not treat her well or accept her and her strange ways.

She was wrong. There were good people in this world, like the Dumont's — Rose's family. Jessie's mother had a bad experience when she was young while helping others with herbs and medication knowledge. Jessie returned to the same place where her mother was at that time, to see, or if possible, to meet her father in person.

No one knew about the bloodline except her mother and herself. Yet, she could never go close to where he lived and refused Lord Jacq once when he asked her to help him heal *her father*. She sent Lord Jacq with the herbs and told him what to do. Thankfully, he never questioned her. Jacq saw the scared look on her face and just left it at that.

Her father had no knowledge of her existence; just the thought of that man violating her mother at an innocent age made her blood boil. To think she was the result of such a bad experience and not a product of love saddened her. Her mother loved her and always protected her through everything that happened — she missed her so much! Maybe she would go home in the near future, but not yet, she still had a lot to do, and it felt as though she was just getting started.

Jessie was at a loss and didn't know where to go from here. It was a dead end. She ate her food, and when the woman came to fetch her bowl, she asked her about the strangers.

"Yes, ma'am, they were here, but not for long. They hired a few horses for a few weeks; however, they came back soon afterward. Their ship was waiting not far out, and they sailed straight away."

"Did you speak to them? What did they say?"

"The man I spoke to was incredibly gorgeous — if you don't mind me saying. He said there was a virus spreading, and they would return when it was safe again. I hope it doesn't reach this side of the island!"

"Have you seen them before or know who they are?" Jessie hoped that the young woman knew them and could get some useful information pointing her in the right direction.

"No, ma'am, I've been working here for many years and have never seen the likes of them before. They were new to these parts. They also asked for directions to the castle and enquired about possible trading locations."

Jessie was a little confused with this information and could not guess who they were. They could have been anyone from anywhere in the world. Her worries grew more for Rose.

"Oh! Have you seen a young girl with them?"

"No, ma'am. Sorry!"

There was no way for her to purchase a passage on a ship in search of Rose. Jessie had no idea which way they went, where they were going, or who they were, but they did say they would return. She would wait for as long as it took to find her again. It was driving her insane, not knowing and not being able to do anything to save her precious Rose.

When she first arrived at this place, she was alone; it was just her and her steed. The Dumont's were the first folks to accept her ways and healing techniques. She had the utmost respect for the family and would do anything for them. Everything that has happened between them, united them in a close bond. They automatically made her a member of the family and treated her as such and nothing less. Now, she lost their little girl and felt beaten. Jessie found a nice safe spot for the night and rested her weary head.

After many agonizing months, the epidemic was finally over. The sick were getting better, and the dead that were locked up in certain houses were cleared and were burnt or buried.

TEN

Every morning, Sigrid and Cnut took turns to fetch Rose, and on some occasions, ride around the island. She eagerly wanted to learn and understand their language; thus, she would point at something during these adventures, and they would say what it's called. Rose would then repeat it, trying her best to pronounce the word correctly. This way, she learned the basics of the language, enabling her to understand the gist of conversations even though she did not understand it all. Her strong will helped her to learn at a fast pace, and she was a quick study.

The season celebrations were close — you could feel the anticipation in the air. Everyone was helping where they could — everything needed to be prepared before then. Rose always helped Popi in the kitchen when she needed an extra hand.

Rose could not sew like most women on the island and considered finding a profession to suit her so they wouldn't think she was spoiled and of no use. She could cook but not that well. Fieldwork was not permitted for women – only at harvest time when the extra hands were needed.

She always had an interest in herbs and healing. She wondered if she should ask Popi if it would be all right to teach her the trade alongside Sigrid.

On one occasion, Popi sent Rose out to deliver food to Var; at the time, Rose thought it was his lunch. However, thinking back, she knew Popi did this on purpose for her to see what he was doing and to get used to their customs.

When approaching, she found him digging a hole in the middle of the field. He took the food that contained the fresh bread and eggs, placed them in the hole, and poured the honey over it. He recited a prayer for Freya and then closed the gap. Rose witnessed Var send a gift to a god named Freya. He told her that Freya was a fertility god and was mostly called upon for their crops to grow. Var explained that in doing so, and if the gods were satisfied with the offerings, the crops would grow satisfactorily.

After the hole was covered, he laid rocks around the offering area. This will be his ritual place from now on. Whenever it was needed, he would come to give offerings and thanks to his god. Rose did not believe in such things but respected his beliefs. She was brought up to believe in one God, the maker of all things. They believed in more than one, and it muddled her brain to try to understand them all.

While riding around with Sigrid and Cnut some afternoons, she found many of these sacred ritual sites. If she hadn't witnessed Var's offering, she would have thought nothing of it. She heard they were everywhere and anywhere, in meadows, fields, groves, hillocks, and shores of swampy lakes. These ritual areas were sometimes enclosed with a simple fence made of ropes or huge stones. They had no statues or idols of their gods or a special place like a temple. They did not need a priest to tell them what or who to worship. They had their own beliefs and were happy that way. Who was she to judge? She was fascinated with these people, with how they lived, and all the gods they worshipped. She wished she believed in something so strongly!

The rides around the island were exciting for her — she had never seen so many different flowers and exotic birds before. It was beautiful and sometimes dangerous with the wildlife running around. One had to be careful!

It was two days before the festival, and there was no work for Rose indoors, so they sent her to work with Var. It was not permitted now, but he gladly put her to work. He gave her a hard workout in the fields that day. The seeds were sown and covered.

Var preferred to stay outdoors through lunchtime. He explained that being inside made him lazy and he tended to stay longer than was necessary — wasting time. She understood and enjoyed the peace and tranquility as well.

Early in the afternoon, she was resting under a tree, enjoying the cool shade and eating a sandwich, giving a person time to think or just be. Var was busy with a water system that ran from the stream to keep the crops watered. He told Rose it mostly only rained in spring and autumn. That's when the hard work started — this was child's play. She took the last bite of her sandwich when Cnut approached.

"Fancy a walk with me, Rose?"

"Would your father not mind?" She did not want to upset Var.

"I spoke to him, and he said it's fine. He said he had a lot done with our help, so we can relax for the day."

"In that case, I would love to!" When they started walking, Rose said, "It's easier working for your father. Your mother would never say anything like that!" They both chuckled with the truth.

Rose asked, "Where are we walking to?" She was always pleased to see him, and it was pleasant to be in his company. They have grown close in the short time since meeting.

"Nowhere in particular, just feel like walking." They walked for a while before Cnut spoke again, "Rose, do you miss your island and the people?"

"I think I do — I mean, I grew up there. To be truly honest, Cnut, I feel there's nothing there for me anymore. I wish to see my parents again someday and share all this with them. I do miss them even though I can't remember them so well. I so love it here, and strangely enough, I feel that I belong here and feel at home. Does that sound silly?"

"No, not at all. We all feel that you are a part of our family. How is your memory coming along?"

"Not as much as it used to, and I don't know why? I'm not letting that bother me, though. Your mom said to let it come on its own and not to force it. The last one was my name, and that was it." She thought back to that moment. They were all so happy, especially Sigrid. She said 'Rose' in every sentence; Rose this and Rose that. It made her laugh every time.

"My memory of Jessie, if your mother told you, also has the healing powers. I can't see her face, which is weird, but I remember what she taught and shared with me about certain herbs. I remember them just by looking at the herbs, and I still find that very interesting."

"Do you think you'll want to be a healer one day like mom and Sigrid?"

"I believe that I could be good at it, yes, but we'll see what happens. For now, I am just happy to be part of something and having a family again." She smiled sweetly at him.

Cnut was confused about his feelings towards Rose. She was a stunning girl and easy to get along with — he felt protective of her.

"Rose?"

"Yes, Cnut?"

"I want to be serious with you for a minute, and please don't laugh or be angry!" He always seemed to upset his sisters. They were hard on him most of the time. However, lately, Sigrid was cooling down toward him. It was hard for him to be so open with a girl, any girl for that matter, who was not his sister.

"What do you mean? I will never be angry with you! Just tell me what's on your mind." She saw the serious look on his face and said, "I promise I won't be angry!"

"Well, I want to tell you... Um... that I care about you and that I will always be there for you if ever you need a friend!"

"That's so sweet, thank you, Cnut. I care for you too. Why should I be angry with such kind words?" Rose could understand why he said, don't laugh. If she laughed at his sincere attitude, he would probably have difficulty sharing any serious words with a girl in future.

"Don't know. I have not told anyone before how much they mean to me. I guess you might have taken it the wrong way or something like that?"

"Never! I'm touched that you care so much."

They were silent for a few seconds, contemplating what to say next.

Speaking to him was so easy. Rose felt she could speak her mind and heart, and he would always listen and try to understand.

"It is good to have a friend or any friends at this time," she continued, thinking about Sigrid as well, "It sometimes feels that I'm all alone in this world!"

"You will always have us, Rose. We will always be here for you!"

"Thank you, Cnut. I am grateful to be part of your family. What I'm trying to say, that in my mind and heart, I believe I was an only child, and I never knew what it felt like to have a brother or a sister. Since I met your mom, she has always been so kind to me. Then meeting you all and getting to know you, having you all share your lives with me makes me feel as though I know what it feels like to have a big family, and I love you all so much!

"To be honest with you, I wish my memories stay hidden. I'm scared to tell if they do surface because they will send me back when that happens. So, you see, I'm in two minds. On the one hand, I want to return to see my parents again, and on the other, I don't, so I don't ever have to leave."

"If you feel you want to share a memory without anyone knowing, I'm all ears. I won't tell a soul!" He gave her a naughty smile.

Rose laughed! "I'll keep that in mind and hold you to your promise."

Cnut smiled and looked relaxed again. "Would you like to see my special place? I like to go there sometimes to be alone. It's stunning and is not far from here. We walked halfway into the woods already."

Rose gave him a huge smile, "Lead the way!" She was always excited to see new places.

When they eventually reached the place, Rose thought it was worth the walk — she was amazed once again!

"Are you telling me no one knows about this spot? I can't believe it!"

"Well, not that I know of. No one has bothered me before. Thus, I made it my special place. It could be yours as well if you wish?"

"This is truly amazing, and thanks for sharing this with me. I will never tell a soul about this place – I promise!" Rose would love a private bath and thought this place would be perfect. As agreed, she could not invite Sigrid. She would need to sneak away or leave early to visit here first.

Cnut took his shoes and shirt off and jumped into the water, laughing.

"It's warmer than the ocean; you should try it. Don't worry, the fishes don't bite," he plunged underwater.

While he was swimming, Rose sat down to admire the place. There was a small rocky hill, and it looked like it was easy to climb. A gentle stream was bubbling over the rock, gracefully plunging into the pool below where Cnut was enjoying himself. It was music to her ears. Tall willow trees and bushes were hiding the place nicely – it looked very private. The water looked so inviting, except she had nothing to swim in, and although he was still innocent, his thoughts might not be. She would have to wait!

Rose was thinking of her mother when they were in the river and how she would have loved this place.

Cnut climbed out and sat down next to her.

They were quiet for a while before he spoke up, "I think we should leave. It's getting late, and mom might worry!"

"Yes, I agree." Rose felt she could have stayed all day. She stood to wet her face and arms before leaving.

Before they reached the open field to the house, Cnut said, "Thank you, Rose!"

"What for?"

"I don't know? It just felt right saying it."

"In that case," she laughed, "Don't mention it!"

He hit her playfully on the arm and shouted, "You're it!" —A game they both were familiar with, and he ran away laughing.

"You little bugger! Wait until I get my hands on you!" and ran after him.

Popi stood outside watching the woods and wondered what could be taking them so long; they were gone a long time. She heard Cnut laughing as he ran through the trees toward the house with Rose on his heels, trying to catch him.

Popi cared a lot for the girl and worried about the day when she would need to leave. She believed Rose's parents were dead from the measles and that the poor child must still remember that day and relive the moment once again. What will become of her, and where will she go, with no one out there to care for her? The world was not a safe place for a beautiful and innocent young lady. The men would not be so kind, and there were the jealous wives to be cautious of too. She needed a talk with the chief to voice her concern — for Rose's sake at least!

There was nothing for Rose to do at the main house, and running into Kiti was not the highlight of her day. Everyone helped where help was needed; thus, she always had a good answer when asked during supper what she had been up to all day. Chief Thorarin looked pleased that she was active. He thought he might have made a mistake in saying she needed to stay with them. He could have asked Popi to keep her until the time came for her to leave. However, it was too late now. The girl looked healthy and happy with what she was doing. Having her here kept her safe if any of the villagers harbored any ill feelings toward her.

Having Rose in the chief's house meant she was someone important. She was a proper lady where she came from and needed to be treated that way. He might be old-fashioned, but he was still decent. In a way, she was Thord's pet. He brought her here and would need to take her back when her memory returns.

The day before the celebrations, Rose was at Popi's trying her best at sewing, with her efforts being unsuccessful; however, she enjoyed spending time with the women. Astrid was there as well, mainly speaking about her new husband. Unexpectedly, she said that they were trying to have a baby.

Popi was delighted and could not wait to have a grandchild. She smiled brightly, saying, "About time too!"

Sigrid was trying to teach Rose how to sew while the other two left to make lunch.

"My sister can be a pain sometimes; blah, blah, blah is all she can do. Blab uncontrollably about herself and her new hubby, Arne. I swear her life is more important! I feel sorry for Arne's ears. I hope I'm not like that when I get married!" They both laughed.

"So, when will your day come?" Rose asked through her giggles.

"Not soon, thank the gods. My mother has other plans for me; I'm to take her place as the island's healer. She started teaching me before you arrived and then stopped for a while, but now I'm back to learning the trade. It's funny how a plant or herb can have such healing powers if you know what to do. I wonder who started all this in the first place?"

"I know what you mean. I, too, find it fascinating. I asked Jessie the same question once — she said that their ancestors used to follow sick animals to see which herbs they ate for their ailments. To think that someone actually thought of doing so is incredible."

"And you, Rose, what are your plans for the future?"

Rose shrugged at first, not sure where her future would take her. She never thought about it. "I don't know! Right now, I'm trying to remember who I am and where I come from or belong. What the future holds for me is to be seen. I don't like to think about that. I'm living from day to day and loving each day with you all."

Rose made a little joke to create a lighter atmosphere. She gave Sigrid a playful nudge and smiled, saying, "Maybe I'll be your assistant in healing. What do you say — you want a helper?"

"You, Rose, anytime. We would be great together and heal all the sick!"

They were joking around and speaking about future healing techniques when Popi and Astrid brought in their lunch.

Astrid joked, "What are you girls speaking about working together as healers? The people would die before you get to them!"

Sigrid enlightened her, "We were just discussing our future and what we are going to do one day."

Popi interrupted, "You know what the future holds for you, Sigrid. You have what I have — the healing powers. Astrid is more from your father's side of the family."

"And happy to be on that side!" interrupted Astrid. Truly thankful, she had no time or the patience for herb mixing.

"I know, mom!" Sigrid answered, "Rose is not sure about her future. So, we joked and said she could work for me."

"Popi looked at Rose, "Don't worry, dear. One day, something great is going to happen to you, and you'll be very happy."

"Something remarkable has already happened! I met all of you, and I am very happy at present. It's my long-term future that worries me. You are my family now. What will happen to me when I leave this island? Who says someone is waiting for me or that my home is still my home? It won't be the same; nothing will be the same when I leave!"

All three women felt and understood her feelings; it was distressing. Popi straightened up in her chair. "Enough of this sad talk, and let's eat. Leave everything to Popi; we will sort all that out when the time comes. It is still far off, so hush, little one. Trust in Popi. I will always care for you; we'll never leave you or let you be in any danger. Even if I have to send my Var with you to ensure your safety, I will!"

Astrid left after lunch, and Popi sent Sigrid to take her father and brother's lunch to them.

ELEVEN

The festivities began, and the island was full of hustle and bustle! The villagers were speaking loud with excitement. Smoke was escaping out of the chimneys, and the aroma of all kinds of food was permeating the air. A knock on the door roused Rose from a deep sleep.

Magdalene walked in and started speaking all at once, "Morning, miss, I'm going to explain soon what I know about the festival. We should hurry if we want to catch the main event. What will you be wearing today? They usually wear their best and brightest outfits."

Rose's mind was still foggy; she listened and watched how the hyper woman went about in her room. When she heard the word 'festival,' she jolted straight up in bed and jumped to wash her face. *The day has finally arrived!*

While they both searched for a perfect outfit for her, Magdalene went on explaining, "There will be no breakfast this morning. Soon, there will be a sacrifice held to honor the chosen gods, and then everything will begin."

"What sacrifice?" Rose had to ask.

"A sheep, Miss Rose. It's usually animals." Magdalene could not help but smile. They became close in the short time together. Magdalene liked the young lady; she still knew her place and had immense respect for Rose.

"The sacrifice is called *'Blot'*—they have three celebrations in the year, and each is named after Blot. The first is *'SigrBlot'*—the second; *'VetrarBlot'*—and the third; *'JolaBlot'*—we'll just stick to the first one for now; *'Sigrblot'*—is the first sacrifice held before the celebrations begin. It signifies the beginning of the warm season and the growth of their crops. This celebration will last for two weeks."

Rose was speechless with all the information and felt very excited all the same.

"If we hurry, miss, we'll be able to watch the sacrifice." Magdalene gave one of her biggest smiles, "It is very entertaining!"

When they left the house, they followed a crowd that was walking toward the fields. When they arrived, Magdalene took her a little closer to watch. Five men were sitting in a roundabout pit made of stones neatly packed on top of one another. In the center was another smaller pit filled with wood. The rest of the villagers were watching. She heard Magdalene speak again, whispering only for Rose to hear. She concentrated on what she was saying.

"The pile of stones is an Altar called *'Blot.'* The whole Altar itself is called *'HÖRG,'* – *'Hlaut'* also means blood. The sheep's blood, which is being sacrificed, is held in a *'Hlautbolli'*—

which means 'bowl of blood,' where the blood is poured into. Now, miss, you watch for yourself what happens next."

Rose was baffled by all the weird names. She was enthralled with what was happening and watched with interest. Chief Thorarin stood in the circle; he was busy with the wood, a small flame started to flicker, then the wood burst into flames. Thord came walking toward the Altar, carrying a lamb. He passed it on to his father, the chief, and sat with the other men inside the Altar. It appeared that the person with the highest authority led the ritual; hence, the chief.

The rest of the crowd stood watching. The chief, also still standing, sliced the sheep's neck and poured the blood into a big bowl – the 'Hlautbolli'—the bowl of blood. He then started cutting the meat off the animal. While this was happening, they began reciting a song in honor of the chosen gods. Magdalene couldn't help but explain once again. She was enjoying explaining the rituals to her new misses.

She leaned closer to explain, "They have chosen two gods to honor the sacrifice; the first is to Odin, the chief god, father of many, and the second is to Freya, a fertility god."

Magdalene was quiet once again. The chief passed the 'Hlautbolli' to the man next to him, and he had to pass it on to the next – it went around the fire three times. The same was done with the meat. During this, they recited some magical words.

The chief stood again and sprinkled himself and the others inside the Altar with the blood. He then poured the remaining blood over the dead animal in the fire. With this last act, everyone started shouting in praise and clapping their hands for the ritual was done. The sacrifice was over and it was time to celebrate.

Magdalene turned to Rose, saying, "I will be leaving you now, Miss Rose. Enjoy the feast."

"One more question, please, before you leave! What happens to the dead animal burning? Do they eat it afterward or just leave it there to burn to a crisp?"

"Good question, miss. I did not think to explain that part. When the fire dies, they bury the remains of what's left of the animal. They never eat it as it was a gift to their gods."

"Thank you, Magdalene, for your insight, and you were right — it was very entertaining!"

For the first time, Rose saw Popi and Cnut among the crowd. She walked over to join them and noticed a pile of weapons lying on the ground next to them. It would seem that no weaponry was allowed in the ritual areas. She kissed Cnut on the cheek and greeted Popi too. Her husband, Var, was speaking to Chief Thorarin.

Cnut asked, "So, how did you enjoy the 'Blot' sacrifice?"

Rose smiled at his sweet face; Cnut was Cnut; there were no two ways about him. He had a charming and open personality and got on well with others; everyone loved him.

"Oh, it was new and entertaining, indeed! Nothing that I have ever seen before — it was wonderful!" She looked around and asked, "Where is Sigrid?"

Cnut smiled, "At home. Mom gave her a few things to do before joining us."

The men that took part in the sacrifice started to collect their weapons.

Popi led them both away toward the activity that was beginning and said, "Now, little one, we will enjoy the day and eat and drink our fill until we can't anymore! You are going to meet my tribe and taste many wonderful things. Let's go — I'm starving!"

Cnut agreed and was famished as well.

The day so far was a bliss; the whole island was vivacious. There were various fish and meat dishes with many different vegetables, fresh bread, and butter. There was a choice of drinks for everyone's thirst. While enjoying their meal, they sat around a big fire listening to the older people telling stories of the past.

With much alcohol going around, there was laughter, singing and dancing. It was a joyous day! Rose voiced her doubt that they did this for two weeks — it was unbelievable! Cnut assured her they did, and they always looked forward to it.

There was a particular area allotted for the main dancing. When they reached it, Cnut grabbed Rose's hand and swirled her onto the dance floor; she laughed with delight.

Popi was swaying her hips and clapping her hands to the music while watching them dance. She wanted a partner to dance with and wondered where her husband was. She was about to turn and search for him when he appeared from behind and gave her a joyful fright. Var whispered something special in her ear that made her giggle like a young girl, then led her onto the dance floor.

Thord watched Rose dance; he wasn't jealous, just envious that Cnut could dance with her. He wanted to have some fun but knew she was not the person to give attention to so early. His father might misread his actions, and there would be talk amongst the tribe as well. It would upset his father if he gave her attention, which might shorten her visit. He couldn't allow that. He liked having her around and wanted to get to know her better. His best friend, Olaf, came and stood by his side.

"Hey, my brother, why aren't you dancing?" he teased, knowing full well where his thoughts were. Thord ignored the remark, slapped Olaf on the back, and laughed. They watched Cnut and Rose dance. He was teaching Rose a Viking dance, and everyone joined in.

"The next dance is mine," laughed Olaf, "Or not, I can't wait, watch me!" Thord knew he was trouble. Olaf had crude manners. When Cnut swirled Rose once again, Olaf grabbed her. "How about a new partner, little lady?" He smiled his crooked smile.

Rose laughed and looked back at Cnut. He waved and said it was fine, but it was not! He experienced a feeling he was not familiar with and stood on the side to watch.

Thord joined him, ruffled his hair, and said, "You dance well for a young man, Cnut. Never knew you had it in you." He was trying to make small talk. Cnut just shrugged and kept watching the two dancing. Thord saw the expression on the lad's face.

"Are you OK, is something wrong?" Thord knew he was jealous. He tried to soothe the moment.

"We all know how Olaf can be, nothing personal. We are all just having fun, nothing wrong with that, is there? I'm soon to be chieftain, and I must advise you not to set your hopes on her. She's an outsider and will be leaving soon. Nothing good can come of it." Thord knew it was the truth but had no idea why he voiced it out loud — was he trying to convince himself of that fact?

Those words upset Cnut; he was tired of hearing that she was an outsider. Thord might not grasp that Rose was one of them. She was probably not a real Viking, but she was part of his family; she had no one else right now.

"I know, Thord, you are right! I do care about her and wouldn't want any harm to come to her. She is not an outsider for my family and me; she is one of us, whether you like that or not. We all love her! It's not jealousy that you see, but your friend Olaf can be vulgar sometimes, that's all." He didn't know what came over him.

Thord was shocked at the boy's outburst and agreed that Olaf can be a handful. Cnut was still young and his cousin. Thord knew how Popi's family felt about her. Even Var protected her name in town when someone said something that he disagreed with.

Cnut, too, was shocked by his outburst. He meant every word, though; he stood his ground and would repeat it. Before Thord could respond, he left and asked his mother to dance. Popi was delighted, and Var was relieved; he wasn't as young as he used to be.

Everyone was dancing now, even Thord. He asked his sister, Kiti, for a dance, then Astrid and even Sigrid. Rose had a short dance with Var, and to Cnut's delight, she asked him to dance again — and so it went on into the night. Not once did Thord ask Rose to dance. She was slightly disappointed. She pushed it aside and enjoyed the festival with her friends.

Her learning of their tongue became familiar to her, thanks to Cnut and Sigrid, and she could understand most of the elderly that could not or weren't interested in learning English. She could communicate a little with them, and they were pleased with her efforts.

On the fourth day of the celebrations, there were fights between the men. Rose was standing close to where Popi was, and Var was having a conversation with Olaf. It happened so fast; she noticed an angry man walk toward Var and Olaf. He said a few words to Olaf, and they attacked each other.

When Var realized what was going to happen, he forewarned Popi, and she took Rose further away from the tussle that was about to unfold. Rose was half-standing behind the older woman; she was shocked at the fight's fierceness and wondered why no one was trying to stop it. She was so scared for Olaf; he might get severely injured or worse!

"Popi, why are they fighting, and why is no one trying to stop it?" Rose asked.

Popi tried to explain, "Well, dear, if someone tried to stop the fight, then more would join, there would be a fighting horde on the island, and my work cut out for me. It's the Viking's way of letting off steam. They don't really hurt each other, per se; if this were a real fight, one of them would be dead by now. It's almost like a sport among the men. You'll still encounter many on this island, just ignore it and step away."

Rose noticed that Olaf was more vigorous and got most punches in. In a way, she was happy with the outcome. Just as fast as the fight started, it abruptly stopped by both men laughing with bloody noses and slapping each other on the back. It went on all through the celebrations – even Thord and Olaf had a go at wrestling.

Popi explained that the two were very close brothers in arms, which was evident to anyone who saw them interact when they were together. It was not as fierce when Olaf and Gier had fought, but more like a friendly game between the two. There was much laughter.

Olaf was Thord's protector from a young age, and it became second nature over the years. He spent most of his time at the main house and had his own quarters. His parents still had the old version house they built and will not accept the change as yet, being too old in their years to even consider expanding, as most have done with extra rooms; they still had one huge room where they all slept together. Olaf would inherit their house when both passed, but he was content with his living arrangements for now.

When Helga was allowed to join in battle with the men, she took it upon herself to protect their young chief, next to Olaf's side. Helga and Olaf became close friends and arm-wrestled a lot. All the men wrestled with her and lost, except Olaf at times, and Thord.

Rose got to know some of their ways during the feast, and surprisingly, started to enjoy herself. Thord had a run-in with Cnut again. He was watching him teasing the girls and acting playfully with Rose. She laughed a great deal and punched him often. They seemed very relaxed with one another. When Cnut went for a drink, Thord decided to have another talk with him.

"Cnut, may we have a word before you run off again?"

"Sure, Thord." He was not expecting another lecture.

"Well, I've seen how you are with the girls and with Rose and want to ask if you're in love with her?"

"Who? Rose? Who isn't, right? She's a wonderful girl and so easy to get along with," he said, laughing at the games they were playing.

"Cnut, please..." was all Thord got in before the boy interrupted him.

"Thord, please! Spare me the speech again. Yes, I love her, but I'm not stupid. Yes, she loves me too, but not that kind of love, but as a sister loves a brother – one she never had. I know I'm not her type – that does not bother me. I'm not dwelling on it. So, please, let it be! Or are you bothering me because you have feelings for her?" Cnut gave him a quizzical look. Thord did not answer, so Cnut left him there to return to his game.

"The little bugger!" Thord said to himself. He thought about it and decided to let him be and never bring it up again. He had some nerve talking to him that way. However, he smiled at how bold he was and how he stood his ground like a true Viking. He couldn't be prouder. He would have to share this with Var one day. He did not dwell on Cnut's last words, as he believed he had no intimate feelings for her.

A week into the celebration, Rose had too much to drink and was feeling tipsy, so she decided to retire. The sun was rising, and everyone was still eventful as though the evening never ended! She first said goodnight to Popi and Var, and Cnut offered to walk her to the house. She wasn't used to partying so late into the night. Rose was laughing non-stop to the house, leaning on Cnut for support.

"My word...! I don't know how you people do this for two weeks, though I must admit, it is fun, and I'm not sure if I'll survive!"

"Of course, you will! You have so far, and in time, you will get used to it."

Rose liked the sound of that. That meant remaining longer on this island. She couldn't bear to leave now! She loved life and never had so much fun living. Rose kissed him on the cheek when they reached the house and went to her room to pass out.

So far, they were on the tenth day of the celebration and coming close to the end. Rose could feel that she picked up some weight, which complimented her figure. The chief's family, including her, was invited all over the village to celebrate with different families each night. They all sat at long tables to eat, and some sat outside around bonfires telling stories, which she truly enjoyed listening to.

On other occasions, during the day, competition games were held. They all had a wonderful time. Thord spoke to her often and was her mentor most of the time. His father thought nothing of it and enjoyed her company as well. Kiti was still aloof toward her and always hard to please. Rose tried to make friends with her and kept walking into a brick wall. Whenever Rose got too much attention, Kiti would flaunt herself to turn the attention toward her. Rose did not mind; she never liked attention that much. There was only one person's interest she wanted, and that was Thord's.

Nearing the end of the celebrations, they went to Popi's place. Even though she saw her every day during the festivities, she still could not wait to visit. At times, she would run off on adventures through the island with Sigrid and Cnut. They would jump on their horses to explore the island and showed her the wonders she hasn't seen before.

At their house, Cnut got all of Rose's attention. She loved him as a little brother and thought nothing weird. She loved them all and took them as her new family. They *were* her family!

Thord had no chance to speak to her that night, but he did not mind. He knew now what they meant to each other, and for the first time, the chief saw it too.

The two weeks flew by with amazement. Rose could not believe a typical day would begin. Like most of the villagers, she was a little disappointed that it ended. The fact that she survived the festival at all was a miracle. She did more drinking and eating during these few days than she had ever done in her entire life! She never thought she had it in her to party just as hard as them, except with some respect for herself as well, to retire when she had enough. You could still hear some of the villagers singing. Rose wondered how they stayed ongoing throughout the entire night into the next morning.

With this celebration, she discovered that all the settlers liked her. None had ill feelings toward her, which made her ecstatic. She could roam the island on her own and be free; Sigrid and Cnut were now off duty to fetch her each morning.

Sadly, Rose had no serious memories of her parents in the two weeks during the celebrations. Nothing triggered a memory either. There were so many things she would have loved to tell them. From what she can remember, they were close as a family and always shared their stories. It was their ritual at night before bedtime to discuss the day's events or tell a story, which Rose missed a lot! She knew her mother would have loved to hear about these people and their way of life. Her father had more of a serious nature; it would have fascinated him, but not as much as it would her mother. He was always cautious with strangers and protective over them both.

TWELVE

A few weeks after the celebrations, Rose laid awake in bed, knowing she would have to get up soon and greet the new day. It was still early, and she could hear that some of the villagers had already started with their daily activities. To Rose's pleasure, Popi offered to teach her the healing trade with Sigrid. She was delighted with the news and was having so much fun learning.

It was a peaceful morning, and she was contemplating when to rise and start dressing. In the quiet early daybreak, with the sounds of the birds chirping away on her balcony, came a scream and a lot of shouting. Rose jumped out of bed and ran to her small balcony to see what the commotion was.

She saw Olaf running out of his parent's house and shouted to call Popi. Rose could hear the dismay in the crowd and wondered who was ill. She decided to go down to see what was happening. When she reached the village, everyone looked forlorn. Someone was saying that Olaf's mother had passed away.

Olaf was kneeling in front of the door, not wanting to go in. This huge, rough man had tears in his eyes — Rose's heart went out to him. She wanted to console him; yet, she knew it was too soon for comfort. She looked over the crowd to see where his father was. Olaf's father was sitting at his usual spot outside his house, leaning forward with his head in his hands. At a loss at what to do, Rose walked over to the old man and took a seat next to him; she just sat there, not saying a word.

Gudrun, an old fossil of a man, told many stories around large fires at night about the olden days and the years gone by, which everyone loved to hear. He was ninety-five years old and his wife, Turid, was ninety; they were the oldest couple on the island. He owned the blacksmith, where Olaf took over when his father became too old to work. Gudrun and Turid were married when she was fourteen, and he was nineteen; they were married for seventy-six years. In the old days, they went on raids with the old chief — Chief Thorarin's father, and they survived through everything.

They had two children; Olaf, the eldest, was not married yet and had his sights on Helga, the tallest woman Rose had ever seen. Olaf's sister, Torhild, was in her third trimester. She was married to Bui, a giant of a man, and they had a beautiful twelve-year-old daughter with long dark hair and big brown eyes. Turunn called her grandfather, Papa, as well. She walked over to her grandfather and knelt in front of him.

"Papa, are you sad?" Tears were swimming in her big brown eyes. Gudrun looked up, and for the first time, noticed Rose sitting next to him. His granddaughter was staring at him and crying. He picked the child up, put her on his lap and hugged her. She hugged him back and started to cry more as Gudrun fought back his tears, to no avail. He was trying his best to soothe the child by telling her that everything would be all right.

Rose sat there watching the scene; her heart was breaking for these people. What a sad moment for the Vikings to have lost someone so loved and respected by all. The Vikings were indeed a close-knit tribe! Everyone lost a mother and a dear friend that day.

Popi came along with her whole family; she alone inspected the body and declared her dead. It was customary for a medicine woman to examine the body before announcing a death. The women would wash and dress her in her favorite outfit for her afterlife. It was not typically done that way; you were buried as you were, no matter what state you were in or looked like. However, Turin was old and wise, just like her husband; they wanted to send her clean and suitably dressed for her journey into the next. Some of the women joined Popi in the house to wash the deceased's body. A few men took their axes and went into the woods.

Rose saw her handmaiden and walked to where she stood. Magdalene was her confidante and taught her many of the Viking ways. The two women spoke more often as equals than as a mistress and servant.

"Good day, Miss Rose. I came to see what the commotion was about and will have to get back to my duties soon. It is a sad day to lose such a dear woman."

"Good day, Magdalene. It is sad. I wonder if you can cure my curiosity. Why have most of the men gone to chop wood? Are they going to build a casket for her?"

"No, miss. She will be burnt on a pyre. It's held either in the morning, but mostly in the evening when the day ends for most. The Viking's beliefs about death and burial are much different from yours — or so my mother told me with her stories. It is important to bury the dead in the right way, to join the afterlife with similar social standing, and avoid becoming a homeless soul that wanders eternally. It is common for them to leave gifts with the deceased as well. Both men and women receive grave goods."

The two were standing next to each other, watching the people around them and their goings-on on this tragic morning, with Magdalene talking away. She enjoyed telling stories to her mistress.

"Long ago, ancient burials were different from the way they do it today. A Viking could also be buried with a loved one or a thrall such as me. Thralls were sometimes buried alive with the person or sacrificed on a funeral pyre. It depends on the deceased's status; if they had a favorite horse, they would kill it first and bury it with that person for the horse to take them on their journey. The old chief was buried with his favorite ship; it is said that it would ease his ride to the afterlife. You should go see the burial site — it is amazing!"

Magdalene gave a side-glance at her mistress, then looked back at the town's activities and went on speaking, "The amount and the worth of goods depends on which social group the dead person came from. As you might have heard, old Miss Turid and her husband are held high in the social group. They were close friends of the old chief and looked after Chief Thorarin when his parents died. He was not young; however, they helped him grow to become the Chief he is today. As his father would have, they helped him by giving advice and teaching him what they knew. It was his choice to decide on his own. They are two wise old fossils." Magdalene stared at her mistress again and saw disbelief and puzzlement on her face.

"Are you all right, miss? Does that answer your question?"

Rose cleared her throat before speaking and tried to smile at Magdalene, "Um... Yes, thank you, Magdalene. There's always something that surprises me. I don't think I'll ever get used to it. You may return to your duties now."

"Good day, miss." She walked back to the main house.

Rose watched her walk away. She had a soft spot for her. One thing about Magdalene; when you asked her a question, she was always honest and brutally open with her answers — saying more than was necessary! She was in semi-shock; not from the burial and the goods, which they burnt or buried with the dead, but from learning that they took a human life or any other living creature and buried it 'alive' or killed it, just to join the deceased for some afterlife journey. It was demoralizing — inconceivable!

Much has happened since Magdalene first told her about her life as a thrall. With the celebrations that came and passed, and now, she was learning the healing trade. She never took notice of the slaves, or thralls as they called them. Rose took the time to look around and noticed that they, too, were sad about the old lady's loss. If she thought back, she could remember finding them laughing and talking amongst themselves during the celebrations.

Time had changed for them, and Rose felt relieved that she happened to be present at this time, to share this experience, and could not think how it would have been if the old ways still existed. She could never think of Popi and her family as being so cruel to any human being. Even though their religion was so strong, she did not want to think of them in that way. She put all that behind her and took it on as history and nothing more.

It was late in the morning, and Rose had not yet eaten breakfast. She felt somewhat peckish. When she saw Sigrid and Cnut, she wondered whether they had eaten and went to ask them to join her.

They were sitting with Olaf's father and his granddaughter. When they were about to leave, little Turunn asked if she, too, could join. She was probably starving as well, as this happened early, and her mother had no time to make anything. Rose smiled at the girl and stretched her hand out to her. The little girl beamed and grabbed her hand.

THIRTEEN

That night, Rose had a flashback of her parents and their last days together. It was the longest one yet. The death on the island must have triggered it.

Jacq Dumont was glad he was home safe. He sat at the table eating supper with his beloved wife, Sara, and his beautiful daughter, Rose. The war took a toll on France against England. England kept invading France, and so far, they had been ready for them and won each time — not leaving much time in between to recover or go home to their loved ones. In their last battle, England was badly defeated and lost many of their men. They needed to first recuperate and build their army before attacking again.

It gave them time to recoup as well. His presence was not required at the base camp; thus, he could take a break after so many months away from home. His men could handle anything further on their own, as England was weak. This meant a few months at home.

The Dumont residence has a small 'family' staff in their employ since moving into their home. They had a father and son. Mr. Alfred and his son, Joseph, both worked together in the stables and the gardens. Mrs. Alice, the cook, and her two daughters, Charlotte and Lucy, worked in the house and kitchen.

At times, Sara would be in the mood to cook for her family and today was a special occasion; her husband was coming home. She made his favorite dishes; roast lamb with potatoes, sweet carrots, and green beans with fresh bread. On the table, fresh strawberries and peaches were cut into bite-size pieces, and for dessert, there was an apple pie with fresh cream. Jacq felt like the king himself feasting on this meal.

Rose could not stop giggling while staring at her father, whom she loved dearly; he devoured his food like a man who had not eaten for months. He stuffed his mouth and chewed with relish, often drinking the wine to wash down for the next bite.

Rose could not help to comment, "Papa, the food isn't going anywhere; did they not feed you at the regiment?"

Jacq stopped halfway with his meat and bread to his mouth and gave his daughter a loving smile, "I'm sorry! Am I offending you with the way I'm eating, Rose?" he teased.

Rose laughed, "No, papa, you seem very hungry – that's all."

"They fed us, my Rose, but your mom's cooking beats the meals they offered us by far. I guess I got used to eating fast because there was not nearly enough time to eat and enjoy with the war going on. It's a habit I will need to unlearn, mainly when I'm home with my two favorite women!"

He took a deep breath and looked at his family; how he missed them. He didn't know if he'd ever see them again — the war was fierce!

His wife looked as beautiful as ever, and his daughter was growing up too fast. He was proud of them both!

Taken – Part 1

"So! Why don't you tell me what the two of you were up to while I was away, keeping the whole of France safe?" Jacq picked up his glass of wine, took a sip, and tried to eat slower. He enjoyed each bite while listening to his wife and daughter as they shared their adventures and hobbies, trips to town, and the latest town gossip. They were all laughing at the end of the meal.

The table was almost completely bare; they will use the leftover meat and bread for tomorrow's lunch. They were drinking wine and nibbling on the fruit. Rose was allowed one glass of wine while her parents were going on their second bottle.

Later, they retired to the parlor, where a fire was kindling in the hearth that kept the room warm and cozy. Mrs. Alice brought a pot of tea for them with the apple pie and bid them a good night. It was getting late and Rose was sleepy — her stomach wanted to pop after a generous helping of the apple pie. She would have stayed longer, for she missed her father dearly, but she decided to leave them alone; her parents were sitting side by side, her father holding her mother's hand like it was his lifeline and kept kissing it.

Rose went over to her father and kissed him on the cheek and then her mother.

"Bonne Nuit, papa, I'm so glad your home. Bonne Nuit, mama, love you both and sleep well."

"Goodnight, my dove, sleep well," her mom answered.

"Night, my sweet Rose, we will go riding tomorrow morning, just the two of us," her father called out before Rose closed the door behind her, not taking his eyes off his wife.

Taken – Part 1

When Rose left the room, she heard her mother giggle and laugh out loud. Seeing her parents so happy made Rose happy too, and she wished she could be just as close to her husband one day.

On other occasions, Jacq would have asked his daughter to stay; however, he wanted his wife for himself tonight. He missed her at nights when he had to sleep alone and cold in his tent, dreaming of her. When Rose left the room, he grabbed his wife, picked her up and put her on his lap, and started kissing her on the neck, how he missed the sound of her laughter. If he could not make his wife laugh at least once a day and smile most of it, then he felt he was not worthy of her. They kissed passionately for a long time.

In other circumstances, Sara would have stopped her husband and led him to their room to finish what he most of the time, always seemed to desire. Tonight, she missed him too much to stop their passion. They ended up on the rug close to the fire, where he undressed her slowly, admiring his wife's gorgeous body. Just like the food he devoured earlier with hunger, so he devoured his wife's body with a different kind of hunger, this time slowly, enjoying the taste of her and the moans of passion.

The next day, after breakfast, Rose and her father went for a long horse ride through the village. They were frequently stopped as everyone wanted to greet, chat, and welcome Jacq back home. He was well-loved by the people.

He made a turn by his assistant, Anthony, who took care of his finances while he was away. Before his next meeting with the king, Jacq wanted to have a quick peek at the books to see if everything was in order. He wanted to know how things were going and how Anthony was handling all the responsibilities by himself. He was satisfied and voiced his gratitude.

When they returned home, there was a messenger from King Louis waiting for him. The messenger had to wait until he read the message and replied to the king.

They took the horses to the stables and walked through the kitchen, where Mrs. Alice was starting lunch. When Sara saw Jacq, she gave him the sealed letter from the king. They both knew what the letter was about and stared at one another, not saying a word.

Rose saw the exchange between her parents, wondered what was going on, and voiced her concern, "Is something the matter, papa?"

"Not at all, my love; let me read the letter and answer the king so that the messenger can go on his way. Not to worry, I will meet you both in the parlor and will explain soon."

While reading the letter, Jacq felt regretful. He had agreed to a betrothal with his Rose and the king's second eldest son, Philippe; however, thought it was too soon, and his daughter was still early in her years. Maybe he could discuss this openly with King Louis; their friendship and trust have come a long way. It was through him that he met his beloved Sara.

He would need to explain that Rose was still needed at home. Sara would be alone and needed her daughter close to her while he was often away to war. Jacq decided that Philippe would be welcome to call upon Rose and start courting her slowly, and hopefully, they would fall in love. He wanted nothing forced upon her.

The letter was an invitation for his family to visit in a fortnight, to stay for two weeks through the hunting season and the Ball, which was in his honor and his men. Jacq wrote back, accepting the invitation and thanking him, also stating he had an urgent matter to discuss with him in private.

When Jacq entered the room after sending the messenger on his way, his wife and daughter were sitting in silence. He first stood there, staring at them and wondering how to explain this to Rose.

He gave them a huge smile to say all was well and sat next to Sara, picked up her hand, kissed it, and placed it on his lap while still holding onto it. He stared at the fire and then at the rug where he made love to his wife the night before. Jacq looked at Sara and smiled; she knew what he was thinking and blushed. He always wanted his wife; at his age, his libido was still healthy and his wife, thankfully, was always ready and willing. They had a good relationship, but for now, his mind needed to shift to another matter – his daughter and her future.

Rose was staring at her father, and when her parents had a moment, she looked away. She could not keep her silence any longer.

Looking at the flames, she asked her father, "Papa, what did the letter say? What does King Louis want from you this time?"

She hoped it wasn't one of those times when the king called him to ask for advice on some issues that kept him away from home for long periods. He just got home! As she waited for her father to reply, Rose continued staring at the flames.

Jacq took a deep breath, then asked Rose to look at him and said, "It's nothing important; the King invited us for the hunting season and to attend a Ball in my honor and for a few generals as well."

Rose smiled, "So, we are going with you this time?" Not taking a breath, she smiled at her mother in excitement, "And a Ball, which means a new gown!"

Rose knew her mother loved to design new dresses. It would make her happy and occupied until the time came to leave. She was just glad to be going out, meeting, and socializing with new people. Spending time at the castle also meant many outdoor activities – she could not wait!

Jacq was happy to see his daughter smile, but it was time to speak about marriage and a family of her own. "There's something else I would like to discuss with you, Rose."

"Yes, papa?"

Just then, Mrs. Alice walked into the parlor; she announced lunch was ready and that they had a visitor. "Miss Jessie has called to welcome my lord home."

Sara stood up and told Mrs. Alice to place another seat at the table and send her in.

Sara walked over to Jessie and welcomed her by taking both her hands in hers and saying, "Jessie, you've been scarce lately; are the villagers keeping you busy and away from us?" She gave her a friendly smile.

Jacq stood too to greet Jessie. "Ah, Jessie, what a pleasure seeing you again! How have you been?"

Rose ran over and hugged her like an old friend who's been gone for a long time. Jessie smiled broadly at everyone and felt at home.

She then said to Jacq, "Good day, Lord Jacq, I have come to welcome 'you' home. It feels as though I've just returned from a long journey myself with this warm welcome, though I saw the two of you not so long ago! Merci! I hope everything is well with you all?"

"We are all fine, thank you, Jessie. Please, you must join us for lunch. Mrs. Alice has placed a seat for you. We should not keep her

waiting, come." Sara hooked her arm through her husband's and took the lead out of the room.

Jessie had come a long way with the Dumont family. She stayed with them when Sara was sick and with child. Her birth was very complicated. She had done everything in her power and used all her knowledge of herbs to save her. She became a member of the family and a very close friend.

When they were seated at the table, Rose started to tell Jessie of the king's invitation, and the excitement was all over her face with this new adventure.

"That sounds fantastic, Rosy, you will have so much fun, and when you return, you must come visit and tell me everything that has happened."

Jessie was excited for Rose's part. She also knew the meaning of this visit as Sara had discussed it with her a long time ago. She hoped the girl would take it well when they tell her. As she could see, no one had yet; otherwise, she would not have been so excited.

Jessie took leave after tea in the parlor and promised to make a turn before they left. Sara and Rose went straight to the dressing room to design dresses for the Ball. Jacq went to sit outside with his pipe and enjoyed a glass of wine. He knew that Rose had forgotten all about what he wanted to discuss with her. He was unsure if he was happy about the delay or making it worse to prolong it. He decided to leave it for now and discuss it as soon as they were settled in the castle.

The day finally arrived for the long trip to the castle. Mr. Alfred and his son, Joseph, loaded the bags onto the carriage and had trouble with the heavy ones. Rose stood outside with her father – ready and excited to leave. Depending on how fast they rode, they would sleepover in at least two inns on the way. It was a long journey to the castle in a coach. On horseback, it would be much quicker.

Her father looked at her with a twinkle in his eyes and asked, "What have you two women packed in your bags, rocks? The poor men are having difficulty loading them, and why so many? A person can swear we're going away for months the way you both packed!"

"Oh, papa!" Rose said, shaking her head as though her father had no clue what a woman needed in society nowadays. "It's a visit to the castle, which means a dress for every occasion; tea dress, picnic dress, riding dress, evening dresses, and don't forget the gown!" Rose smiled. She rarely got out of the house. If she could, she would be jumping up and down with excitement like a silly girl. Rose hugged her father. "Jet'aime, papa."

He hugged her back. "I love you, my bug – more than life itself! Now, I'm going to help those poor men before they injure themselves!" They both laughed.

Everything was ready for their departure. Rose, more than eager to leave, was wondering why her mother was taking her time. She started calling out loud, "Mama! Come, it's almost time to leave."

Just then, her mother walked out of the front door and stared at her daughter.

"Rosaline Labella Dumont, a lady never shouts!"

"Yes, mama!" she said, feeling embarrassed.

Sara was worried about her daughter; how was she going to handle the news of marriage? She was not ready. Perhaps the marriage would mature her some; if not, it could go either way and break her. No! She brought her child up to be strong. Rose could handle anything that *came her way. Jacq was putting these thoughts in her head because he was scared to tell Rose. Their daughter would be fine!*

Putting the last bag on, Jacq asked if they were ready, and if so, they should climb in.

Rose gave a worried look toward her mom, and Sara asked, "What's wrong, dear? Have you changed your mind about going?"

Rose gave her mother a quizzical look, "No! I was wondering where Jessie was? She's never been late before. I wonder if something is wrong."

"She's fine; it must be an unexpected patient that's keeping her. She will be here."

Jacq walked over to them to find out what the holdup was and asked if they still wanted to leave.

Rose looked at her parents, wide-eyed, and said, "Why do I have this feeling that you both don't want to go?"

They laughed and said she was imagining things. Of course, they wanted to go! Jacq made another joke by asking them if they packed everything or misplaced a bag, or forgot something. The three of them laughed and made the workers around them laugh as well.

Rose told her father that she was worried about Jessie, so he suggested waiting a while longer. When Jessie wasn't close to coming, Jacq left a note with Mrs. Alice, and they were underway. The two women sat in the coach while Jacq rode alongside on his horse.

They were on the road for about an hour when Jacq saw someone approaching them from afar, riding the poor horse like a crazy man. He told them not to worry; he would meet the person halfway and hear what he wants. When he started getting closer, he saw it was a woman – Jessie!

Rose and Sara were hanging out of the coach, trying to see what the matter was. When Jacq returned, he told the coachman to turn around and go back home.

"What's the matter, papa? Who was that?"

"Not to worry, I'll explain at home."

"Jacq! Who was that?" Sara's voice sounded stressed.

"It was Jessie, my love; she will meet us at home. I can't explain now, wait until then, it won't be long. I will ride ahead and meet you there."

They could hear Jacq was troubled about whatever news Jessie told him. The fact that she rode all the way to catch up with them must have meant something awful has happened. With haste, the coachman made a turnabout to return home.

When the two women arrived home, Jacq's horse was in front of the house, not the stables. When they entered the parlor, Jessie was sitting, and Jacq was pacing. For the first time, Sara saw that her husband was exhausted – a look she was not used to.

She looked straight at Jessie and then at Jacq and asked, "What's the matter? What happened, Jessie?"

Jessie was always straightforward with them and never kept anything back. It was how they knew her and accepted her that way.

"It's the measles, Sara. The castle is rampant with it, and it's spreading throughout the villages. I've come to make up a remedy for you all. You will need to ask Mrs. Alice to close all the windows and curtains. Maybe we can all help her. It's imperative to stay in the dark and not go outside."

Sara just stood there staring, not knowing what to say.

Jacq walked over to his wife and held her. "Sara! Are you all right? We will be fine, my love, I promise you. Please do as Jessie suggests. We should all start closing the house up."

"Mama?" Rose was listening to what Jessie was saying and was scared. Her mother was scaring her more with the look in her eyes, just standing there frozen!

Sara came over her shock after a few long seconds. It was hard to take in this bad news, and she was worried about her family. She started taking control; everyone in the house began running and doing as they were told.

Jessie went to the kitchen to put a pot on the fire and washed her hands before handling the herbs. When Jessie heard about this, she picked what herbs were needed and was glad she caught up with them. She would have ridden all the way if necessary, just to help them.

Rose's parents died. First, her mother, and much later, her father. Jacq was more worried about his daughter and tried to fight it – a battle he could not win this time! Rose had not had time to mourn for her parent's death, for she fell ill as well.

Rose could not sleep. She remembered her parents now and what type of people they were – loving and caring. The last memories of her parents and the days that followed up to now went through her mind. She was emotionally disturbed and heartbroken. She had thought and hoped they were still alive. There was so much she had wanted to tell them. Her night was restless and gloomy.

Turid's burial was held the following evening and was burned on the pyre. Each person placed a gift either next to her or in a hole where her remains would be placed. It was sad and beautiful to witness such an occasion; their prayers to send her off and all the gifts were fascinating.

Rose stood on the side and watched it all; she was not allowed to participate. They were very superstitious; they believed it was vital to bury the dead in the right way to avoid becoming a poor soul that wandered eternally. The pyre was made from eight layers; the bottom started with wood, the next layer thickly stuffed with twigs and dried grass, then wood again, and so on. Turid lay on top of a soft bed of hay.

The family nominated Olaf's father to light the fire – it was a massive blaze and extremely hot. Everyone took a step back to watch the scene. Long after watching the fire still blazing away, everyone went back to the village. The weather was perfect – the fire would last a long while. The family would return later to pick up the remains, scrape them into a fern or scuff them all inside the hole with her gifts.

Rose watched Olaf as everyone left the burial site. He was sitting on a large stone looking out to sea, not ready to leave yet. Olaf was kind to her when she first met him, and they became close friends. Rose felt she could not go without saying something to him. He looked heartbroken! Rose wanted to comfort him with a hug but knew it would be improper. Vikings don't act on their emotions.

She contemplated telling him a secret and believed he would not speak out. She went and sat next to him on the boulder; looking out to the ocean as well, she started the conversation, "I had another memory last night."

"So happy for you, Rose. Do you want to share it with me?"

"Not sure. It's not a nice one. I was not ready for it and so soon."

"That bad, hey? You can tell me, I'm a good listener – or so I've been told."

"Only if you promise not to tell anyone until I find the right time to tell Popi."

"I promise, lass. Now, what was it?" He needed the distraction from his thoughts.

Rose took a deep breath, "I guess you can say death triggered a death memory." There was a pause before she went on, "I think both my parents are not with us anymore. I mean, I know they are not. My mother was the first to go, then much later, my father. I was too sick to remember much then."

"I'm so sorry, lass. That is not a nice memory to have returned to you!" He knew how she felt. Losing a parent was not a nice feeling, and she lost both. Though it didn't happen recently, but with her memory loss, you can say it was close enough.

"What's worse is that I was just remembering who they were as people and parents, and then to find out that it was all for naught and that I'll never see them again."

156

"No, you should never think like that! Remembering your parents is a good thing. They still live through you and in your heart. They will always be with you. Sorry to say not in person, but in good memories that you had with them."

"I guess you are right. It's just so much to take in after all that's happened."

"You'll be all right. Give yourself some time. You're a strong lass."

"Thank you, Olaf." There was a pause.

"I'm so sorry for your loss, Olaf! If you need anything, please don't hesitate to ask!"

He looked at her and gave her a small, sad smile, "Thank you, Rose! If I need anything, you'll be the first person I ask."

They were both quiet again. Rose stood and remembered how the Vikings showed their affection toward one another.

She hesitated for a second, then without thinking about it, she playfully punched him on the shoulder and said with a shy smile, "OK, then. Are we going to follow the others, or are we camping out here tonight?"

Olaf was shocked at her actions. He looked at where she hit him and burst out laughing! He stood up and saw Rose was blushing. She felt awkward, so he punched her back as lightly as he could, and still, she stumbled back. Olaf knew what she was trying to do and was thankful for her kind affection. As they walked off to join the others, he put his arms around her shoulders. Olaf was himself again, and in a playful mood, he was joking around with Rose.

"I should teach you to punch harder, my little lady! Your sting is like a mosquito bite!"

Rose laughed and played along, "Oh, is that so?" She wiggled out of his arms and punched him as hard as she could.

He roared with laughter and rubbed his other shoulder. "Ouch! That hurt!" They were both laughing when they reached the village.

"Thank you, Rose! I needed that." Olaf was sober again, "I'll be seeing you around. I'll be leaving you for now."

"I understand," Rose replied.

He strolled off to where his father was.

The day was almost over, and everyone retired to their homes.

FOURTEEN

When Olaf worked, he worked hard — when he fought in battle, he fought tough — when he drank, he drank hard. Life for him was easy and straightforward. There were no complications. The only loneliness a Viking felt was without a companion. Aside from that, they were constantly surrounded by people all day; the town was always buzzing with life — they were a close-knit tribe. The only thing missing in Olaf's life was one particular person, a woman — Helga. His problem was making the first move to show his true affections, and he hoped she shared the same fondness for him.

The proper and only way was for him to go to her parents and ask for her hand. He also had to explain why their marriage would be good for the family and him. Olaf believed Helga would give him strong and healthy offspring.

The codes of Vikings were about honor, justice and truth. While they rode the seas and fought their battles in fierce abandon, they trod with great care regarding courtship and marriage. Both sexes were expected to marry to secure peace or greater prosperity and power, never for love. It was almost unheard of to marry for the sake of the heart. For Olaf, it was different. He could not see himself marrying any other but Helga. Love or not, he had great respect and a strong fondness for her.

The two had been friends for a long time and fought together in many battles. When a Viking woman loves, she loves forever. Once you have your sights on a woman, the battle begins! Viking women are hardheaded, but once you break that barrier, you have a partner for life. The most challenging part of a relationship was keeping her affections and satisfying her, making her always feel special.

Helga was not like other women. She was equal to men in prowess. Because she was a warrior and a good one at that, most men feared her. However, in battle, they would follow her anytime.

Olaf was making something special for her. It was a small pocketknife that was as sharp as possible, and it had an ivory handle with Vik's carvings on it. With it, he made a leather pouch so Helga could carry it on her person. He hoped she would love it and felt a bit nervous giving it to her. He was good at his trade — a born professional. He could build or make anything out of iron and sometimes wood if needed. He made all their weapons and helped to build their ships, just as his father had done. It was in their blood.

While busy with his task, to his surprise, Rose walked in. "Well now, hello to you, lass! You not working today?"

"Hi, Olaf; I'm taking a break and curious to see your workshop and what you do." Rose looked around and asked,

"Is this all your handiwork?" She was impressed with what she saw.

"Most of it, yes. Several are my father's toil as well."

While she was walking around and staring at everything, Olaf thought of what they had spoken about at his mother's funeral three days before.

"Have you spoken to Popi yet?" While Olaf was talking, he continued on his project.

"About what?" Rose was lost in thought; she was searching for something specific, hoping to find one.

"You know what! I've noticed you haven't been there since you received that last memory. Instead, you've been playing with the kids and helping the folks in town with small chores. It would seem that you are trying to avoid her?"

Olaf was right, but Rose was not going to admit it. She was worried that Popi might see through her lies if she asked questions about her memories returning. They have – almost all of them, with a few bits and pieces needing to still fall into place. She was scared it reached the chief's ears, and he would send her home. Rose knew she couldn't avoid Popi for much longer.

She saw Cnut only once in the village when he ran an errand for his mother. They fooled around with the kids playing sword fights with wooden sticks before he ran off again. Thankfully, he was not like the others to ask questions. They just enjoyed each other's company. Cnut must have told his mother that she was helping in the village, so Popi knew she was busy with other things.

Rose tried to explain, "I'm not avoiding her per se. I was going to make a turn today, much later when I have time."

"Was? You can't evade her for long. That woman ain't stupid!"

Rose gave a nervous laugh, "I know. I might go later. You haven't told anyone, have you?"

"No, I said I would not, and I've kept my word. It's for you to tell, not me." Olaf decided to drop the subject. Rose would go when she was ready.

"Thank you!" She stopped searching. She could not find what she wanted and stared at what he was doing instead.

"What are you busy with now?"

He finished his last stitches on the pouch and made sure the knife fitted in nicely.

"It's a gift," was his only reply.

Rose noticed how nervous he looked and wondered if she should ask whom it's for. Being as inquisitive as she was, she would. If he said it was personal, then that would be fine. She'd soon find out anyway.

"If you don't mind me asking, who's the gift for? It's lovely!" Olaf was blushing, and Rose was sure she was the first to elicit such a feeling from him. She wanted to laugh but kept it in. Teasing him about that would not be good for his ego. So, she just smiled and waited for him to answer.

"It's for Helga." Olaf gave her a bothered look. "Please don't tell her or anyone! No one knows. I want to present my gift first and see if she shares the same affections before I meet with her parents." He knew he could trust Rose with this secret. It was also all still new and nerve-wracking for him.

"It's fine, Olaf; your secret is safe with me. I'm sure she would love it! What do you mean by meet her parents? Are you going to ask for her hand in marriage?"

"Well, that's the whole idea with this gift. To be honest, Rose, I'm a bit tense. I'm not sure what her feelings are toward me."

Touched and honored that he would confide in her about something so personal was sweet.

"Well, I've noticed how she steals a look at you sometimes; any girl would be flattered to receive a gift like that, and from a man like you! Don't be scared! Follow your heart. You might be surprised."

Olaf was grateful for her kind words. It gave him some courage and confidence to face his fears. He smiled at Rose – she was a sweet girl, but she still had a lot to learn about their ways and the way to a person's heart. Or confessing such feelings aloud could get one killed! He knew he had to say something.

With a stern look, he said, "Rose, I need you to understand that declaring your love for someone may get you in deep trouble! Our way is very complicated; you should ask Popi to explain this to you."

Rose was grateful for the advice but also confused. Olaf looked very serious! What could be so different from the Viking's kind of love and her kind? Love was love, wasn't it?

He completed the job and packed the gift safely away, then gave her all his attention.

"So, Rose, what can I do for you today?"

While fooling around with the kids, Rose noticed them playing with all sorts of wooden toy weapons and thought she would like one herself — not a toy but a real one. She came in to see if there were any lying around but saw none. Rose wanted to ask; however, she was unsure if she was allowed to own a weapon. She heard that everyone owned some kind of weapon and had to carry it on them at all times. The Viking's rules were so confusing sometimes. Everyone else had a weapon, so why couldn't she?

Rose started by flattering him, although, in fact, it was the truth, "I hear you are the best marksman on the island?"

Olaf, pleased with himself, said, "Yes, I am!"

She was going to be forward, "I would like to learn to shoot a bow and arrow! Unfortunately, I would need to own one first. I wondered if you could make one for me — not too big, though!"

Olaf stared and smiled at her, "And who's going to teach you to shoot the thing?"

"I don't know yet! Just getting the bow was my main goal."

Olaf thought about it for a while and said, "It will be my pleasure to build you a bow, and I shall teach you as well."

Rose beamed with excitement. "Oh, thank you, Olaf! You'll let me know when it's ready?"

"Yes, as soon as it's done!" He laughed at her excitement.

On her way out, she said, "Good luck with you know what."

"Thanks!" Olaf needed all the luck he could get.

It was close to supper time. Rose finished the chores in the village and went to wash up in her room. She was not yet ready to face Popi.

The following day, Rose decided to heed Olaf's advice and ask Popi about the Viking's love behaviors. She was a little intrigued to hear what Popi had to say on the subject.

At midday, when Rose entered the house, she called out, but there was no answer. She had a flashback with her mother scolding her for shouting and not acting like a lady. What point will it achieve by being or acting like a lady on this island? They freely shouted as they wished. She was no different from them, so there was no point in acting differently.

Rose was learning their ways too easily! If, or whenever she leaves, she would have to act on the manners her mother taught her and was not looking forward to it. Being a Viking meant to let your hair down and enjoy life, with certain rules and regulations, which she could live with. You were free to roam the land and find yourself, whereas being a lady meant staying indoors and being someone else altogether to please others. That was not for her. It was as though she was born to be a Viking. The thought thrilled her. Now that she knew her parents weren't alive, she never wanted to leave.

Rose searched inside and found no one. Her next best option was Magdalene. While walking out of the house, she heard laughter. Following the sound, she found Popi and

Sigrid busy in the herb garden. Her mind was so occupied that she never thought to look there.

Sigrid saw Rose first, "Rose, thank sweet Odin, you're here! My mom's impossible this morning!"

"Don't be silly, child; I'm trying to teach you about herbs!" Popi gave Rose a welcoming smile, "She's the one that's impossible, trying to argue with me about something I lived with my whole life. The first thing any mother teaches her child about herbs is monkshood; it's deadly if you don't know how to use it right — use too much and the heart will stop!

"It should not grow close to your other herbs either, but at a distance, and always wear gloves when picking the plant. Never pick it with bare hands or near wounds, and always," she stared at them both and said, "wash your vegetables and herbs *properly* before cooking or before making *any* concoction!"

Rose laughed at the two women who were down on their knees, discussing herbs.

"Yes, mom! You keep telling us. That's imprinted in my memory forever." Sigrid then asked Rose, "Where have you been? I thought this was what you wanted? Mom did say she would teach us both if you are still interested?"

Rose felt guilty for staying away, "Yes! I am interested in learning! I will be here early tomorrow, I promise. I'm still helping someone in the village today, just taking a break, and I thought I'd ask Popi about something I've heard."

"Good! Now Rose," Popi said, trying to get up. "Why don't you give me a hand and help an old lady to her feet. I'm getting too old for all this bending; it should be left to the young ones."

Once inside, Popi made lunch and poured milk for the three of them to drink. While eating, Popi asked, "So, Rose, what have you heard? How can I help?"

Popi knew Rose always asked her handmaiden for advice to explain their ways. She was happy to explain anything to this young lady — not to say of late! Popi smiled. Rose was a free spirit; she could not help but love her more for her different ways of looking at life.

Rose did not know where to begin or how to ask. Asking Magdalene was easier. She felt silly asking, but Olaf thought it was necessary. She could have waited and asked Magdalene; however, both women were now staring, waiting for the question. Popi saw that Rose was hesitating and wondered if it was personal.

"Would you like to ask me in private? If it's personal, Sigrid can leave for a while?"

"No, she can stay." Sigrid looked relieved. "It's just that someone told me to ask you how the Vikings go about their love affairs — of declaring one's love to another?"

"Oh, who told you about this, dear?" Popi wondered.

Rose could not say without implicating Olaf's secret.

"Does it matter? I heard that declaring your love for someone is dangerous. Is that true?"

"Well..." Popi thought about how to explain this in a manner that Rose could understand, "Marriage is not just for love, but for power, to secure peace between the two families, and for greater prosperity. Marrying for love is unheard of; however, the young couple also has a say since a good relationship between the spouses is crucial. If a man sends poems of love or declares his love openly for a woman, it's interpreted as a scandalous slur toward a woman. It's believed; 'How could a man know a woman so deeply without tasting the wine?' Do you know what that means, Rose?"

"Yes." She blushed.

"Good. Going into that subject is another matter altogether," Popi laughed, "Well, where was I? Oh, yes, if this news of love becomes known, the man dishonors the woman and the entire family as well. I'm not just talking about her parents and siblings, but aunts, uncles, cousins, etc. A man who professes his love for a woman does so with great risk to his life."

Popi could see that Rose was not happy with this news and looked more confused. She tried to lighten the subject.

"It's not as bad as it seems; both parties have to agree to the relationship for it to work. No one is forced into marrying someone they don't like or agree with. It is also understood that a disapproving bride would result in utter disaster towards the groom; he could lose a body part or worse – death. Your parents must have had an arranged marriage for you, Rose?"

She looked at Popi and thought it was absurd. Her parents would have told her! Marriage was important to her, and it definitely involved love. She wanted the same relationship that her parents had.

Rose answered, "I think they would have told me if such arrangements were made. We might have arranged marriages, but the man courts the woman for a while before the wedding. I feel and hope there is love and that the man would declare it to me, if to no one else. I do believe in love, Popi, and want nothing else. I want what my parents had; they had the whole thing – love, friendship, a partnership and understanding – everything!"

Popi was sincere, "I hope all those things for you one day. I believe you shall have them and more!"

Popi stared at her daughter with love in her eyes and said, "For you, Sigrid, nothing but the best! If a man declares his love for any of the two of you, I will know he took time to know the woman you will become and fall deeply in love with the thought of spending the rest of his life with that one woman – is fine by me! We shall keep that to ourselves." Both girls were giggling by now.

"Though..." Popi lengthened the word, "We should watch out for the trolls if that should ever happen."

"What trolls?" Rose was lost.

"Yes, trolls," Sigrid said, still laughing, "It's also believed that if one addressed one's betrothed with an endearment that it weaves a spell capturing their intended – one the other would be unable to break."

Rose laughed and thought that was the silliest thing she had ever heard. She left soon afterward to finish her task in the village. She said her goodbyes and promised to return early the next day and was looking forward to learning the healing techniques again. She was glad Popi never asked if any memories had surfaced.

They were having lunch the following day, and Rose was enjoying her first day of serious training. The first week would start with basic training about knowing your herbs and washing them. After that, they would begin to crush and boil the herbs for specific ailments. A crucial point as well was the quantity to add to create certain potions. Sigrid was far ahead of her; still, she was catching up nicely.

Popi was busy with her sewing while the two girls ate. When they finished, Popi sent Sigrid out to deliver food to her father. When she returns, the two girls will finish washing the herbs so that Popi can start the next lesson. No time for lounging! It was only now, during lunchtime, that Popi had some time to speak to Rose.

"Ah, my *Lillé*, it's always a pleasure having you around." Popi was happy she was back.

"I was worried at first, then Cnut told me you were helping others in the village. That's kind of you." While she was talking, she continued with her sewing.

Feeling guilty, Rose said, "I'm sorry I never came sooner or to let you know."

"It's fine, love. How have you been? Any new memories?"

Here it was. Rose knew Popi meant well by asking all the time and was worried. Her memories returning meant she was recovering.

"Yes, kind of."

"I'm so happy for you, dear. Share and spare no details. I'm always glad to hear your stories."

Rose already had the story she wanted to tell. She had to think before she spoke in case she had a slip of the tongue.

"It's not a pleasant memory to remember!" Rose took a deep breath, "Both my parents are gone. They passed away with the virus; first, my mother and then my father."

Popi stopped sewing, "Oh, dear! I'm dreadfully sorry, love. That is not a nice memory and to feel the pain all over again is very sad. How do you feel about your loss?" Popi wanted the girl to be open with her feelings, and crying was one of the healing processes.

"Well, I was just starting to get to know who they were as parents and people. I was happy and excited thinking I might see them again, and now, knowing that it will never happen…" Rose was looking down at her hands, not wanting to face Popi.

"Yes, I see how that may hurt a lot. If you don't mind me asking, what was the memory about?" Popi wondered.

"Not much, just two graves and bits and pieces of that time. I was sick myself, so I can't remember much from that period." She hoped that Popi would not ask any more questions. She did not want the chief to find out or wish Popi to lie for her either. Whether she would lie or not, she did not want to take that chance. Rose felt awful for not telling her dear friend the truth.

"That's not much of a story, but better than nothing, even though a sad one."

"I'm sorry, Popi; I don't want to discuss this particular subject right now. I'm still trying to come to terms with it." It was true, in a sense. She hoped it would be enough for now.

"It's fine, *Lillé*; maybe next time, when you are up to it — I understand. So, tell me who you've been helping in the village and the chores you've been doing?"

She had a feeling the girl had not cried over her loss yet. She was bottling up all her emotions. Popi knew that when that day came, there would be a flood of tears.

They were both laughing when Sigrid came walking in from the fields. It was a hot day, so she poured them each a drink before returning to work in the kitchen.

While they were washing each herb to perfection, Sigrid said to her, "You've missed a lot the past few days that you were not here. I've been making all kinds of ointments. Not mature ones yet; however, still important ones."

Rose was a little disappointed that she missed all that. At first, all she had been doing was pulling weeds, learning the names and what they were used for. She smiled at Sigrid and was happy to be back.

A week had passed since the funeral — Rose noticed that little Turunn, Olaf's sister's daughter, followed Cnut everywhere. At such a young age, she had a crush on him. It was sweet to watch, though Cnut was getting a little irritated with her constant closeness.

Popi sent the two girls out early to pick mushrooms and certain flower roots. Rose always enjoyed their outings. Cnut wanted to join, but he had to drop something off in the village for his father. He was going to meet them at the stream to ride out together.

When he neared the stream, Rose noticed he was not alone and couldn't help smiling at his new companion, or should she say Cnut's shadow. He did not look happy at all. The only reason he agreed for her to tag along was that her mother begged him. Little Turunn frequently wanted her mother's attention – Torhild needed a time out to lay down for a few hours as her stomach was getting bigger each day.

After picking what they needed, Rose offered to drop the young girl off and would meet them later. Cnut was thankful and relieved to get rid of his escort. Rose dropped little Turunn off before going to wash up. Her hands were filthy from the soil while trying to dig the roots out correctly.

Once inside the main house, she noticed all the women were preparing the Chieftains Hall for an event. Something big was happening again, and no one told her – not even Sigrid or Cnut on their ride. They probably thought she already knew.

Rose was searching for Magdalene, knowing she would be able to explain what was happening. She could not find her and decided to wait. She was hoping someone else would enlighten her. The day's activities were normal; everyone was still working and going about their duties.

Rose decided to stay at the main house and not go to Popi's. She had a feeling she would be seeing them soon. To let the time pass, she played with the kids for a while on the beach, where most of the fishing took place.

At lunchtime, she went in to eat. Everyone from the main house was seated. Usually, no one ate at the same time at lunch; it was always with one leaving and another entering. However, that was not the case today! It also did not look like a lunch meal, but more like supper. Rose wished she knew where Magdalene was. The table was filled with food, and everyone ate their fill. She decided to do the same and ate until she could no more.

After such a big meal, Rose decided to take a walk in the garden. While she stood looking out at the ocean view, she heard someone approaching. She turned to see Thord walking toward her, stunning and gorgeous as always.

She smiled at him, "Good day, Thord."

"What's the matter, Rose? I could see something was bothering you at the table. You kept looking around."

"Have you seen my handmaiden today? I searched everywhere and can't find her."

"Do you need her to help you with something? I can send someone to find her if it's an urgent matter?" He did not want to intrude in her personal business.

Rose did not want to bother him with all her questions.

"No, no urgent matter. Thank you, all the same. I'll wait; I only wanted to ask something."

"Maybe I can help?" he offered with a smile.

Rose was hesitant to ask him, though it was just a question she was sure he wouldn't mind answering.

"Well!" Looking up at him and feeling embarrassed, she continued, "It's about today's event. I'm not sure what is happening, and Magdalene always explains things to me. Why was lunch turned into supper?" She gave him a questionable look. His smile always affected her, so she looked away.

He laughed, "Well, that one is easy to answer, and I don't mind at all to explain."

He gestured toward a garden bench; they both sat, and he turned slightly to face her. It was too much for Rose being so close to him. He dominated the bench so that their legs touched.

"Well, Rose," he began, "A week from today, Turid was buried. She was very important to all of us and was held high in my father's favor. She knew the majority of our history by living through most of it. She was very old, as you know! We give the family a week to sort their things out and to mourn her passing.

"We have what you call 'ceremonial drinking.' All the villagers meet in the Chieftain's Hall for one of our many rituals – this one is for Turid. It is customary for the remembrance of her. We choose a drink, ale or mead – we chose ale – the head of Turid's house, her husband, gives a speech, or recites a poem, and then drinks out of a drinking horn. You may only speak up when you are holding the drinking horn to honor her life, which you should empty afterward. Then it's passed to the next person, whoever wishes to say something.

"When the evening is close to an end, there are many formulaic boasting and oaths. Eating and feasting are excluded; that is why we ate so big a few minutes ago. It changes from household to household. We don't always do this. It only happens when the head of the family changes or inheritance is passed on. Also, sometimes gifts are given to people. It's more serious than mere drinking or celebrating." He stopped speaking; his arm was resting on the back of the bench.

In the beginning of the speech, he spoke to her face-to-face and later looked away in the distance when he got into his Viking history. He stopped to give her a chance to say or ask something, except she was quiet. Rose couldn't help staring at him while he was explaining.

She tried to keep focused on what he was saying, except his glorious face distracted her. When he looked away, she had an open invitation to admire what was in front of her; his full lips and the way they were moving with each word. She never had this opportunity before — and the freedom to do so without anyone noticing, not even Thord — was thrilling.

The scenery was so romantic — sitting on top of the hill in a beautiful garden, looking out at the ocean and sitting next to this stunning, amazing man! Thord was still busy explaining, so Rose went on to examine more parts of him. His arm that was resting on top of the bench was so close. She could see every dent and contour of his muscles. It was very distracting and made her stomach flip. She heard everything he was saying. When he stopped, she froze and stared at him like an Idiot.

"Rose? You have nothing to say or ask me?"

"Oh! Yes," she answered, blushing, "Will there be gifts given today?"

He laughed and said yes. Just then, they heard Sigrid calling for her. When she saw them, she ran toward them.

Thord stood up and greeted Sigrid, "I'll be seeing the two of you soon." Before leaving, he turned to Rose, "I hope that answered all your questions?"

"Yes, thank you, Thord." She showed her appreciation with a shy smile.

"Rose! I have been searching everywhere for you. Cnut is searching in town. We better go find him – he won't stop looking." They both laughed and walked arm in arm in search of her brother.

"What were you and Thord discussing before I arrived?" Sigrid wondered what she asked him.

"About the upcoming event."

"It's exciting in a way and sad at the same time, don't you think?"

"No...! Maybe if I knew earlier, why did you not tell me?" She playfully scolded her.

"I thought you knew; that's why you offered to take Turunn back? Even so, Magdalene always explains everything to you, so... we thought...!"

"Well, she forgot to inform me about this one, so Thord offered. Not complaining though..."

"Yes, I can see that..." They ran off giggling and laughing, calling for Cnut.

The ceremonial drinking was about to start, and the main hall was slowly beginning to fill.

Rose woke up with a massive headache. Sigrid was sleeping next to her; they both had too much to drink and were sick in the gardens – this was the first time for both girls. Fearing being caught, they went straight to bed to pass out. Not to wake Sigrid, Rose got up quietly to drink water. She felt very thirsty and cold, not feeling too well. She climbed back into the warm bed, placed the jug of water on the bed stand close to her, and tried to sleep further.

They woke up near noon, washed up, and rode out to Popi's. Sigrid thought she was in trouble for not being there for her chores. Rose kept trying to reassure her that her mom would not be hard on her, and she was right.

When they entered the house, Popi had a big breakfast ready to help settle their stomachs and gave them something awful to drink for their headaches, which worked wonders! She gave the girls the day off to relax, which was exactly what they did – nothing!

Rose was proud of the gift she received last night from Popi and her family. She did not expect anything and was thrilled when they surprised her with it. Var made it himself in Olaf's shop and was pleased with her reaction. Now, she too had a weapon to carry on her person at all times. It was a small sharp

knife with a pouch, and Sigrid showed her where to hide it —
around her thigh. Rose knew she would never take it off! She
was still waiting on Olaf for her bow. She could not wait until
she had that as well.

While sitting and daydreaming, Rose wanted to hear more
of the wonderful stories of the Viking history. She remembered
the one that Magdalene said she should listen for — about the
thrall who was buried with her master. She wondered if Popi
would tell the story. She was busy sewing as usual when Rose
asked, and Sigrid begged her to tell.

"OK, you two! It is a long story, so sit back and relax and
listen carefully." Popi began,

"A long, long time ago, a great chieftain died. His villagers
— very much loved and respected him. He was deemed highly
as their Chief. Thralls those days knew the risks of sacrifices
and very much feared it. However, one brave thrall woman
volunteered to join him in the afterlife. This was a first for any
Viking colony for a thrall to offer themselves freely. On her
request, she was guarded day and night. An old woman
referred to as the 'Angel of Death' was called upon to facilitate
the ritual to its proper order. It was a great honor for the
Vikings. A small feast was held, and the slave was given an
enormous amount of intoxicating liquids while she sang
happily.

"Meanwhile, the dead chief was put in a temporary grave for
ten days until his people had sewn new clothes for him. When
the time arrived for cremation, they pulled his longship ashore,
put it on a wooden platform, and made a bed for the dead

chieftain on the ship. The old woman, Angel of Death, put cushions on the bed. She was responsible for the ritual. She was a dreaded old woman; everyone respected and feared her at the same time.

"They disrobed the chieftain and dressed him in his new clothes, then laid him onto his new bed with all his weapons around him. For his afterlife, he was given all kinds of grave offerings; intoxicating drinks, fruits, bread, stringed instruments, and much more. They made two horses run themselves sweaty, cut them into pieces and threw the meat onto the ship. Next, they sacrificed other farm animals as well. You never questioned the old woman's methods.

"The thrall was sent from one tent to another and had sexual intercourse with the men. Every man told her, 'Tell your master that I did this because of my love for him.' In the afternoon, after that specific activity, they moved the girl to something that looked like a door frame, where she was lifted on the palms three times. While still being intoxicated, this put the slave in an ecstatic trance that made her psychic, and through the symbolic action with the doorframe, she would see into the realm of the dead.

"In her trance on the doorframe, the thrall told of what she saw. She first saw her parents. The second time, she saw all her relatives, and the third time, her master in the afterworld. There, it was green and beautiful, and together with him, she saw men and young boys. She saw that her master beckoned for her. They were satisfied with the results.

"Before taking her to the ship, she removed her bracelets and gave them to the old woman. Then she removed all her finger rings and gave them to the old woman's daughters, who had guarded her. She was then allowed to board the ship. However, they did not permit her to enter where the dead chieftain lay — not yet. She first received several more alcoholic drinks, and she sang and bade her friends' farewell.

"Only then was she taken to the dead chieftain. The men started to beat on shields so her screams could not be heard. Six men entered to have intercourse with the girl, after which they put her on her master's bed. Two men grabbed her hands, and another two grabbed her ankles. The old woman put a rope around the girl's neck, and while two men pulled the rope, the old woman stabbed the girl between her ribs with a knife. When the ritual was complete, and everyone was satisfied, the dead chieftain's relatives arrived with a burning torch and set the ship aflame. It is said the fire facilitates the voyage to the realm of the dead. That was the first and last time any thrall offered themselves in such a way. The end!"

Popi kept on sewing; everyone was quiet and left to their thoughts.

Rose thought she understood why the thrall offered to be buried with her master. She must have been secretly in love with him, been under his command for years, and could not declare her love or have him because she was not a Viking by blood. The only way to show her deep respect toward her master and to be with him was to offer her life to join him in death. The pain of losing him must have been excruciating that she came to that conclusion. However, the way they conducted the whole ceremony was inconceivable. Moreover, the pain that the poor girl must have gone through was dreadful!

FIFTEEN

During Olaf's spare time, he started carving Rose's bow. It took him over a week to finish it all, and he enjoyed doing it. It was small and dainty to fit her person, and it was easy to pull. At the ends where the strings were attached were two beautiful flower shape designs. It was sturdy and thick — not easy to break. In the middle, where her hand was going to clutch, was tightly wrapped with leather for a comfortable grip, and her name was branded on it. He was proud of his craftsmanship. The arrows were a bit tricky; they were thinner than the regular ones and very sharp. It would fly far and true if she aimed right. He made thirty of them with a quiver to carry on her back for easy access.

Rose asked Olaf to keep it a secret until she was skilled to surprise everyone.

Thus, the next day during breakfast, he gave Rose a wink and a nod, and she understood. With an eagerness to see how it looked, and with excitement, she ate fast, tripled out the door and ran to his shop — knowing he took his time in the mornings, but she was too animated to care.

The shop was open at all hours, and she wasn't sure if he ever locked the place. Why would he need to! You could sleep with your doors open; no harm would come to you. Rose's life changed drastically, and she learned to deal with the ups and downs — challenges of life on the island. She loved life here; the feeling of not wanting to leave became stronger each day, as did the love she had for the people. Olaf was approaching his shop and saw Rose waiting outside.

"Why haven't you gone inside, lass? The door is open!"

"It just felt right waiting outside." She followed him in, and there it was, on the table waiting for her. It was indescribable, and it was hers!

"Well, don't just stand there staring! Pick it up and see how it feels." Olaf was happy with her appreciation.

Rose was speechless as she admired the tool with wide eyes. She noticed her name on the handle and could not help showing her gratitude for all his hard work. She hugged him and thanked him profusely.

He looked a little uncomfortable at first, then lightly hugged her back and said it was nothing.

"Now," he took a step back, "When would you like to test it?"

Rose could not wait to try it out. She would have a sleepless night if she had to wait any longer. Giving an innocent look, wishing and hoping they could go this instant, she said, "Maybe today some time, as soon as it suits you?"

Olaf laughed at her sly expression, and seeing how eager she was; he added, "The folks in town need to be out of harm's way when you shoot that for the first time. My morning is free. Go off and fetch your horse!" He laughed when she squealed with delight and ran to get her horse. Olaf just shook his head and smiled. It was so easy to please her and a pleasure to have around. He was fond of her and became protective without realizing it.

When they arrived at the spot Olaf had chosen to shoot, she noticed Helga was waiting for them. She completely forgot to ask Olaf how it went. Helga had the pouch around her waist and the knife resting in it. No questions were needed. She could see it went well and was happy for them.

Olaf looked at Rose and asked, "You don't mind her being here and helping along?"

"Not at all. It will be fun," she answered, then whispered, "I'm so happy for you both." Rose greeted Helga, and she blushed for the first time.

Olaf made a target for her to practice on; it was pegged far away on a tree. The bow was perfect and easy to hold; however, her first arrow went entirely the wrong way.

Helga was enjoying herself and said to Rose, "You'll get the hang of it. You just need to practice a lot! Stand a little closer to the target at first, then slowly move further away." She gave her a few tips on how to hold and aim accurately too.

At the start, Olaf and Helga helped, then left her to practice by herself. After shooting all her arrows, Rose had to go search for them. The two sat one-side and chatted in private, shouting comments at Rose at times. Olaf was a skilled teacher. After a while, Rose's arms were getting tired. She was not used to so much pulling in one day. She was getting better at aiming, but still not well enough.

Olaf eventually called the day to an end. Rose could come back to practice tomorrow until she got the hang of it. They were in the woods for close to two hours; he had to get back to work. A new moon was almost upon them, and hopefully his pending marriage to Helga, which he still needed to ask her parents' permission. Olaf was confident they would agree to this union. There was much to prepare. The day to set sail out to sea for trading goods was also coming nearer, and by then, a second season celebration — a lot had to be done before then.

On occasions, Thord would keep an eye on Rose's daily activities. He always wondered what she was up to. At first, he noticed she avoided going to Popi for a few days; however, she was back to that routine. During her days helping the villagers, she entered Olaf's workshop. Since then, she's been full of anticipation, and he couldn't help but wonder why. He had been watching her like a hawk since.

They spoke to each other, as they often do — nothing odd. Rose had her usual routines; she went to Popi's, rode around alone, sometimes with Cnut or Sigrid, and on rare occasions, with them both. She played around with the kids in the village and helped the women bathe them on bathing days. Olaf never left his workshop during the day. Thord thought he was being silly and saw something that was not there. When he decided to stop spying on them, he witnessed something bizarre, which changed his mind.

During breakfast, he noticed that Olaf winked at her, and she smiled broadly. That was not normal behavior! He wanted to confront them but kept quiet, as they were not alone at the table. Rose ate so fast she almost choked, which was unusual manners for her. And in such a rush to get out that she almost tripped as well; if it weren't so serious, he would have laughed.

He, too, stood up, his appetite gone. Maybe he could catch Rose in the foyer and confront her while Olaf ate. When he got to the entrance, she was already gone. He went to the gardens for a better view. Olaf was still eating. That man had to fill his belly before his day could start and needed to wash it down with mead.

When Olaf eventually reached his shop, they both entered. The sun at this time of morning always shines halfway into Olaf's workplace. Thord could not see their full figures, only their feet and shadows. They moved closer together as though they – gods forbid – kissed! He could be guessing wrong! Thord hoped it was nothing more than just a friendly embrace for some reason. It took a few minutes before Rose came running out toward the stables. Olaf was on his horse with a package, and they were off toward the woods.

Thord thought to follow them but decided to wait for their return. He did not want to intrude – he could not imagine what his actions would be toward his best friend. His thoughts were eating at him! To calm down, he went about his everyday activities. However, it did not help! They kept invading his thoughts. He would have to have a long discussion with his friend when he returned.

He could not understand why — Rose was not Olaf's type. He contemplated who would be and was sure Helga was a perfect match as she was more 'woman' for Olaf. He must have judged his friend wrong. Either way, they were both irresponsible in their actions.

Two hours later, Rose came riding out of the woods toward the house by herself. When Rose walked in all flushed and happy, Thord was waiting for her. She stopped dead in her tracks and almost ran into him when entering.

"Thord!" Rose still felt uneasy in his presence, although it was getting a little better. She had gained some self-confidence to stand up to him and not feel intimidated. He could not manipulate her feelings as much anymore — or so she would have liked to believe.

"Where have you been this morning, Rose?" he asked in all seriousness and not smiling or being polite as he usually was.

Rose was so animated with the days' events that she did not take note of his mood. All she thought about was keeping her secret until she improved at the sport. She wanted to surprise them all at the games during the festivals. She heard they had many on wedding days as well. It was too embarrassing to admit, even to him.

Rose did not want to lie either, so she avoided answering his question with a question instead, "Why, did you need me for something?"

"No! Just wondering. I saw you riding into the woods, that's all." He did not mention that he saw Olaf riding with her, not letting her know he knew something!

"I'm actually in a hurry; I'm expected at Popi's. Will that be all?" She was ready to leave to wash up.

So, she's keeping her affair a secret, he thought. Why would she tell him?

"No, just wanted to warn you to be careful. The woods aren't safe! There are always wild and dangerous animals roaming around."

"Thank you for your concern, Thord. I'll keep that in mind." She started to climb the steps.

Thord let her go and decided to get at Olaf instead. She was the innocent party in all this. Olaf knew better. He turned and left so quickly that he didn't hear Rose shout after him.

"See you later at supper!" she shouted over her shoulders, but he had already left. She shrugged and went to her room. She did not like the confrontation and was glad it was over.

While walking toward Olaf's workplace, Thord's thoughts drove him mad; he was all worked up by the time he reached the shop — fuming — and ready to face Olaf when he entered the shop. This could not go on any longer and had to stop today. Was he jealous? *No, of course not!* Thord knew that if this news reached his father's ears or the tribe, he would not be sure what would happen.

The tribe liked Rose; they had already accepted her. He was unsure what their actions would be, and it was up to him to fix it. He would have no choice but to send Rose back to where he found her, whether her memories returned or not. His father would demand it!

Olaf was singing while working, which pissed Thord off even more.

He was busy burning iron and hitting it on a flat surface when Thord entered. Olaf greeted him joyfully then saw Thord's expression. He stopped halfway with the hammer aloft, wondering what was amiss. Olaf put the hammer down and walked toward his friend.

"Thord! Are you all right? What's wrong?" He was concerned for his friend and was always ready for any action.

Thord had not seen his friend this happy before and felt a bit guilty for what he was about to say. He knew this was not going to be easy – Olaf was a very determined person, but it has to be said!

"I know what you've been up to!" he said, not beating around the bush and getting straight to the point. He hoped he'd do the same. "Have you no shame? How dare you keep this a secret from me! We've been friends forever, and you have disappointed me. So... explain yourself!"

Olaf was confused by this sudden attack. He thought that maybe it was about Helga, and Thord found out somehow. That would be very dangerous since he had not talked to her parents yet.

"Relax, Thord. I was going to tell you! I wanted to do this on my own before the news came out. I wanted to see how things develop in the relationship first."

Thord was shocked to hear this. "So, you are going to tell everyone?"

"Yes! Why not? I have strong affections for her, had for a long time now. Thought you'd be happy for me?" He was upset and puzzled by Thord's response.

"Happy? Have you gone completely mad? You can't go on with this; you must end it now!"

Both were in a tizzy and raised their voices at each other.

"End it? What's gotten into you this morning? I will do no such thing!" Olaf shouted back.

"Yes, you will if you know what's good for you!"

Olaf, having enough of this nonsense, attacked Thord. They started fighting, which attracted a few bystanders.

Rose was eventually on her way to Popi's when she heard the commotion and thought nothing of it. Vik's will be Vik's; they were just fooling around and blowing off some steam. Though, Olaf always seemed to have more issues than most! It sounded as though they were breaking down the shop. She was already late; thus, she rode faster.

Olaf was pinning Thord down, then shouted at him, "What's the matter with you? Why can't I see her?"

Thord wrestled Olaf off him and reversing the position, "Because it's not allowed and doesn't seem right! Since when is she your type anyway?"

Still in a tussle with each other, Olaf replied, "Helga is my type, and if I want to see her or ask for her hand, I will, and you can't stop me!"

Thord froze. *Helga?*

Olaf punched him in the face. "Have you had enough?" Olaf growled!

Thord was baffled and felt embarrassed. With the last punch he received and deserved, the fight was over. He was sitting on his behind on the floor.

Olaf saw that his friend was more relaxed and offered him a hand to be lifted. Olaf, still slightly worked up, asked, "So, what's this really about? I never thought you'd be against me marrying Helga?"

"No, my friend, I'm not. I always thought you'd end up together. I'm sorry, really, I am! So, you and Helga, right? How serious are you?" Thord started smiling for the first time.

"Oh no, you don't! Don't go changing the subject. Explain your actions!" He was ready to attack again.

Thord lifted his hands in surrender; he had enough sports for one day.

"Relax, relax," he said. Through awkwardness, he explained everything.

When he finished, Olaf stared at him for a few seconds, then laughed at such a silly notion. He was shocked that Thord could think such a thing.

"Hey, Rose is sweet and all that, but far from my type. Helga is my kind of woman, one hundred percent, and I thought you knew that!" Olaf explained the whole situation to him from the first moment Rose walked into his shop. Leaving out her secret about her parent's death, this was for her to tell.

"She wants to keep the bow a secret for now and later join in some games. She's very determined to perfect the skill and mostly surprise Popi and her family. It means a lot to her, so Helga and I are helping," Olaf showed him the bow he made. "She leaves it here with a sore heart until next when she wants to go practicing."

Thord felt like an idiot for thinking what he did. Thank the heavens he faced Olaf first. What would Rose have thought of him if he confronted her with these notions he had. She came here all ladylike and decent, but now, she was changing. She was more open and free-spirited. He had to admit that he liked her more this way.

Olaf wondered about something and asked his friend, "Are you sweet on the young lass?"

"No!" he answered too quickly. He wanted to explain why, but somehow, it would seem more like an excuse than the truth. He did not know what he was feeling; however, knew it could never grow into something more than a friendship. Him becoming chief forbade that. Even so, he would *never* disappoint his father in that way. They could only be friends!

Thord was about to explain his feelings when Olaf put his hands up and said, "No, my brother, no need to explain. I understand more than you know." —And he did. Olaf and Thord spoke a lot during their years of friendship, and he knew Thord's family history. He knew the respect he had for his father and would never break that. Both nodded and agreed to continue the day as though nothing had happened.

"See you later," Thord said and walked out.

Olaf replied, "Yeah," and continued hammering away.

Olaf went over to Helga's parents early the next day. The marriage was permitted. Helga's parents never expected their daughter to get married, mostly because she was part of their comrades – she was one of the men – and all the men feared her most of the time. They were happy with the choice and always liked Olaf.

The bride's price was settled upon and broken into three payments; the first was to be made before the wedding. The second after the union and the third was like a dowry controlled by the husband, but one he was unable to spend – the gods forbid that something evil should befall him, then his wife had money to care for herself.

The wedding day was set on a Friday –'Frigg's Day'–a tribute to Frigg, the goddess of marriage – it would be held outdoors and in the fall. The wedding plans would be ready before the next season's celebration.

Rose never missed practicing archery. She was getting good at aiming. Helga or Olaf accompanied her in the evenings before supper. They were proud and amazed at how quickly she learned.

The wedding was scheduled in two weeks. There were still a lot of preparations before then. The wedding festivity would last for four days; any less than three were considered paltry. Traditionally, there was a feast ahead with loads of food and drinks. A lot of mead would be available and necessary for the ceremony. Popi explained to Rose that the newlywed couple would be sharing a certain amount of the honey-based ale for a month after the wedding; thus, the 'honeymoon.'

If the honeyed mead ran out before then, this foretold a great displeasure to the gods and a powerful curse on their union. Rose prayed that Olaf would be kind toward this threat — he lived to drink. Maybe they should give them more, just in case.

Eventually, the time arrived. The whole village attended the wedding and would be witness to their nuptials — that everything was done correctly. The two were dressed in their best outfits.

First, they exchanged swords. Olaf entrusted Helga with his ancestral sword; she would hold onto the sword until their firstborn son came of age to pass it down. Helga, in turn, gave Olaf the sword, bearing the crests of her family. The rings were given next; each held the ring before the other on the swords' tips just presented. This act emphasized the sacredness of their union. The couple then joined hands to recite their vows.

After the ceremony, everyone rushed back to the keep for the great feast, except for close friends who wanted to congratulate them personally. For Rose, it was something to behold. She was excited for them and their future together as man and wife. If what Popi said was true about the mead, Rose feared they still had a way to go.

The feast was held at the main eating hall. Olaf blocked Helga before entering, took her hand, and led her safely across the threshold. Popi was Rose's mentor that day and made it clear, once again, that they feared the gods' powers and omens so much that they believed that if a bride should trip or stumble as she crossed the threshold, so would their marriage.

Popi told her that witnesses with torches would lead the couple to their chambers after the first night's festivities. Helga would be prepared for her new husband with her hair spread in a veil around her. Olaf would then enter with a grand fanfare, taunted by well-wishes and ribald cheers. They would be left alone to consummate their union.

It was a memorable event, and the fun began. There were many games and challenges. A few participated in sword fights and other competitions. This time, Rose was also entering and waited for the right time to walk forward. She was still unaware that Olaf told Thord during their brawl in his shop about her bow – in her mind, no one knew except Olaf and Helga.

Rose was on edge. Olaf reassured her that she was good enough to participate and should not be worried. When it was announced, who would enter the challenge with sharpshooters, Rose stepped forward, proudly clutching her new bow, and before the games began, she waved at the newlyweds and to her favorite people in the crowd. Sigrid and Cnut ran closer to inspect her bow in awe and to cheer her on. Many were at first astonished; however, they were cheering loudly afterward. Popi's family made the most noise. She came fourth in the games and was thrilled with the outcome. Olaf and Helga were very proud!

On the last day of the wedding festival, Rose was staying at Popi's later than usual. Var told stories of their gods, how they rule, and how they appreciate sacrifices to appease them. He explained a little of the gods and their children, although not enough to cure her curiosity. She did not want to ask any questions and had them all bottled up for Magdalene.

It was dark by the time she rode back to the main house. The village was quiet as most of the people retired early. Rose had so many questions about their religion and was fascinated with all the gods they worshipped. The Vikings had so many, and one could choose which one to worship and change at any time, depending on the situation. Everyone had a favorite one; some were even named after their chosen gods. Odin was the chief and father of them all, then his two sons and their wives. She knew Thord's mother favored Thor – naturally. His father favored Odin, which made sense, with him being the chief and Odin being the chief god.

Rose was dizzy with all the questions and thoughts going on in her head. She had questions about her own religious beliefs too. That night another memory surfaced while relaxing in bed. The *god stories* must have triggered it. Most of her memories have returned, but there were still bits and pieces that were falling into place.

She remembered sitting with her parents one evening reading the Bible. Her mother always did the reading. While reading, many thoughts went through her mind, so when her mother stopped, she asked both her parents, "Why do we go to heaven?"

"Why do you ask?" her mom asked back.

"I don't know? It doesn't sound right that we all go there. The earth was made for us to enjoy and live on, so why do we go there when we die? I mean, what is there, what do you do all the time, and does everyone go there?"

"I believe so. I guess God gives you an assignment, and you must obey. No one knows."

"But mama, this world has been here for centuries and centuries – forever – and many, many people died. Do you know how crowded heaven must be? What's the point?"

Sara looked at her daughter sincerely.

"Wouldn't you want to go to heaven when you die?"

Rose thought about that, "No! I'd prefer to stay on earth forever."

"No one lives forever, Rose. Everything dies eventually. That's nature – life!"

"I know, mama, but if I had a choice, I'd stay on earth and try to make a difference here and not in heaven."

"My sweet child! Some people find it comforting to know they will see their loved ones again. It's a nice thought, don't you think?"

Rose's mind was on another matter that confused her. Her father listened to their discussion and did not interrupt; he enjoyed the conversation between mother and daughter.

"Rose, dear, do you have any more questions before bedtime?"

When Rose started to think about things, she couldn't help herself. She had a curious mind about everything since a toddler and has not lost it as most children often do when older. She was bright and caught on quickly. The questions just came bubbling out.

"God? Where does He come from? Does He have parents and siblings, and if He does, where are they? Who made him? I mean, if you think about it, He can't just be there, can He? Everything exists through life. Someone must have given Him life as he gave us! It makes no sense! He was all alone, and He decided to make the world and fill it with things. What did He do before then, and how long did it take him to come up with the world idea?"

Her mother unintentionally slammed the Bible closed. Rose stopped talking and stared at her mother.

"Good heavens, child! You're giving me a headache with all your questions, and I must tell you, you will never find the answers you are looking for – no one knows the answers, and no one ever will. You will drive yourself insane. Just let it go!"

Jacq burst out laughing and spoke for the first time, "You have to admit she had good questions there, dear."

"Yes! Still, they are questions that no one can answer!"

Her father gave her a sympathetic look, "Maybe you can ask the priest and see what he says?" Jacq would love to be present for that, to see the priest's expression and hear what he has to say.

"Oh, Jacq, don't encourage the girl!"

Rose looked down at her hands, and in a low voice, said, "I have already asked him."

"No!" Her mom was shocked, and Jacq laughed once again. He was enjoying this very much.

"What did he say to you?" Sara knew she had to apologize to the priest when she saw him next.

Rose looked embarrassed when she told her mother. Her father had a huge smile on his face, and she could not help but return the smile.

"He was quiet for a while; I guess he was trying to comprehend what I was asking. Then he said God works in mysterious ways and all we can do is believe in Him. The priest said he would help me to understand the Bible more. So, I can understand God and how He works, but he seems to be avoiding me."

Jacq could not help himself any longer and tumbled over with laughter; Sara and Rose joined in.

Sara gave her daughter a fond look. "Rose, you have an extraordinary mind – inquisitive and beautiful. Try not to voice your thoughts so openly to anyone. No good will come of it. I say this because I love you and worry that some people might not like what you ask and might question you. It will get you in trouble one day. Next time, please ask us before you ask other people, no matter who they are. Will you do that for me, my dove?"

"Yes, mama, I promise to ask you or papa first," smiling fondly at her father.

He voiced one last thought before bedtime, "I can't imagine all the questions you will have after studying the Bible. You will have the priest go insane, and your mind might burst."

It was Sara's turn to burst with laughter, picturing all the questions she'd ask and the poor priest trying to answer them all. The priest would not last long with her inquisitive mind.

Back to reality, Rose was satisfied with her one God. There were no complications; well, not really. To have so many gods would confuse her altogether. Jessie also had a different religion. The little she knew of what Jessie told her, the Indians' religion was not complicated, and it was easy to understand. Rose thought what they believed in was beautiful, including their rituals. It was a congenial culture.

She still wanted to understand the Viking's religion and all their gods. It might help her to understand them as people. She decided to ask her handmaiden if she wanted proper answers to all her questions. Popi might not want to explain everything, though she would not mind if asked. However, Rose preferred Magdalene with this dialogue.

The days flew by on the island. The next festival was close at hand; it was a few weeks away. The village was full of activity once again. They always prepared a month before the time to get things in order. The second celebration means the harvest will start. It was called '*VetrarBlot*,' where lots of food would be available. Each celebration always began with a sacrifice.

During the harvest, Var gave Rose a sickle to cut the corn. She never used this kind of tool before – it looked dangerous. It had a short handle and a curved blade that looked sharp. Var showed her how to use it before he handed it over. She was clumsy at first, but she got the hang of it after a few tries and enjoyed the workout. Popi explained that they would be working harder to preserve most of the food for the months during winter. There would be no time for loitering.

The 'VetrarBlot' celebrations began early in the morning, same as the first, with no breakfast until after the sacrifice. Everyone was relaxed and in a jolly mood once again. There was plenty of food to consume during the first few days. After that, families were invited to visit certain homes for meals.

One evening, Olaf wanted to have some fun, so he made it his mission to get Rose drunk. In all innocence, he started a drinking game. It started slow, then progressed in more different games that more people began to participate. It turned out to be entertaining with many laughs. Rose drank her fill in mead and soon could not walk straight. She decided to disappear before Olaf found her again and walked as best she could to her room to pass out.

Thord noticed and decided to help her in case she took a slip down the stairs. He wanted to ask Cnut, but he was nowhere in sight. He caught up with her as she was climbing the stairs, and as he guessed, Rose swayed slightly backward, then forward, and as she came for another backswing, Thord ran up and caught her in his arms.

She looked up at him, "Thord, once again, you saved my life. Thank you!" She smiled playfully. When he put her upright, her legs were no more useful to her and she fell flat on her tooshie. He gave a light laugh. Rose felt a little embarrassed, though not as much as she would have if she were sober.

He lifted her off the floor and put her back on her feet, and asked, "Can you walk?"

Rose was in a teasing mood now, "I hope so, or you'll just have to carry me to my room." She giggled, experiencing all the confidence the alcohol brought on.

"You should be more careful; you drank too much, and the stairs can be a deadly place for tipsy people." He was smiling at her expressions.

"Ah, I'll be fine, no thanks to Olaf, though. He's a cruel man to do this to me!" She pouted her lips.

Thord was fascinated with this creature. She had a wild and outgoing personality and cared a lot for others. He was sometimes aloof in case she got the wrong idea; she was not easy to ignore. He was not sure what he felt for her, though. It was a dangerous feeling to have with him becoming chief. Pleasing his father always came first. He had to disregard whatever he was feeling. It had to stop before it got out of hand.

At her door, also being good-humored, Thord gave a slight bow as a gentleman would do and said, "Goodnight to you, Lady Rosaline Dumont."

It was the first time he ever said her full name. As he bowed after saying those words, Rose flung her arms around his neck and kissed him full on the lips!

Thord was staggered at her actions – and intrigued. At first, he paused, then went straight in and enjoyed the sweet taste of her lips. Not long after, reality kicked in, and he pushed her lightly away.

"I'm sorry, Rose, but this cannot happen." He thought a kiss could be an exception, but that was it. "You understand, don't you?" Rose was so drunk, he thought she might not remember, and there was no explaining anything to an intoxicated person. He must advise Olaf not to get her drunk again.

Rose felt slightly embarrassed with her forwardness, but just as fast as it came, it passed. She had no care in the world.

"I'm so sorry! I have no inkling what came over me?" She tried her best not to smile and show some remorse, except it was her best first kiss ever!

"Go inside and sleep this off. We can discuss what happened at a later time." Thord was demanding and sounded stern but still had a hint of a smirk on his face. He was trying his best not to laugh.

"Yes, Sir!" She saluted him and closed the door. Giggling and was pleased with herself, she wobbled to her bed and passed out.

Rose tried her best to avoid Thord for the rest of the celebrations and stayed away from all alcohol. Thord also thought it best to ignore her for now, though he badly wanted to be in her company. Any feelings toward her, apart from being friends, were dangerous.

A week after the festivals, Thord noticed Rose was still practicing archery every day, either early in the morning or in the afternoon when she returned from Popi, before dinner. He was impressed with the way she handled it at Olaf's wedding. Thord decided to wait for the right opportunity to follow and give a few pointers on aiming. He thought she would not mind his input on the matter. He preferred early in the morning than later and slowly followed her into the woods the next day. Rose was surprised when he came riding toward her. Thord smiled and said he was here to help if she did not mind.

She said it was all right and felt a little awkward being alone with him, and even felt uneasy practicing with him staring. Her arrows were all over the place, and she felt embarrassed. They haven't been alone since 'the drunk' episode. It wasn't just her; he, too, was keeping his distance. So far, everything was going well. He gave some excellent advice, and she was happy with the outcome.

Thord stood close behind Rose while she aimed to help with her posture and to keep her arms steady. They were laughing at one point, and she turned smiling — his smile was enthralling; they stared for a few seconds before he leaned down and kissed her!

While the gentle kiss was progressing, she had to lean closer in case her legs gave way. He was holding her, but not securely enough. Rose could feel her legs shaking, and just like that, the kiss ended with her falling on her fanny. She just sat there, dazed and embarrassed. She didn't know what to do or say next, eventually looked up and saw his broad smile.

Thord wanted to laugh, though he kept it in. He extended his hand to pull her up. "Are you OK?" he asked with a huge grin on his face.

She was perplexed. All she said to him was, "You kissed me!"

"You don't make it easy for me, Rose. I see why everyone loves you. You are like an intoxicating drug; a person can't get enough of you."

"What does that mean?" She looked puzzled by his words, knowing their different status and his feelings to please his father. She felt excited but kept her feelings hidden.

"Rose, sweet Rose, I'm sorry for confusing you. I don't know why I kissed you; it just happened. It was an impulse at the time. I'm not sorry I did!" He smiled, "I wish I could explain further. I can't defy my father when I'm so close to becoming chief."

"I know the rules, but won't or can't it change like everything else is, especially when the heart is involved?" She was trying and holding onto hope.

"No, I'm sorry! I can never discuss this with my father and won't. I can't do that to him even if I do have feelings for you. It must end here — we may never repeat this. I wish you could understand. I'm sorry, it was not my intention to mislead you."

Rose stared at him and tried to give her best smile to show that she was fine with what he was saying, except she was breaking inside. She was happy to know that he had any feelings at all and that hers weren't wasted on him. They weren't the same feelings though, but something. Rose had no right to fight this or demand anything from him.

She pushed the subject aside as best she could, and to show that she was OK, she resumed practicing. It did not last long when both agreed to stop for the day. To distract her mind and thoughts, she went straight to Popi's place to continue learning the healing trade with Sigrid. Rose tried her best to accept her life on this island and not have the man she so wanted and desired.

SIXTEEN

Popi was demanding on everyone. They worked harder now to preserve food for the upcoming winter and accumulate enough stock for a trade ship that was planning to leave soon. Rose prayed she was not on the vessel as well. She made plans to meet Cnut in the woods at dawn, to have a little freedom before the day started. If Popi knew, she would have a fit! Working was essential than needless activity. It was pointless riding before supper; she was too exhausted by then. She loved her morning rides when the air was fresh and crisp.

Var went early to the village to give Olaf a hand in his shop. While Cnut's mother and sister were distracted, he sneaked away to meet Rose. She was already waiting for him when he arrived. She was so excited for this free time and took her bow with for practicing as well. They started by pushing their mounts as fast as they could. The wind in her hair was wonderful; it felt like she was flying.

Thinking back to her parents, her mother was always strict on tidy hair — as ladies should look. It was only at night that she was allowed to let it hang free. To be saddled like a man was not permitted for a young lady or riding fast either; it was side saddle all the way. Her father trained her on how to handle a stallion. Now and then, without her mother knowing, she could saddle properly to learn how to control the beast. Rose was an excellent rider, thanks to her father.

The forest was filled with shadows so early in the morning, and the rays were streaming through the branches. Without warning and not expecting trouble, Rose's horse stopped abruptly, started to dance nervously, and wheeled about. She was trying to soothe him, but to no avail. Cnut's face showed pure fear of what was about to happen.

Two snakes were hissing around her horse's hooves. Rose tried to steer the mount away from the danger. Stomping around was its way of defending itself, but it would not obey. The snakes began attacking the horse. Rose swiftly removed her bow, grabbed an arrow from the quiver, aimed and let it fly towards the snake, and missed. The mare would not idle. With luck, she shot one in the middle and it slithered away. The other one was fiercer and came higher for its attack. Rose was aiming when the horse reared up and threw her off. At this period, Cnut was trying to distract the snake by throwing stones at it and shouting.

Thord avoided Rose since their last encounter when he kissed her. Not by choice though, because he had been working just as hard to get the ship ready for trading. That morning, he needed a distraction from his labor, and Rose was a good diversion to unwind.

While he was getting ready for the day, he noticed Rose riding into the woods again. Thord wondered whether he should tag along to give more guidance. He was positive he would not repeat his actions as last. He was still puzzled by his manners. He knew in his heart that they could never be an item; he could never disappoint his father. Thord didn't want to add on to the pain that was already festering there. He did enjoy her company though. He thought he was over it and trusted himself not to repeat a kiss. He was fond of her — that much he knew.

Thord rode in the direction where Olaf put shooting posts up for her training — she was not there! He hoped she did not go further into the woods on her own. He stood there, trying to guess where she might have gone. Maybe she had a quick practice and left for Popi's house.

He was about to turn back when he heard shouting in the distance. He pushed his horse toward the sound and found Cnut throwing stones and shouting. When he took in the scene, he saw Rose lying on the ground, and a snake was about to attack her. Thord acted straight away; he took out his knife and walked carefully forward.

The snake went straight for him, but he had plenty of run-ins with these creatures and killed it with well-skilled moves. He ran straight to Rose and asked if she was bitten and where. She said yes and showed him; it was slightly above her left knee. He took his knife and lightly cut over the two bite marks. Thord immediately sucked the poison out and spat it out on the ground. He did this a few times before looking up and told

Cnut to ride as if Loki was chasing him and to tell his mother what happened. Cnut was beside himself; his eyes were huge, wide with panic. He was worried about Rose and rode like a madman.

Thord sucked again and spat, "Rose, what am I going to do with you? How many times must I save your life?"

"I'm sorry!" was all she could say. At that time, she was not afraid for her life, but this man holding her leg and sucking on it was all she could handle.

Thord helped her stand and called his steed closer. The thought of losing her was too much. The impulse to kiss her was intense. He had his hands around her waist and was about to lift her onto the saddle when he surprised them both and kissed her full on the lips. It was deep and passionate. Just as quickly as it started, it stopped! Her mouth still hung open from the kiss, speechless once again. He did not say a word either.

Thord threw his legs over the horse and leaned down to lift her to be seated in front of him. Securing her on his horse, he rode off in haste, leaving a cloud of dust behind them. They were both silent. The feeling of his arm tightly around her and the closeness of their bodies after that kiss was too much to bare. Rose felt faint and wondered whether it was the kiss or the bite that was affecting her.

When they arrived, Popi was waiting outside and told him to take her straight to Sigrid's room. While Popi was busy with her leg, she voiced her disapproval of how careless they were.

"Child, what am I going to do with you?"

"Thord said the same to me."

"Don't interrupt me, young lady! I'm very angry with you and Cnut, and he had his ear full. You can be glad Thord was there to help. By all the gods, how many times must I save your life?"

"Thord said the same as well!"

"Well, with the two of us saving you all the time, I don't blame him! We don't want to lose you, little one. You mean too much to us! You know this could get worse, and if you're lucky, you'll survive." Popi was trying to scare her, and Rose knew this.

"I have you, don't I? You're the best there is," she smiled.

"Oh, *Lillé*, you'll be just fine, thanks to Thord." She wrapped the wounded area and left to fetch a herbal tea for the girl's nerves. The aftershock has not yet kicked in.

"I'll be right back."

Thord walked in with Popi when she brought the tea. Rose was not feeling that well and took the tea from Popi and almost dropped it. Thus, Popi had to feed her until she emptied the mug.

She could not look at Thord. Still, she had to say something. "I'm sorry, Thord, and once again, thank you for helping me in my distress." She felt a little uncomfortable and wondered what happened between them with that kiss. She was not going to ask why or bring it up. Somehow, she knew what he would say — it would be a repeat of his last explanation and why it can't happen again. She was just glad it did and won't question him.

Thord felt apologetic himself and was baffled by his actions. He had no idea why he kissed her — again! He would not try to explain either. He would leave it unspoken this time and said, "It was nothing, and those things happen to most of us. You should stay until you are well."

Popi ushered Thord out for Rose to rest. Much later, she woke up and felt a presence in the room and opened her eyes. Cnut was sitting on Sigrid's bed, watching her. He looked upset and started to apologize for his cowardice and not acting as Thord had.

"Don't be silly; you were brave, and I'm OK, aren't I? How is the horse?" she asked.

"I'm sorry, Rose! It was in a bad state and had to be put down."

She felt heartbroken and blamed herself for being so irresponsible. She felt as though she had put the poor mare out of its misery. Cnut hugged her and left again, and Rose slept further. Popi came in before supper and brought her food.

"Popi, I killed your horse. I'm so sorry. I feel terrible!"

"It was a good horse; however, you are all that matters now. How are you feeling?" Popi felt her forehead and realized she was growing a fever.

"Tired!"

Popi did not want to stress her further. She fed Rose some more, called for Sigrid, and said, "Sit with her for a while and take that bandage off. I'll be right back..."

One evening, after supper, they were all sitting outside listening to Var's many stories as they often do. At one point, everyone was quiet with their thoughts. Rose was healing well after the snake incident. Thord insisted that she stay at Popi's to recover and mainly to be close in his aunt's care. He often visited to see how she was recovering. Still confused about his feelings, he knew he had to stay away but could not.

Rose would be returning to the main house the next day. No one spoke for a while after Var's story. Rose decided to speak – it was time to tell them the truth.

"I have something to share," Rose spoke up and felt the courage to be honest at last. No matter the outcome, they were her family and would understand. She could not keep it to herself any longer.

She had everyone's attention and went on to explain, "So much has happened after the celebrations and then the death and so on. I had no time to share my news, except with Popi once, and I only told you half of it. I'm so sorry. I was scared!" Rose stared at the four people that meant so much to her.

Popi stopped with what she was doing, and the other three sat up straighter, waiting patiently for her to continue. Rose began to tell them how her memories returned after the first celebrations. She explained that death triggered a death memory. They left her to speak in silence. She talked about her parents, how loving they were, and of the days ending to where Thord found her.

Popi put her sewing on one side and listened intently. The poor child! Such a sad story, and she was acting so brave. She wished the child would cry and let it all out.

Poor Sigrid was feeling the pain and had tears running down her cheeks, frequently wiping them away.

Cnut could not help himself. When Rose finished her story, he got up, sat next to her and hugged her. Rose liked the comfort and hanged on to it for as long as possible.

Var just sat there, drinking his ale and listening. He felt sorry for the young girl and had no idea what to do or say.

"*Lillé*, my dear child, I'm so sorry! We are always glad when you remember things. However, this one is hard to be delighted about." Popi went on, "I'm sorry you had to go through all that pain, but I don't understand why you were scared to tell me?"

Rose explained, "Scared that if the chief found out, he would send me back. I'm not ready to leave or feel I ever want to leave. It felt wrong not to tell you. Keeping it to myself for so long was not fair to you. I guess I'm OK with it now. I hope you understand and forgive me for not telling you sooner."

Rose liked that Popi kept calling her *Lillé*, even though she had a name now. It made her feel special somehow. She went on to explain, "I had a few weeks on my own to take it all in. There are still some blanks in my memory of the last days during my illness; however, I feel they have all returned."

Popi answered, "I'm so happy to hear that! Don't fret by not sharing this sooner. What you must be feeling or going through is hard. No one can imagine your pain. To ease your mind, of course, I forgive you!"

Sigrid still had tears in her eyes. "That is such a sad story, Rose. My heart goes out to you. You are so strong! I would break into pieces if I lost my family."

Rose took Sigrid's hand in hers and held it tight, and said, "You are so dear to me, Sigrid; you are like a sister to me. I would not have changed anything that has happened to me if it meant not meeting you all. Except for my parent's death, I do truly wish they were still alive." She stared at Popi.

"Of course, dear. We all feel the same having you here with us. Do you remember Jessie now as well?" Popi wondered.

Rose gave a slight smile, "Yes, I do. Would you like me to tell you about her?" They all nodded. Rose explained who Jessie was and of her parents once again.

"Jessie was like an aunt and close friend, but we were not related. I don't know anything about her past; she never spoke about herself and always changed the subject when I asked. Not that she was hiding anything; I think it was too painful for her to talk about it. She spoke about her mother many times and how she taught her the healing techniques. I've known her my whole life. Jessie was there at my birth, and while growing up, she was constantly around. I went to her place a lot on the other side of the river. She was always happy to see me. I often helped her to weed her vegetable and herb garden."

This Jessie woman intrigued Popi. "So, Jessie was a good healer?" she asked.

"Yes, as you are. That's why I remembered the trade. Jessie used to show me what she did and taught me a little about it. She saved my mother's life twice; however, could not the third time, or my father."

Rose was back there and felt the pain of losing them. She could remember her mother being sick, but not much her father. She became ill herself by then as well. Her mother died first and then her father, but she was not sure how long afterward. She was too sick to remember. Jessie tried her best to save them, but nothing helped. Jessie did all she could, trying to save her family, and hardly slept. Rose missed her so much. Jessie was the only family she had left.

Rose suddenly looked worried. She looked at Popi and asked with a frightened voice, "Do you think she's all right? Perhaps she got sick and could not take care of me and left me there for someone to find and maybe care for me?"

Popi leaned forward and took hold of her hands — to put the girl at ease, she told her,

"I think she's well, dear. We can't jump to any conclusions at this time. She must have had a good reason for leaving you where she did. The way you speak so fondly of her, I think she felt the same about you. I heard of that day when Thord found you that you were hidden well, which means she was coming back for you. I guess Thord was too hasty when he took you; however, I can't complain. Having you in our lives is the best thing that has happened to us."

"I feel the same. Thank you, Popi!"

Rose relaxed a little, and after a few seconds of thinking, she went on speaking, "Jessie is a kind and wonderful person. She loved my family; we respected her and her profession. My father was Lord of Chinon. King Louis gave the title to him. He was highly respected in our village, and everyone looked up to him. He was general to the king's guards and the army. He was strong in war and steadfast in rules. My father allowed me to sit in a few meetings when the villagers came with their problems. He was a kind man and always gave them enough time to pay their taxes, which the king never knew about.

"My mom, her name was Sara, loved the people just as much and helped where she could. She saw them all as equals. She was an educated woman and raised me to be the same. My father was the first one to accept Jessie in the village. At first, everyone called her a witch and feared her, saying a woman can't be a healer like a man. My father disagreed and said that every community needed a healer. The people slowly started to accept her. We were a happy family before this evil sickness came along.

"My father told me stories of when I was born — how sick my mom was after giving birth, her complications, and how Jessie saved her. I felt sorry for them when they told me how she could never fall pregnant again. I was their only child. My most favorite stories that my father used to share was when he had to babysit me while my mother was recovering."

Her parents loved her very much. Her father was protective of her and always made her mother laugh; they still loved each other after all their years together. As for Jessie, she wished she was well.

Rose's eyes were tearing up for the first time, but she still did not let her emotions out. She was also smiling with fond memories. Her parents were the best! Her life seemed to go on without them around, which seemed weird now. It felt so surreal sometimes that they weren't alive. She felt alone with them not being around anymore — it was a different kind of alone, but she did not share this.

SEVENTEEN

King Louis recuperated from his illness. News arrived that England was building an army to attack. They were on full demand to fend his land against England. No one knew when the attack would be; the king had spies watching all parties and had to inform him of their arrivals. He put his son, Philippe, in command of the military. He wanted him to grow up and become a man instead of drinking every night and spending all his time in the brothels. There would be enough time for that in the future, but for now, he needed to fight and save his birthright that he inherited after his eldest brothers' death, and in time, a good wife. That was still in the future and not important right now.

While he was ill in bed, he was informed of Jacq and Sara's demise. He asked Philippe to send someone to fetch Rosaline. His deceased comrade, Jacq, was a good and trusting friend. He would look after his daughter.

When the messenger eventually returned, he informed the king that Rosaline was missing and presumably taken. The messenger explained that even after hearing this from a woman on his departure, he first went to the village to see for himself and asked around before relaying the news to them. She was indeed missing, and her whereabouts were a mystery to everyone.

Rose was promised to marry Philippe when she turned eighteen. They would have been engaged by now if this misfortune had not fallen upon them. She comes from a decent family, would have been a good and honest woman for his son. However, things have changed, for the future king must marry in his status. He has not discussed this with his son yet.

Her father was a steadfast person. He knew Jacq was very protective of his daughter and made it his duty, as a tribute to Jacq, to find her and bring her home wherever she was. King Louis put the word out for any information about the young Lady Rosaline and her whereabouts, promising a reward for her return. Antoine, Philippe's younger brother, would need to wait until his time comes to marry. If this war turned out to be a disaster, he would have to offer his sons' hand to one of the Brit's daughters to join houses, if he had any.

Philippe knew about the marriage to Lady Dumont and was not disappointed with the arrangement. When he last saw her, Rosaline was very young and pretty. She must have grown into a beautiful woman. He, too, was asking around and trying to find her. He became half-obsessed in searching and made it his mission to bring the people down who took her.

The young Prince Antoine was a quiet boy; as a young lad, he kept to himself most of the time. Now, as a young man, his father allowed him to join in on the council meetings and become acquainted with the work. Not that he was not strapping like his brothers were at his age. His father wanted him indoors, and he was happy to comply. Antoine was a straightforward person; he was honest and open. He was doing well in the council meetings, and his father was proud of him.

He was keeping a secret from everyone; he was gay, or thought he was. He didn't act gay or over-dressed. Like any other man, he acted normal and spoke like every other man, but he knew his thoughts were different. He felt more attracted to men than women.

One evening, to be sure of his feelings, he went to one of the brothels his brothers went frequently. The way they boasted about some of their evenings there, you had to be open with what you desired. He acquired a room for the night and asked for a woman companion with small breasts since big and oversize puts him off. Surprisingly, an attractive woman arrived. He was not sure what to do or how to begin; thus, he poured them each a drink and decided to be honest and told her it was his first time.

She did not laugh at him as he thought she might; however, she was determined to make it memorable for the young man. She decided to relax him first by ordering a bath. She undressed him slowly, and while he was soaking, she made him watch while she also undressed and joined him. She sponged him intimately and allowed him to wash her too by taking control of his hand and moving it around her body. Deciding it was enough foreplay, she climbed out; still wet and dripping, she poured him another drink. After she dried herself, she dried him too and led him to the bed, where she had to lead most of the way.

Antoine was glad for this experienced woman; he was nervous at first. Without her help, he would have given up long ago. It took a while for him to get aroused; thus, she did a particular activity to help him on. He went through the romp to the end, paid, and thanked the woman. They had not spoken much during their intercourse, and he never asked for her name.

While lying in his own bed that night, he went over the evening and his feelings. Not that he had a bad night; the woman was good at her work. However, he still felt the same. He got no arousal looking at women, but it often happened while looking at men. If this ever reached his father's ears, Antoine was sure he would be furious and would likely kill him! He loved his father and would never disappoint him, so he made a vow to keep his secret forever.

Sometimes, he thought his mother knew when she used to look at him, or maybe it was just wishful thinking on his part. He needed someone to talk to and felt that she would have understood or hoped she would. He missed her terribly at times.

Philippe was in the same area where Jessie was. He was traveling all over the Kingdom looking for recruits for their army. Anyone willing to fight for their king — young or old, they are always useful for something.

Arriving at a tavern, Philippe and his men ate and drank their fill and hired rooms for the night — some will camp outside to keep watch. Philippe took his role seriously and was respected by all his comrades. He was growing into a tall and handsome man. He had picked up weight and muscle from all the training he had been given. Most women heard about the lady he was searching for and wouldn't give up until he found her. As women, they found that very romantic, felt attracted to him, and they all tried to share his bed. He was not interested in any of them. However, he was still a man on all counts and had a lady friend he visits at times.

Jessie was still camping and waiting for any signs, trying to decide what to do next. It's been months now, and still no sign of newcomers or any helpful information about Rose's whereabouts. When she decided to give up and return to her home, she heard Prince Philippe was nearby. The news got around that the king and his son were also searching for Rose.

She packed her belongings, and before leaving, she wanted to address the future king. She waited for him to settle before approaching. She was a bit nervous, but she had to tell him what she found out for Rose's sake. When Jessie entered, she went straight to Philippe and gave a slight bow.

"Prince Philippe, good health to you."

One of his men stood up, "Be gone with you, peasant. The prince is resting and wants nothing to do with you!" With authority, he tried to push her away.

She side-stepped before he could touch her, and she went on speaking, "It's about Rose; I might know something that may help in your search."

Philippe stood up, and his man stepped aside.

"Come sit with me, please, and have a drink." While he poured the drink, he looked her over before speaking. She did not look common as most villagers. She was clean and well-mannered. He also wondered how she knew the Dumont family. She was probably another attention seeker as most.

"Who are you, and how do you know Lady Rosaline? What news do you have? And don't bullshit me! I will know if you are lying." He heard many tales about people wanting rewards for their information. In all the stories he heard so far, nothing led them closer to her whereabouts.

Jessie felt uncomfortable sitting across from this young man, keeping an old secret that only she and her mother knew and could not tell a soul. She was also not sure if she was doing the right thing. She might be held accountable and be blamed for losing Rose. She started this, and now she had to finish it.

"My name is Jessie; I used to work for Lord Jacq and his family. I am the town's healer and was asked by my Lord to look after Rose after his death."

Philippe interrupted her, "I remember you, or your name, that is. I overheard Lord Jacq speak about you when my father was sick and what you've done for his town."

"Yes! Lord Jacq was very kind to me and trusted me with the care of his daughter. I'm sorry to say that she was taken from me. By whom I don't know. I heard from others that it was outsiders and people from another land. They looked different and dressed differently to us. I was told they left by ship and said they would return, and I've been here ever since. Waiting for a blessing, or answer to where or who took her, so I know where to start looking."

"Explain to me what you've heard of these people and leave nothing out."

She was feeling hopeful at last until she started to explain. Jessie told the prince everything she heard. When she finished, he sat back in his chair and gave a long sigh. He had a frightened look in his eyes. Jessie saw the look and asked him, "Do you know who took her?"

"Sadly, yes, Jessie, and it ain't good news at all! They are called Vik's, Vikings — they have a bad reputation and are all roughnecks. They are savage people! If they took Rosaline, then she's gone for good. She is probably a slave somewhere on their island."

Jessie was shocked and almost in tears. "Oh no... Please don't say that! There is always a way. If she's still alive, we can maybe try to save her. Will they hurt her in any way?"

Philippe thought before answering, "I do not think they will harm her, for they do not touch a slave. It is forbidden in their culture. They stick to their kind, though some tribes don't care for rules — just pleasure. We can only hope she was not taken by one of those."

Jessie heaved a sigh, "Thank the heavens and pray that she's unharmed! So, there is still hope?" she asked, hoping he would get started and fight for his future wife. If everything was true, Rose was still innocent. Jessie was waiting for an answer from him and maybe hear his plans to save her. He was silent.

"Please tell me you're going to do something and not leave her there?"

"I'm not sure what to do or know where to start looking. I must first discuss this with my father and hear what he thinks about this matter. For now, we must be patient and pray that all is well with her. That is all I can say for now. Would you mind keeping this to yourself? Don't tell a soul what we just discussed. Can you do that for me, your future king?"

Jessie agreed and promised. It must have something to do with Rose's past. She was excused and left the inn.

After the discussion with Jessie, the prince went to his room to be alone. They would leave at dawn to return to the castle to discuss this new information with his father. Standing up to the Vikings would not be an easy task. He feared he had lost Rosaline forever.

EJGBTEEN

Rose could not believe she was on the island for almost a year! Also, the fact that she endured the active lifestyle the Vikings kept. She had learned a lot about this tribe and herself and felt that she belonged. It was late morning, and she was still in bed, feeling lazy and relaxed.

Yesterday, Popi pushed them hard at work. She was very demanding and hardly let them rest. A lot was done — and she gave them the day off today for all their hard work. She and Sigrid were getting more familiar with the herbs and mixing techniques for each different kind of illness. Popi was an excellent teacher, with lots of endurance for the two of them.

Astrid, Popi's eldest daughter, came over for lunch two days ago and announced she was pregnant. The joy was all over her face. Popi was ecstatic and almost in tears with the good news. She hugged her daughter and congratulated her; the girls got up and did the same. Popi voiced her excitement by saying she could not wait for little feet to run all over the place.

It was a beautiful day outside, the aroma of flowers wafted into her room, and Rose was wasting it in bed. A bird came and perched on her balcony and started singing a beautiful tune. She decided it was time to get up. She was going to spend the day with Sigrid and ride around the island.

While washing her face, she heard a knock on her door. Thinking it was Magdalene, she called out, "Come in!" To her surprise, Thord entered.

"Thord! I thought you were Magdalene." She quickly dried her face and felt the heat growing. Realizing her mistake – Magdalene always entered after a quick knock – too late now.

Thord was standing there smiling at her and gave a small laugh, "Sorry! I thought you were already up. I can come back later?"

"No, it's fine, was there something you wanted?" She was embarrassed by his intrusion and smiled shyly.

"No, not really, as you know, it's bath day today." '*Laurdag*' (washing by day) was held every Saturday. "And we are all going for a swim and was wondering if you wanted to join? Kiti was supposed to invite you but said she forgot."

Yeah, sure, Rose thought. She had entirely forgotten about bath day as well.

"It sounds great, and I would love to go." She wondered what she should wear to swim in. While she changed, Thord waited outside the main house for her.

Rose thought they were going down to the beach to swim, but he led her to another place — a place she would never have thought of going or be possible to have fun.

The mountain where she spent her first weeks on the beach between the fishing moors was used for diving games. They started the steep climb, which was not that difficult, and had a narrow path. Rose noticed how high it was and decided to sit and watch rather than participate. The place became crowded, mainly with the young. Everyone was jumping and screaming with joy. Rose felt their enthusiasm.

Thord took his shirt off, and Rose's heart skipped a beat. She had never seen a man's bare torso and gawked like an Idiot at him, then quickly looked away. She was acutely aware of his presence beside her — *he was a god!* She thought. Kiti was there waiting for him. When they both dived together, her heart stopped.

When they returned, he was ready to jump again. He turned and looked at Rose first, gave her a thumbs-up, and dived backward. Her stomach flipped as though she was falling as well. She waited to hear a splash before she could exhale.

Kiti was next; she gave Rose a look before turning and dived. Rose smiled at her. She had no ill feelings toward her and hoped that maybe one day, Kiti might come to know her, and hopefully, they would become friends. Not the way she and Sigrid are, but at least smile and greet each other kindly. What was she thinking? That would never happen between them! She shifted her thoughts to Sigrid and Cnut. *Where were they?*

When Thord retraced his steps back up, Rose noticed Kiti had left. She was in awe of this man. Oh, but what a sight he was! He was all wet and laughing with joyous pleasure; she could not help but laugh too. Kiti was all forgotten, with her fastidious mood.

Thord sat next to her and smiled, "Well, Rose, you have two options. One, you can jump down with me, or two, you can meet us by the shore? We are going to swim for a while before jumping again, and if you want, you can swim with us."

Rose smiled at him and watched how his dripping wet hair hung about his handsome face. She gave a nervous laugh. "No, thanks; I'll meet you down there instead."

Thord wondered, "Are you scared because you can't swim?"

"No... Yes..." She was afraid and was not sure what his actions might be if she said she could swim. She was scared he might take that as an invitation to grab her and jump.

"Well, what is it?" He was staring at her, and it made her nervous.

"I can swim, not as well as you, and I'm a little scared of heights."

"Well, that's fine. I'll meet you down there." He ran to dive in.

When she got up to walk down, Cnut came walking toward her. "And where do you think you are off to, Sir?" She stared at him.

"Hi Rose, going jumping, where else?" Cnut smiled innocently, thinking there was nothing wrong with it. However, Rose would not allow him.

"Oh no you're not!" She grabbed his hand and held it tight, then led him away from the edge. "You are walking down with me so that we can go swim."

"But Rose, I'm fine. I've done this many times!"

"Well, not with me around; my nerves can't handle that."

He did not protest further, and hand in hand, they walked down the mountain, with him laughing all the way.

Rose was sitting on the sand, perspiring a lot while the sun was beating down on her. The water looked very inviting, and on occasion, Thord or Cnut would call on her to join. She could not handle it anymore and walked into the water.

It was so much fun until she noticed Cnut was missing and looked around frantically. She saw him on the edge, ready to jump. She shouted up to him as loud as she could, "Cnut, you little bugger!"

He shouted back, "Sorry, Rose!" He laughed and jumped.

With that, the jumping started again. Rose stayed in the water and watched them drop. It was scarier from that view, and every jump created a massive wave, which made her float further away from shore.

It was almost lunchtime, and Rose had nothing to eat all day. She was starving by now and decided to swim back to shore and sit down to dry before calling it a day. While slowly paddling to shore, out of nowhere came loud screaming and shouting. It was not the cry of joy.

Rose knew something was amiss. All she could think about was Cnut and was frantic with worry. She stopped swimming and looked around to see who was in trouble and noticed everyone was swimming faster to the shore. She looked up and saw Cnut with Thord staring at her from on top of the mountain; however, could not see the horror and fear on their faces.

Rose was relieved and waved; they both shouted back and said she had to get out. Just then, Thord jumped in, swam toward her and told her to swim.

"Swim Rose, swim!"

"Why, what's going on?"

"Swim, in Odin's name, I'll tell you onshore. Swim!" he shouted.

He stayed by her side until they were close to shore while everyone waited for them, staring. Rose had no idea what was happening and wondered why they were so worried about her – she could swim!

Thord stood next to her, and Cnut came running toward them.

"Are you all right, Rose?" Cnut shouted in concern.

"Yes. Why? What's going on? Why do you all look so worried and frightened?" She was utterly perplexed.

Thord explained, "There was a shark swimming toward you! There's no escaping them without losing a limb or arm, even your life!"

"Shark?" Rose just stared at him. She had never heard of a shark before – no one told her. She knew about fishes and so on, but not the real dangers of the sea. Cnut decided to inform her about the subject, and she was shaken. *Why do they swim and take the risk if there are creatures like that in the waters?* She was never going in again!

The days' swimming was over, and everyone left to have a late brunch. The next day, the trade ship was departing. They had to pack all the stock today and would be leaving very early in the morning.

Cnut was all keyed up; his father allowed him to attend this trip with Thord. The chief was supposed to attend as planned. However, he announced he was not feeling well or up for the long voyage and decided to stay. Popi went over to see how he was feeling and what she could do, knowing it was a waste of time. Chief Thorarin did not like to take any medication and always allowed whatever was ailing him to pass on its own.

Everyone was carrying stock to the landing to load onto the ship. The men that were leaving in the morning were spending the day with their families. The voyage and trade always took a long time, probably three to four months,' maybe longer. It was hard to predict when they would return.

Cnut was genuinely excited. He could not stop speaking about what might happen, the places he would see and experience. He could not wait for morning to arrive.

After supper, Thord offered Rose a walk in the gardens. There was a light breeze; you could feel winter was almost upon them — it started getting chilly in the evenings and early mornings. Although it was slightly nippy at this hour, Rose was feeling warm inside while walking with Thord. He spoke about his other voyages and the people he met on the way and knew

Cnut would love it. She was going to miss them while they were gone and felt Cnut's excitement.

He walked Rose to her room, and when she opened the door, he stepped slightly inside, so there were no witnesses to relay his actions. He surprised Rose by grabbing her and kissing her passionately. It was with hunger at first, and then it slowed to sweet nothings. It made her knees weak, and she felt a little faint — always regretting the end!

He gave his irresistible smile, and his last words to her were, "Look after yourself! I'll be seeing you soon." He then turned and walked out.

She was up early to greet Cnut and to wish him well on his trip. When they all left, it was still dark and freezing; so Rose stayed at Popi's, climbed into her old bed and slept further.

NINETEEN

The two girls were busy picking herbs when a rider came rushing toward the house calling for Popi. It was Bui, Olaf's brother-in-law. He sounded stressed and went straight into the house looking for her. Soon, Popi came out with Bui, and he left immediately again. Popi called and told them to get their horses ready. Torhild was in labor; they were both going with for the experience of the birth. She ran back inside to get a few ready-made bottles for what she might need. The girls looked scared and excited and were ready when Popi emerged.

When they arrived at the scene, Torhild's water had just broken, and a pool of clear water lay at her feet. She was sweating and moaning from the pain that started building up again. Popi got straight to work. The girls were standing there like two idiots with their mouths open, shocked at what they saw.

"Come girls; I need you now more than ever. Snap out of it! Torhild needs us." Popi shouted at them.

"Yes, mom — Yes, Popi," they said simultaneously.

"Rose, fetch blankets, and Sigrid, run and get me hot water, and Rose, I will need rags as well," Popi ordered them around while she went to inspect how far the birth was and how Torhild was coping. Rose brought the blankets and rags and helped Sigrid fill the pot with water to boil.

"Rose, bring me a wet cloth and wash this mess on the floor," Popi called out, "Bui, come here, I need you!"

The poor man looked stressed. You would think this was his first child.

"Bui, lay the blankets over there and put your wife gently on them. Thank you, you may leave." He kissed his wife on the forehead and stepped out.

Popi placed a cool cloth on Torhild's forehead and held her hand, and called out, "Sigrid, how far is the water coming along?"

"Almost done!"

"Good!" Popi let go of Torhild's hand and went to see how far the baby was coming along. "You're almost there, my love, the baby wants to come out, but you will have to help it as you remember with Turunn. So, when the pain comes again, I want you to push, OK?"

"Yes... yes... I remember. AAHHHH..." —she shouted in pain.

"Push, child! You are doing well. I can see the head. OK, it's time to breathe and relax. When you are ready, once again, push with the pain."

The pain was intense, "AAH – AAHHH... This is my last child! MMMM... phoo... phoo..."

Rose helped lift the pot when the water was warm enough. The girls brought the water over; they held hands and stood looking at the new baby arriving. There was singing outside; it was getting louder and louder. Rose wondered what they were singing but would ask later. Right now, a miracle was happening in front of her. It looked unbearable — she was amazed how women go through with this repeatedly.

"I see the baby, one hard push, Torhild, then all this will be over and you can hold your baby in your arms."

Torhild gave one hard push and the baby slipped out. Popi held it upside down and gently slapped it on the arse. It gave a loud cry — mother crying too with joy. Popi asked Sigrid to call the father in for a quick peek at the new member of his family.

They covered Torhild up for now, and Popi told the proud father, "Congratulations to you both, it's a boy!" He was beaming with pride. He kissed his wife and whispered something private in her ear. Then Popi added, "Bui, you will need to leave soon, so I can finish up and wash them, OK?"

"OK," was all he said. When he stepped out once again, he shouted, "It's a boy!" There was more cheering.

"OK, girls, it's not over yet. Come closer and see what I'm doing." Torhild was holding her baby while Popi made plans to cut the cord. She measured from the child's end of the cord at the belly button with her index finger's length and tied a knot with a piece of string, then cut the cord above the knot.

"Torhild, one small last push for the placenta to come out, there it is, thank you!" Popi was in her element. Both girls were bending over to see what Popi was doing and when the

238

afterbirth came out, they took a step back; it was a ball of veins or something, and it was disgusting!

Popi took a big bowl, filled it with warm water, and poured something into it from one of her bottles, and said, "Sigrid, you saw what I've just done, please do the same, then you and Rose wash Torhild for me. Start from the top and go down while I clean the baby."

She took the baby to be washed and wrapped it up nice and warm, then took the infant back to the mother and placed him close to the breast to feed.

Torhild looked worried, "He will not suck — why not? I had no problems with Turunn!" She sounded stressed.

Popi took another bottle, which contained honey, rubbed some on her nipple, and said, "It takes a few tries for some babies, but he will suck soon."

She was positive, and they all waited and watched. It did not take long before the baby took the nipple with relish; they were all relieved and laughed with joy.

Popi went to inspect if the bleeding had stopped and made a warm herbal tea for Torhild to drink. She would be just fine. She covered Torhild up decently and was proud of the girls for cleaning up so nicely. She smiled at them and nodded and was pleased — everything was in its place. They would make exceptional healers one day.

"Thank you!" Torhild smiled at them too and thanked them for everything. The two girls went over to admire the baby before everyone else walked in.

"OK, my work here is done; I will come see you both tomorrow and if there are any problems, let me know." She kissed Torhild on the forehead. Popi was satisfied, and the three women left the room for the rest of the family to enter.

When they arrived home, Astrid was waiting for them. Popi went to pack her bottles away while the girls got a drink for everyone and sat down. Sigrid could not help but tease her sister.

"Oh, you are in for a huge surprise!" she teased.

"What are you talking about?"

"All I'm saying is that you are in for a huge surprise!" Both girls laughed except Astrid.

"Stop saying that – Ma...! What are they talking about?" Astrid called out to her mother.

Popi walked in. "Never mind them, how are you feeling?"

"I'm fine, and where were you? I was waiting a long time!" she complained.

"Torhild was in labor and gave birth to a healthy baby boy," Popi explained.

"Oh!" Now she knew what Sigrid meant and looked at her.

"Told you, surprise when that pops out." She could not help teasing her sister. It was too easy.

"Stop it! Ma, she's scaring me. What happened over there?" She looked worried.

"Sigrid, stop this nonsense! Nothing happened; it was like any other birth. Everything went fine."

"If that is like any other birth, then I don't want any of it!" Sigrid answered.

Rose could not help but laugh at them all. She looked at Astrid and said, "It was beautiful and wonderful all at once, and yes, to be honest, it's a little scary too, but with your mom around, you'll be just fine."

That did not help Astrid, and she started crying. Rose felt terrible as she never meant to upset her. She was trying to console her with her fears. "I'm sorry, Astrid! I never... I was trying to help!"

Popi spoke, "It's fine, Rose. You said nothing wrong. When you're pregnant, you are very sensitive and emotional since your body is going through many changes. Now, you two go out and finish your work, and leave us alone for a while. Go now!" Popi ordered.

The two girls sat under a tree and spoke about what happened.

Sigrid asked Rose, "Do you think you'll ever have a baby and go through all that?"

"I don't know! I might say no now, but maybe one day and just one baby," she laughed, "I think going through that once is enough, and you?" she asked Sigrid.

"No, never! Not even once! Being pregnant is too much stress. It's the crying and what else that comes with the pregnancy, then the birth itself! Not looking forward to it at all! However, I do feel guilty about teasing Astrid. Let's be more understanding and maybe help where we can. What do you say?"

Rose laughed with the 'we' in her sentence, almost as though she teased Astrid as well, but agreed to be more sympathetic toward her in her condition. Rose had always been friendly but said nothing. She remembered the singing outside while Torhild was in labor and asked Sigrid to explain.

"They send a prayer to the goddesses, Frigg and Freya, then sing a ritual to protect the mother and child. In nine days, there will be a gathering to bless the child. You should perhaps bring a gift. It will be held in the chief's main room." Both girls sat there with their thoughts until Popi called them in for lunch.

After the baby was nine nights old, he was given a name and became a legal member of the family. It was the public naming ceremony of the child after ten days.

Bui was sitting on the chief's highchair in the main hall waiting for everyone to arrive and be seated for the ceremony to begin. Magdalene explained earlier that they would sprinkle water on his head or dunk him in ice-cold water. The purpose was to protect him in battle when he was older.

So, it began. Bui sat waiting for his wife to come forward with his new son.

Torhild walked forward with her baby in her arms, stood in front of her husband, and said before presenting his son to him, "I have borne you this bairn, hale and whole. Will you know him as your own, born of your clan? Or shall he be cast out of the garth, to live or to die with troll and warg?"

Bui inspected the baby, then accepted him and took him in his arms. He lifted him high and said, "All worthy in might ween I the bairn, come he now, the clan of my blood. High ones and holy hear now my words, this name I give—Rurik—my child—my son!"

Bui was smiling. He was a very proud father of a healthy boy. They sprinkled water on the infant's head, which he was not happy about. He was named Rurik, after his great-great-grandfather. Rurik was a fierce warrior and a great man to be named after, and everyone was pleased.

One by one, they brought the child gifts and wished him well. Rose went forward and gave a soft doll-like shaped toy. It was made of thick material and stuffed with sheep wool; she gave her best sewing ever, with much-needed help from the women! Bui said, thank you. She smiled at him, then looked at the baby and took his hand.

"Hello, Rurik, do you remember me? Aah... he's so adorable — and so big!" Bui beamed with pride at those words. People came forward and gave their blessings. Rose stood close to hear what they had to say, and Magdalene stood beside her if she needed to explain certain words.

Kiti walked forward and said, "May great Thor protect you with his strong arm and his mighty hammer, may the good Mother Holle (Odin's wife) embrace you, and bestow all blessings upon you, small and holy one!"

Chief Thorarin came next, "May the father of all the gods give you knowledge on your journey. May Thor grant you power and courage on your way, and may Loki give you amusement and laughter as you go about your days."

Popi and Var went forward to bless the little one and said, "May the gods and goddesses smile on him. May our father, Odin, guard and guide him, and may the Norn's grant him a fine orlög." Bui was satisfied with the blessing. It was an honor to his ancestors and the name he was carrying.

Rose looked at Magdalene with a questionable stare and said, "Orlög?"

"Oh, miss, that's a very complicated thing to explain and a very long one as well, but I'll try to make sense of it in short for you." She thought of how to explain, "Well, orlög is the same as karma or fate — it's more or less the same thing but are slightly different. Part of orlög is inherited — it is believed that it's passed down through your ancestors. It will mostly come from your parents, lesser down to your grandparents and still further down, and so on. You alone are still responsible for the actions you take. In theory, this part of inheritance stresses the importance of family in their beliefs. As I said in the beginning, orlög is the same as karma and fate, in that; there isn't automatically the idea of good or bad.

"It states that things will happen to you, regardless. The part of orlög determines is built through the actions and behaviors you show throughout your life toward others and the world, as well as yourself. If you tend to be honorable, you will generally find yourself surrounded by honorable people who treat you honorably. Or doing something undesirable or bad will affect you the rest of your life and your family in a negative way.

"It's what determines your actions or behaviors as a leader, companion, partner, or just someone desirable to others. It goes so far as to say you strive to be desirable to the gods. Norn's play a big part in this, which is a much longer story, maybe for another time. I'll say one more thing before you leave."

Everyone was seated and ready to eat. They wanted to say a prayer before their meal, so Magdalene tried to explain quickly, "The Norn's are responsible for your primal layers or determining your fate. It can be altered, but it is not easy to change." She ushered Rose to a chair and could see she was still a little confused by it all — maybe she explained it wrong?

Rose said nothing during the explanation and was still trying to process it all. Then, the prayer began. The chief stood up and spoke up with his loud voice,

Lord Odin,
We all give our greetings to thee.
Please bless the newborn present,
may he grow to be strong and healthy,
pleased by all the gods.
Bless this bounty set before us
and may we enjoy this good food and drinks
with good company.
Hail and love to Thee.
United, they said, *"Hail and love to Thee."*

TWENTY

At first light, Rose was up and washing her face. She was feeling chilly as the seasons were changing. She heard a commotion outside, and someone shouted that the ship had returned. She knew nothing about the trade market and thought that maybe they forgot something important, or it went well for them to return so soon.

For some reason, Rose went ice-cold and shivered, and not from the cold. She grabbed the first thing she found and ran to her balcony. A single boat rowed to shore. When the dinghy arrived, she could scarcely identify the person; however, she knew it was Olaf. As he climbed out, he leaned over to retrieve something in the dinghy. By all that was holy, he was carrying a person in his arms!

A scream came out of nowhere that reminded her of the day when Olaf's mother passed away. He carried the man into the village and laid him gently on the ground. She heard the stress in everyone's voices and decided to see who it was and what happened.

When she reached the village, a crowd stood around. As she pushed her way through, she was shocked to her core when she saw Cnut lying there. He looked pale, and his lips were blue. Someone shouted that he was still alive. Olaf returned with a blanket he obtained from the nearest house. Rose grabbed the blanket and covered him, then took Cnut's hands in hers and held them tight; they felt cold and tried to warm them. The tears were unable to flow.

Rose shouted toward the crowd, "Has anyone sent for Popi?"

A woman answered and said she was on her way.

While rubbing his hands to keep them warm, feeling at a loss with what to do, Rose whispered close to his ear, "Cnut, sweet, Cnut! It is I, Rose. Your mother is on her way. Please, do not leave us! Your mom will fix this; just hold on a little longer." She could see his eyes flutter, though they would not open.

It felt like hours before Popi arrived. Rose kept speaking to him, not wanting to stop, lest he drifted off. She had a sinking feeling that from this day on, everything was going to change.

Someone shouted that Popi had arrived. Rose kissed him on the cheek, left his hand and stepped aside for Popi. It was fully crowded when she came running through to her youngest child. She pushed past Rose so quickly without seeing her that she almost fell. Rose never realized that Olaf was standing next to her until she fell back against him, breaking her fall. He could see the pain in her eyes as they stood together, watching the scene. There was silence between them.

The distraught mother put her head on her son's chest to listen and then her hand on his lips to feel for any air coming out. He had a weak heartbeat, which was a good sign that he was still breathing.

Olaf was explaining to Popi, and everyone nearby heard; that on their way to the trade markets, and before docking, they were getting the stock ready for loading when they were attacked out of nowhere. An assault they did not expect or were not prepared for, put them at a disadvantage. They lost good men that day, and a few were wounded. Olaf knew he could not tell who had passed until he shared the tragic news with the chief. It was the chief's duty to announce the information to their people.

He was not looking forward to it and wished his friend — brother — was with him right now. No one knew how his heart was breaking at this moment. Helga was still on the ship with the others; she would be arriving with the deceased soon. She promised to support him when he confronts the chief with the tragic news.

Popi wasted no time in caring for her son and taking charge. Not speaking to anyone specifically, she asked for a bucket of warm water and clean rags. She did not want to move him yet. She turned Cnut on his side and searched for further injuries. There was so much blood, and not long after, her clothes were soaked with it too. When the water came, she started cleaning most of the blood away to see how nasty the wounds were; there was one bad cut on his arm and head. His leg was bleeding the most. She noticed his head was sagging to one side, then laid him gently back on the ground. He was losing a lot of blood!

"Come, my baby, don't leave me! Come back to me... please, come back!" She pleaded with him. If she did not act now, she would lose her child forever. The gods may not have him yet — it was not his time!

Popi was speaking to him, trying to encourage him to fight. She was ripping fabric from her dress to tie around his injured leg to stem the bleeding — it was bleeding out of control. Rose also noticed his head limping; Cnut was as white as snow. She had tears in her eyes, watching the scene. Popi started to hit on his chest and was frantic now, thinking she had lost him. She was hoping for a miracle.

The crowd was silent, and Olaf went forward to see if he could help. He believed the child was dead and tried to tell Popi that it was over and wanted to help her up, but to no avail. She refused to leave her son's side. She was kneeling the whole time and felt forlorn, then dropped on her behind, took her child in her arms, and gave a loud, sad shriek.

Rose jumped with fright, and a shiver ran through her body, the tears just flowing down. She felt excruciating pain watching this sweet woman lose her youngest child. She did not deserve this as a mother, to suffer the loss of a child so soon. Rose wanted to go to her and support her but knew Popi was nowhere near to be comforted. So, she silently prayed to her one God to help this family, and if there was any hope, to save Cnut's life.

No one noticed that Popi's family arrived and was watching along with them. Var walked up to his wife with tears in his eyes, kissed his son on the mouth and tried to help her up, to persuade her to let him go. Now, everyone had given up, except Popi, who would not have any of it. She was not the type of woman to give anything up so soon. There was always a way. There had to be. She went on by cleaning the blood and inspecting the wounds.

Olaf was watching Rose; he felt sorry for her. This was her family too. He wanted to console her; however, he knew it was not the time or place – that time would come. He would be there for her if she needed a friend. He knew the pain for her and everyone, has not yet begun. It was yet to begin when the deaths are announced. By the looks of it – once again – she was going to be alone in her pain. He promised himself that he would be there for her when the time came. It was a sad time for the family and the village. Everyone loved him. It felt as though everyone was losing a child that day.

Popi held her child once again and rubbing him to get warm. With her eyes closed, rocking herself and her child, she prayed aloud for all the gods to hear. Not just one, but every god she knew, and she called them all by name; she was begging them to help her and give Cnut strength to fight for his life.

Then, in the quietness of the village, someone in the crowd shouted, "He moved his hand! I swear I saw him move his hand! He's still alive! Praise the gods – praise Odin!" Then everyone saw it happen again, and they all shouted, *"Praise the gods! He's still alive! Praise the gods!"* Rose was so happy and relieved; she, too, cried out with the people.

Cnut was not giving up and was fighting for his life.

Popi acted immediately with new hope and called for Olaf, Var and Sigrid to come forward. Her husband helped her to her feet while she gave them all orders to act immediately. There was no time to take him to their house, so Olaf was to take Cnut to the chief's house, put him in the nearest room on the ground floor and undress him. Sigrid was instructed to pick certain herbs from their garden, and before leaving, her mother asked her to repeat the list — it was imperative that she remembered each herb. Rose was listening and wanted to contribute somehow; when Sigrid left, she went along to help her with her task.

Popi looked at her husband and gave him a quick hug. While walking toward the house in haste, she gave him orders as well.

"My husband, while I'm busy in the kitchen with my herbs, I need you to bathe our son. I need him clean before I can see to his wounds and inspect his leg, which I shall need more warm water for." Var just nodded, and when they entered the main house, he was off in the other direction to get buckets of water, rags and soap while Popi went to her child. She could do nothing until Sigrid returned with the herbs.

Olaf did what she had asked him; Cnut was on a bed, laying there naked with a blanket over him to keep him warm until she arrived. He started a fire in the hearth to keep the room warm. Popi was thankful for all he had done for her son. She could see in his posture and the look in his eyes that he was contrite.

She gave him a sincere smile and said, "Thank you, Olaf, you may leave now. I have everything under control."

He was sure she had and left the room. He stood outside the chief's main room, dreading what he had to do next, and wished that Popi had more chores for him. Olaf stood and waited for Helga to accompany him.

Chief Thorarin attended the scene at the village; no one noticed him, and he left soon afterward. Everything that happened on this island concerned him and always touched him personally. No matter who it was, they were his people — his family! He was at the shore waiting for the other boats to arrive, to hear from his son what had happened. No boats were coming in anytime soon, and he wondered why. The ship should have been docked on the landing as well, to unload the merchandise, not out there — and why was Olaf the only one here? He was stricken with worry and wanted to know what was going on.

He walked back to the village, planning to call Olaf and question him, but noticed he was busy with Popi, trying to help her up as she refused to obey. Thorarin felt sorry for his sister and knew she would not give up fighting for her son's life. He decided to wait for answers in his meeting chambers where Kiti was waiting for him, not wanting to go to the village. She was waiting to hear the news from her father as to what was happening in the village. Kiti was in no mood for another tragedy, so she stayed away from the scene. Not that she did not care; she loved her people, but whenever there was a death, she lost a part of herself. She had lost too many people close to her heart in her short life on earth.

Helga was taking her time — Olaf decided he could not wait any longer and had to face the chief alone. Just then, Rose and Sigrid came riding up close to the house, jumped off their horses, and left them unattended while running toward the entrance. Helga was right behind them. Instead of scolding her and asking where she was, he forced a smile and thanked her for coming.

Sigrid ran to her mother with the herbs, and they left for the kitchen straight away.

For some reason, Rose stood rooted in the main entrance passage. She was at a loss as to what to do. Odd, she felt she would be in the way. An extra hand was always good in this kind of situation. However, she decided to wait until they returned and ask if there was something she could do to help.

She noticed Olaf and Helga enter the chief's room. They did not look too happy; she thought they were afraid of being scolded for whatever happened to Cnut and for being blinded by the attack.

Var came through with a big bucket of water and went into Cnut's room. He was going to bathe his son while Popi was busy in the kitchen.

"Can I help with anything, Var?" Rose called out, wanting desperately to keep busy.

"Not now, Rose, thank you. Why don't you wait for Popi and hear if she needs your help."

A few minutes passed when Rose heard Kiti scream and heard a thumping sound as though someone threw an object against a wall. Rose wondered what the matter was. Not long after, she heard the chief's loud voice but not the words. Helga came out with Kiti in her arms, carrying her to her room.

"What's the matter Helga, is she all right? What happened?" Kiti was as white as a ghost and wished Helga would tell her.

She did not want to say and asked Rose to send Popi in to see the chief when she saw her.

Rose went straight into the kitchen to give Popi the message; as expected, she was unhappy with the news. They were busy with the last concoction, mixing the potion. There were three bottles on the table, one thick ointment, and two liquid medications. Popi informed Sigrid to make sure Cnut's wounds were cleaned adequately before rubbing the salve on and to use a generous amount on each wound. Rose informed her that Var was with Cnut, bathing him.

"Good. Your father can help you while I see what the chief wants from me at this imperative time. He must know how important my mission is. Please remember Sigrid; make sure he drinks this entire bottle of potion. He needs to be completely out when I examine his leg!"

Popi was very upset with Thorarin for calling on her while her son was bleeding to death.

Rose briefed her on what happened so far, "Helga carried Kiti to her room; it must have been something Olaf said? She would not tell me. She just said to ask you to see the chief as soon as you could."

"Thank you, Rose." She looked at her daughter and said, "You will be fine while I'm gone, Sigrid?" Popi was waiting for an answer from Sigrid before leaving.

"Yes, mom, I'll be fine! Go to the chief and come back quickly."

"I'll be back as soon as I can." Popi walked off to the chief's room and entered without knocking.

Rose followed slowly behind, waiting outside. She wanted to hear what was going on. A few minutes went by when Sigrid came out of the kitchen and went into Cnut's room. There was nothing to do; thus, Rose stood with her ear plastered against the door to listen in to what the chief had to say. When she heard Thord's name, she listened more intently!

"Chief Thorarin, I hear you called for me! It must be crucial, for you know I am busy with my son's needs. He demands me now more than ever." She did not want to sound rude; she was just trying to let him know how crucial the situation was.

The chief looked as though he had aged ten years since the last she saw him, and that was yesterday!

"Popi, my sister, I can imagine how you must be feeling, and I know you want to do all you can for your son. All I ask is that you send Kiti medication of the poppy. She is all out of sorts and needs to relax. She needs to sleep it off."

"May I ask why it is so important to call on me for that? There's something you're not telling me!"

Thorarin did not want to tell her now while she was busy with her own child and wanted her to be in full mind for her task ahead. Nevertheless, Popi was adamant and wanted to know now before she left. The chief was fighting to keep all his feelings inside until everything was sorted, and he could be alone to break down.

"My son…" He paused while going on. He was trying to be strong, though he was breaking inside. "My Thord is dead!"

It felt like Popi was slapped on the heart by the way it skipped with those words. She sat there crying for her chief and the loss of such a great man.

Thorarin continued, "Popi, please be strong for your child and bring him back to us. Mine has gone; nothing can change that. Please send some poppy for Kiti to rest. That is all I ask at this time."

Popi stood up, wiping the tears from her eyes, "I'm so sorry for your loss, my brother. I will send Sigrid to Kiti immediately."

Rose's knees went weak when she heard Thord was gone — dead! She sat on the floor, shocked. This day kept getting worse. Rose's own body felt ice cold and dead. She couldn't handle any more news and wanted to hear nothing further; thus, ran to her room in a daze and fell on her bed. In shock, she was trying to come to terms with everything that happened — it all felt like a dream — so surreal, and she'll soon wake up from this nightmare.

Her heart was so tightly locked up with everything that happened to her and her loss so far, and still she could not cry — the shock was too much — her world was spinning — stunned, staring at the ceiling. Rose never left her room that day and slept all night. She woke up in the middle of the night and just laid there thinking about Cnut and prayed that he was all right. The thought of how much she missed Thord and not being able to see him anymore was unbearable — heart-breaking! Moreover, she could not imagine what the family was going through.

For the first time, she heard silence outside, which was not common on the island. She ate nothing the following day and felt a little peckish. She lit the candle by her bedside, and to her surprise, found food. There was bread and a piece of meat on a plate with a mug of mead. The food was cold, and even though she was hungry, she could not eat. Her stomach kept turning. She did try and ate very little, drank all the mead and went back to sleep.

The following day, she woke up with more silence. There was no hitting on metal, calling out oaths, or shouts to the next person. It was as though the whole island shut down. The silence made it all feel so real, and she felt lonelier than she ever felt before. Her handmaiden, Magdalene, walked into the room. Rose was groggy from all the sleep; she sat up and rubbed her eyes.

She remembered the food and said, "Morning, Magdalene. Thank you for leaving food for me last night. It was very thoughtful of you."

"Good day, miss! I have no clue. I brought nothing up; I was told to leave you alone and that you did not want to be disturbed."

Rose looked confused. "Who told you not to disturb me?"

"It was Popi and Olaf, Miss Rose. How are you feeling this morning? Olaf sent me to see how you are doing. I believe he must have brought the food at some point." Magdalene knew how she felt about Thord and how close she was with Cnut. She poured fresh water into a bowl for Rose to wash her face.

Rose was lost in thought; with everything on Popi's plate, she still had time to think of her. How she came to love that woman, she has always been caring and thoughtful to her needs. Olaf's kindness and care touched her even more.

Magdalene went on speaking while tidying the room, "Everyone is going down for breakfast. Will you be joining them, or should I bring you something?"

"Yes, please, and thank you, Magdalene. I don't think I'm ready to face everyone yet. I will go when I'm ready. I am still not in the mood to get up right now. However, I would like to know how Cnut is doing and if they need my help with anything." Not that she could concentrate on mixing herbs right now, but she would do her best if needed. Rose wanted to know about Thord as well, where his body was, and when his burial would be. However, she could not say his name out loud.

"What I've heard, miss, is that he's doing well so far and that Popi hasn't left his side."

"I'm glad to hear that!" Sorrow filled her heart once again as she fought back the tears. Magdalene left her in peace. She slept the day away once again and never left her room. This time, Magdalene brought something for her to eat.

The following day, Rose felt she needed to get up and face the day. She washed, got dressed and went down to eat.

When she entered, everyone was seated and dishing food onto their plates. No one took notice of her, and all had puffy eyes from crying and too little sleep. To her surprise, she saw Popi's family sitting at the table. Rose wanted to run to Sigrid and hug her but did not. Popi was missing; she must still be by her son's side. Kiti was also missing. There was silence in the room.

No one knew what to say, so everyone ate in silence. She went and sat beside Sigrid. They held hands under the table and stared at each other in silence; no words were needed. Rose dished up a little and took a few bites and a sip of mead. She looked over at the chief. For the first time since arriving in this house, Chief Thorarin sat staring and pushing his food around on his plate. He looked pale and heartrending. She felt sorry for him. Not long after, she stood up and left the room. Rose could not handle all the grief around her. She needed to be with Popi, for her sanity. It just felt right to be with her.

When Rose entered the bedroom, she first walked over to Cnut; he was in a deep sleep with the help of all the medication. She inspected his injured leg and noticed that it was gone! She was at a loss for words with what Popi had to go through to remove her son's leg. She kissed him on the cheek and stared at Popi. She was sitting at the window looking out. She hadn't noticed Rose enter the room – spell-bound in her thoughts. Popi looked lost and very tired. She refused to leave her son's side. Rose saw a plate of food on the table, untouched.

Something stirred in Rose's body. Suddenly, it felt like jelly. Her heart fluttered and started to pain for all her loss. She said nothing and walked over to her old friend, sat down at her feet, put her head on Popi's lap, and started crying her heart out. She cried for her father, her mother, for Jessie, for Popi, and for a brother — friends Rose knew and came to love dearly in such a short time. She also cried for the only man she had ever loved, lost so soon.

Popi looked down at the young girl, soothed and stroked her hair, and cried with her. They sat there in silence for a long time until Rose cried herself empty of emotion.

When Thord's mother died, Siv, Popi's younger sister, Popi took on the role of a mother for her kids. The sisters were very close; they were inseparable. Popi put her feelings aside that day to help her sisters' two young children. Thorarin took it badly and was absent for many days. Popi and her family lived with them for a long time until she felt that they could cope independently. Now this, Poor Thord lost to them all. Her heart went out to her brother-in-law and his daughter. They lost so much, and poor Kiti must feel it even more since they were twins.

The separation was not good, and it's not the first time they have lost a family member. Popi wanted to be alone. She wanted no one around her until Rose walked in and started crying. She thought she could cope on her own. Now, she realized just how much she needed her family's strength through all this.

She knew Rose was eventually crying for all her losses — the poor soul. She had not cried over her parent's death, having been sick most of the time, then the change in her life on this island prolonged it — until now. She knew Rose was in love with Thord, as every young girl was on the island. Rose always blushed when he was close. He found it amusing, but Kiti thought it was pathetic. She knew her brother was handsome; as for herself, she had the same features.

Popi was in a daze since all this started. It was as though Rose brought her out of her sad bubble and popped it! She was still heartbroken, but she saw the world again and the living and how they must be feeling as well. Everyone was in pain, and Popi realized that she was not making it easier for the rest. Worse, because they did not know how to handle her. Thank the heavens, Cnut was recuperating.

The hours flew by, and they spoke about nothing specific, allowing the day to pass. Sigrid entered to see how they were doing and brought them something to drink. She knew Rose would want to see her mother and let them be. Rose stood up to greet her, and Sigrid looked at her mother with tears and worry in her eyes.

"I'm so sorry, mommy!" was all she could get out before crying. Popi stood up for the first time and held Sigrid close.

"It's not your fault, my child. I am the one that should apologize for not making it easy for you all to mourn him as well. I see now that we all should grieve together."

They drank their drinks, Rose shared hers with Sigrid, and Popi said to follow her, so they did — not knowing what was on her mind.

When they entered the chief's main room, everyone was there, including Olaf. Popi saw all the sadness and worry in their eyes and spoke to them all.

"I would like to apologize; for all our losses and of fear to grieve openly in front of me. I have been selfish in my feelings. I want to thank Rose for reviving me out of my trance, showing me that we are all in pain. We will all do this together and stand by one another, as it should be, as a family. I know how you must all miss him as I do. Cnut's condition had me busy for over a day, and all reality hit me when I had a chance to breathe."

"How is our Cnut's condition?" Olaf asked.

"For now, he's doing well and sleeping most of the time; when he wakes up, he will be in much pain and shock. All his wounds are looked after and covered. His leg was infected, so I had to do what was needed. He's healing fast; he's a strong kid. The will to live is strong in him. I just hope that it will all pass soon so this island can get back to normal again." Popi looked tired.

Thorarin got up and hugged Popi, and she cried in his arms, "We are all here for you and Kiti."

"Thank you, my sister, as we are always here for yours!"

Kiti stood up, hugged her, and cried with her aunt. Popi asked about the burial.

Var spoke up, "All is being arranged, and it will be in two days. We can discuss that later."

Popi walked over to her husband, sat next to him and kissed him on the cheek. While holding his hands, she whispered something in his ears for him alone. You could see the tears flowing down his cheeks. She looked at everyone and then at Rose.

"This is how it should be. Thank you, little one, for waking me up." Rose just stood there and smiled at her friend.

Through all this, Sigrid was left to heal all the wounded that came off the ship. She, too, was exhausted and stressed out, wondering if she was doing it right. Now that her mother and Rose were back, they could help, especially Rose, as her mother would still stay at her brother's side until he wakes up.

Chief Thorarin offered everyone to sit down and ordered food and drinks. When the food arrived, they all ate to their heart's content. Popi fell asleep on the couch next to Rose and Sigrid while Var spoke to the chief and Olaf.

Kiti and Astrid were having a private conversation. Astrid was mainly talking about her husband and being pregnant. Kiti was envious of her cousin; she always felt so alone and pushed aside. All she ever wanted was a life of her own. Now that her brother was dead, she knew she would never leave the island. Her father needed her more than ever now. She was all he had left — or not! She hoped and wished that not all was lost!

TWENTY-ONE

Rose has been in her room — bedbound since early yesterday and had not left it since. She was despondent and felt drained of all energy. So much had happened in one year, and felt she, too, had changed from the girl she used to be to the one she is now. She could understand their language fluently even though she could not speak it as easily as she would have liked.

Everything was about to change for her once again, and that scared her. Rose honestly thought that she belonged here with these people whom she came to love and respect. She was home! Things had changed since the sad tragedy of losing their beloved Thord, what happened to Cnut, and to all their other losses of the disaster, which occurred at sea. Nothing was the same anymore. The island seemed more quiet than usual.

Chief Thorarin left his hair unwashed in mourning for his son's death. Not to bother him and to keep it orderly, two thralls braided his hair. He would be enduring this rite for a month. This happened after the funeral took place. The

Vikings were very particular with cleanliness and clean hair; this meant a lot in mourning. It's said, their god Odin performed the same ritual when he lost his son.

Kiti joined her father in this ritual. She did not only lose a brother but a best friend. It was not just their looks that were identical, but their minds too. They shared the same womb and entered the world on the same day. They could understand each other's feelings, and at times, knew what each was going to say before saying it. Kiti lost half of herself, and her heart was broken in two.

A few days ago, a week after the funeral, was the ceremonial celebration of Thord's remembrance of the person he was. He was going to be missed! There was a lot of drinking involved, more than they had for the older woman, Turid, and many, many tears. Rose had her share of drinking, even though she could not speak up with the others. She had her memories of him and had a personal celebration of his life in her own way. If it weren't for him, she wouldn't be here to meet the people she came to love dearly. She thought it was fate that Thord found her and brought her here.

Her heart still ached for her parents, but on the other hand, she gained so much more on this island after losing her parents. She felt blessed to have Popi and her family in her life. Thus, with every thought of what he had done for her, Rose took a sip — one for kindness, another for always being friendly, and so on. The fact that he saved her life on numerous occasions meant more.

Rose sat alone in a corner listening to what they were saying about him and became tipsy. She left early to cry herself to sleep.

The story that later arose about the disaster was that England was the enemy that attacked their vessel. England was on their way to conquer France, and somehow, with no explanation, the Vikings were attacked by surprise.

A few days after Thord's memorial, the chief called for her, which was unusual. He never called her before. When she entered, he was formal and straight to the point, and she had been in her room ever since her meeting with the chief.

Magdalene walked in to do her regular chores for the day and noticed Rose was still in bed.

"Miss, are you feeling unwell?" She wondered why Rose was not up and about doing her normal day-to-day activities. Rose had no strength to get up or have a conversation with Magdalene.

"I'm fine! I still feel tired, that's all," she said without looking at her.

Magdalene had not heard what the chief had said, so she did not understand the girl's mood. She tidied a little where she could and filled the jug with fresh water. It was cold outside; thus, she started a fire in the hearth to warm the room up. She did not blame Rose for wanting to stay in. On her way out, she said that she'd return later to finish cleaning up. Rose turned on her side and closed her eyes, trying her best to ignore the world around her.

When Magdalene returned after lunch, thinking Rose was gone by now and was surprised to find her still in bed.

"Miss Rose, you missed breakfast and lunch. Should I fetch you something to eat?" More worried now than before, she wondered what brought this on.

"No, thank you," was all she said.

"If you are not feeling well, I can call Miss Popi for you?"

Rose wanted to see no one and was not in the mood for Popi to fuss all over her.

"I said I was fine, so please don't!"

"OK, I'll be back later then." When she closed the door, she contemplated what to do. Should she tell Popi or just leave it for the time being and see how it goes? When Magdalene returned after supper, she brought a plate of food and a big mug of mead for Rose. She had to eat something or try to at least. Magdalene believed a little mead always brought some life back into a person and hoped it would help her mistress. She put the food on the bedside table, but Rose showed no interest in any of it.

"Please, miss, you need to eat something, or you'll grow weak!" She half begged; she was fond of Rose and wanted her to be her usual self again. "Miss, even if you just drink the mead for now, you can try to eat a little later. It will give you some energy to do a little movement and maybe be up tomorrow."

Rose turned and reached for the mead. She did not want to be rude. Magdalene was fussing too much, and drinking the mead would hopefully make her leave her alone. Magdalene passed her the mug; she downed the whole lot and lay back down again.

When Magdalene returned the next morning, everything was still the same. The food she brought was not touched. She said nothing to Rose this time, and without asking, brought fresh food for her during lunchtime. Magdalene had seen this depression before many moons ago, and it did not turn out so well for that person. She wanted to make sure she was not overreacting and made one last turn to check in on Rose. She had not eaten in two days...

She decided to speak to Popi about this, whether Rose approved or not. Rose would be upset, but she might thank her later.

Popi was busy clearing the dinner table to do the dishes when she heard a knock. She was surprised to see Magdalene at her door at this hour. Magdalene asked to speak in private, so they stepped outside. She voiced her concern about Rose and explained why. She also mentioned that she had seen this before, and there was no need to clarify with whom. Magdalene did not have to, as Popi knew exactly about whom she was speaking. Depression was not a good thing, and Popi wondered what triggered such a thing in the child.

She thanked Magdalene for caring and coming over to tell her. Popi thought Rose was helping in the village again, and that's why she was so scarce. She fetched a potion that she thought might help her to relax.

Popi told her family she would be out on an urgent matter and might be late and told Sigrid to finish cleaning up. She did not tell her where she was going, as she was not sure Rose could handle Sigrid fussing over her. From experience, fussing too much might push her further down. Not saying that Rose was like her sister — everyone experiences their own kind of depression; it was up to them alone to fight it and feel the need to go on. Popi had to find out why the girl was depressed first and then go from there to help her.

Sigrid was always invited to learn from her mother; she felt left out this time and wondered why.

"Should I not go in case you need an extra hand or need to send me back home for extra herbs? You always ask me to learn from you?" She was wondering who was sick.

"Not this time, dear. I can handle this one on my own. Please, clean the dishes for me and off to bed with you." Sigrid looked upset, so Popi gave her extra work to do that would keep her busy for a while.

"If you're not tired, finish the ointment that we were busy with today. I will come back as soon as I can." She then left her daughter staring at her while she walked out.

When Popi arrived at the main house, she made a turn to see the chief first before going in to see Rose.

"Evening, chief." She needed not ask how he felt; she could imagine the pain still burning inside — missing his son. The pain of losing another child and a loving wife soon afterward — it was too much for an old man to cope with. She saw in his eyes that he was not coping well.

"Evening, Popi. What brings you here so late in the evening?"

"I received news about Rose not feeling too well. I've come to see if I could help."

"Ah, yes," was his only reply. He wondered whether he should tell her what he discussed with Rose.

Popi thought Thorarin could do with a good night's sleep. It sure looked like he needed one. She knew how he felt about potions and medications; he was not fond of them and always refused to take any when offered.

"Don't take this the wrong way, but may I offer you a few drops of my relaxing potion? It will make you sleep soundly."

Thorarin mulled over the option before answering. He did not like potions; however, ointments were different. He had a problem with sleeping lately and switching off as his mind was too busy. The dreams were too many, and he felt exhausted.

"OK, just this once. You know how I feel about them!"

Popi poured him some mead and put a few extra drops in the mug. Thorarin was a huge man; it would take a lot to knock him out, and her potion was not that strong. It was more of a relaxant than a sleeping mixture.

"This will make you sleep like a rock. Drink all the mead and have an early night. Go straight to bed afterward." She turned to walk out.

"Thank you, my sister, but wait. Before you leave, I think I should tell you what I told Rose."

Popi turned and waited in silence.

"I think it's time for her to return to her homeland. I told her she would be on the next trade voyage." Thorarin was expecting an earful from her and was surprised by her silence.

"Oh, I see. Thank you for telling me. Goodnight, chief, hope you sleep well." Popi closed the door behind her.

That's why the poor girl was depressed, Popi thought to herself. She was angry with Thorarin for the way he handled it. He could have at least asked her to break the news and maybe lessen the blow of disappointment. Popi was a little shocked, and this was sad news! Attacking him now was not the time, and she was not in the mood to tell him where he went wrong. He was straight to the point and sounded cold and must have expressed the same coldness toward Rose — now she understood the child's mood. Even if she wanted to argue with the chief, she would have lost. She put her anger aside to have a clear mind when seeing Rose.

When she entered Rose's room, it was pitch dark inside. She lit two candles by the door, carried one to the bed and placed it on the side table that still had her untouched food.

Rose thought it was Magdalene again; she tested her patients and tried her best not to be rude. Why could she not leave her alone! She was irritated with her now.

"Magdalene, I said to leave me alone!"

Popi sat down on the bed, "It's me, little one; don't be angry with Magdalene; she just worries about you as we all do. Thorarin told me what happened."

"Oh, Popi. I don't want to discuss this right now." Talking was an effort as well. She loved Popi, but she just wanted to be left alone. Why could no one understand that!

Popi thought for a while about what to say to her, "Oh, my *Lillé*, what can I say to make you feel better? I know the chief was wrong to tell you himself. I believe the news coming from me would have been more soothing. Though I can say, the idea of you leaving is very upsetting. I do so worry about you, but I believe you will be just fine."

"But why? Why now?" Rose was so forlorn; she wanted to stay and assumed she was one of them. She still had not turned around in bed to face Popi.

"Chief Thorarin is still grieving for his loss, and he is not thinking straight. Loss comes in different stages; you feel upset, disappointed, and then depressed, which I think is passing. He's angry now for what happened, and he has shifted the blame to make himself feel better. You must always remember you will forever be a part of our lives. You are my family, and I love you very much. We must try to see how this is a good thing instead of bad." Popi had time to think about the subject before entering her room.

Rose turned around, "Oh Popi, I love you too, but how can this be a good thing? To never see you or anyone again? It's eating me up inside!" She started crying.

Popi moved further onto the bed to be more comfortable and leaned her back against the wall. She moved Rose's hair away from her eyes and wiped away her tears.

"My poor child! Take it as another adventure, to see your old home again and visit your parents' graves. Maybe find Jessie and see how she is? I can promise you this; if you are unhappy there and nothing is working for you, then you come back! I don't care what the chief says then. I do believe this will be good for you to have closure before moving on and deciding what you actually want out of life."

Rose thought about what she said. It would be nice to see everything again and the things she had forgotten when she first arrived. "But the ache in my heart — thinking of leaving you!" She cried further.

"I know, dear, I feel the same, believe me. It's unbearable to think about."

Rose moved closer to hold onto her. Popi went on speaking, "There is also hope; that's what we can hold onto. Hope to see each other again somehow, hope that not all is lost, and hope you find a life for yourself, which you always wanted. Yes...

right now, we must find a way to control the pain and move on. What you are doing is not the way."

"You might be right, but I can't handle the pain! I don't feel like seeing anyone right now. I will think about what you said, but at the moment, I feel exhausted."

"Don't you want to eat something first before you sleep?" Popi was thinking of her food still being untouched.

"No, I'm not hungry. I just want to sleep."

"OK, but before you sleep, drink some mead for me." She put a few drops into the mug and made her drink it. Popi decided to stay the night and made herself more comfortable on the bed. A fantastic idea popped into her head; she decided to share the news before Rose fell into a deep sleep. She was confident it would cheer her up.

"Rose, are you still awake?"

"Mmm..."

"I was thinking, and I believe it would be good for you to move back to my house until the day comes for you to leave."

"Mmm... sounds good." She was fast asleep.

The following day, at daybreak, Popi started to pack Rose's belongings. Magdalene walked in. She was worried about Rose and was surprised to find Popi there.

"Morning, miss, how is she doing?" She realized what the older woman was doing. "Is she going somewhere?"

"Morning, Magdalene. Yes, she's coming home with me and is staying there from now on. Can you please bring something small for her to eat before we leave?"

Rose woke up and was surprised to find Popi still in her room.

"Popi, did you sleep here last night?"

"Yes, dear, now get up and wash. We are leaving soon."

"Oh, why are you packing my things?" Her fear of leaving the island kicked in, thinking she was leaving today.

"Relax, my *Lillé*; you're coming to stay with me from now on. Can't you remember what I told you last night? Never mind, get up and get ready."

Magdalene walked in with the tray and placed it down. Popi decided to eat with her to make sure that Rose ate something. While they were busy eating, Magdalene packed the rest of Rose's belongings and tidied the room. When they were done, she asked Magdalene to take the bags to the stables. They would be leaving soon after they have seen the chief.

The chief looked a little better after a good night's rest. He had an early meeting with a man that Rose had never seen in the village before. She thought she knew everyone on this island.

"Popi, you have come early this morning. What do I owe for this pleasure again so soon?" without any regard, he greeted Rose, by her name – "Rose."

Popi noticed the lack of informality towards Rose and knew she was doing the right thing.

"Morning, chief, I slept here last night, and I have come to tell you that I will be taking Rose to my home until the day comes for her to depart."

Thorarin noticed she was telling — not asking. He was OK with the idea at any rate. Rose spends most of her days there anyway, and with the news he just received, it would seem like the best idea. It was not yet time to inform Popi of this — he would send for her later. On the other hand, maybe he should tell her to prepare for their arrival and warn the girl. It would help to explain to the girl what would happen with the new visitors here. He was taking too long to answer that they thought he might refuse. Popi was headstrong. No matter what he said, Rose was leaving with her today!

Chief Thorarin looked at them and forced a smile, "Sorry, I was thinking of whether I should tell you the news I just received. It's all right that Rose leaves with you, and I believe that it's for the best. I received information that your home tribe is on their way, and another tribe from the east is arriving too. It's debatable whether they will arrive at the same time, or they might cross paths on their travels. Only time will tell. I think it would be best and a good idea that Rose would be at your place, where you can keep a constant watch on her when they arrive. She will be safer with you than being alone here."

"Oh, this is news," she was troubled, "For how long are they staying?"

"I'm not sure. We will hear when they arrive what their intentions are after years of absence. We can only wait and see."

"Well, we'll be off then. Please send Magdalene if you need me for anything."

"Thank you, Popi, and I will. Good health to you both."

When they arrived at Popi's place, Sigrid had breakfast laid out for everyone. She was happy to see Rose and was delighted with the news that she would be living with them again. After everyone finished their breakfast, Popi walked out with Var, and they spoke in the fields for a while. When she returned, the girls had cleaned the morning dishes, and Sigrid was busy discussing the potions she'd been making while Rose was absent. She was glad to see the young girl laugh and smile again.

Var and Popi decided to tell the kids soon about Rose leaving and about the newcomers. That was if Rose did not blurt it out before then. Her children would not remember any of her tribe's people, as they were babies when last they were here. The other news about Rose, they would not take well. They will be terribly disappointed and very much upset, but that's understandable. It was remarkable how close the kids had become. It would be like breaking up a family by taking one away.

Var was a quiet person and kept to himself most of the time. He enjoyed his daily chores and his family's company in the evenings. To him, having Rose was like having another daughter in the house. She was a delightful person and was always willing to work and eager to learn things. She was not a lazy lady. He respected that about her. Rose was not a Viking by blood, but she was one by heart.

When Popi explained Rose's situation, he became angry and thought the chief was unreasonable. He wanted to march to the main house and have a few words with the chief. Popi had to stop him and explain that it would not help Rose in any way – the chief had made up his mind and was sticking to it. So, between the two of them, they decided that when the time came, Var would travel with Rose to make sure she arrived safely at her destination. They would need to discuss this with the chief, and in a way, they knew he would not object to this arrangement. Everyone knew what Rose meant to them and how close they were.

For now, Var had to work twice as hard to get things ready before he left. He would be gone for a long time. When they decide to explain to the kids about Rose leaving and that he would accompany her, Cnut would need to start helping again, though there was not much now that winter was upon them. If he's not back by spring, he would have to ask someone to help his son because of his injuries and can't do most of the work by himself. He also knew that Cnut would plead to go with;

however, that was not an option. Not with what happened to him on the last voyage.

Not now, it was too soon after his injuries; it's still too dangerous on the water with the English all over the place — they were causing havoc on the open waters. One day, he would allow Cnut to travel again. It would be good for him to see the world. He was still young, and in his condition, he was not yet ready for a long journey — his leg was still healing.

The news that the other tribes were visiting was another matter. Some clans were changing their old ways and adjusting well, while others were still set in their old habits and disapproved of changing their beliefs and traditions, though times are still new in this changing period. The kids would need to be on guard for their arrival and couldn't roam freely as they pleased. It could be dangerous for Rose. He would need to make a turn at Olaf's to discuss this matter with him. Knowing he also cared for Rose's safety.

"Var, my old friend, what brings you down to this side?" Olaf was trying his best to act cheerful. He had been having a hard time with losing his best man, his brother in arms.

"I have an issue to discuss with you and some news we just received. Please keep it to yourself until the chief makes an announcement."

Olaf was hoping for a distraction from his daily duties and his depressing thoughts. Something to take his mind off the loss of Thord would be welcoming.

He gave his full attention, and Var continued, "The news is very upsetting. There's another that concerns me more."

"Spit it out, man. What's the news?"

"First, Rose is going home on the next trading ship."

"What?" Olaf's anger was more than he expected. It was too much loss and too soon.

"The chief told her first before discussing it with us and in so, neglected to tell us as well. Rose was in a state and kept to her bed. Magdalene fetched Popi as she was worried about the girl. The same thing happened with the chief's wife. At least Popi could get through to Rose. She's living with us now until the day of her departure. Her spirit seems lifted a little."

Olaf was fuming, "How can he do that? He probably blames her, which is stupid. Can't he see that she belongs; she's our people now? She has no one out there, and everyone loves her here! I think I should talk with him!"

Var answered before Olaf stormed off to face the chief, "I was about to as well when I heard the news, but Popi said not to and to leave it as it is for now. She thought it through, and as much as it hurts to see Rose go, Popi thinks it's best that she goes back home to see the place and people again. When the time is right, she believes Rose will return — she was sure of it, and then it will be for good. I just hope she's right. Popi says she doesn't know why. She has a feeling Rose will come back, and with that thought, it will be easier to send her off.

"Another matter that brings us to the present; two tribes are coming to visit straight after each other, and Popi fears for

Rose's safety with the one. She wants Rose to be kept away from her tribe — they do as they please and care for none, as you well know."

Var still couldn't fathom that Popi came from that type of tribe. She was different and had more caring in her right arm than ten of their men put together. He told Olaf about the eastern tribe that was next, and they discussed the matter in length. They both agreed to keep a close watch over Rose.

Olaf made an oath to see her person unharmed and was glad about this distraction. He was eager and very much prepared for a good fight.

Var explained it all to Popi in bed that night.

"Thank you, my husband! I feel much better knowing the two of you will be by her side. We must discuss a way for her to contact us whenever she feels the need to reach out. I'm going to miss her so much. I'm worried about the child, although I believe it will be good for her, and if she needs to come back, I will do everything in my power to make that happen. Even if I must go over the chief's head to do so."

"I know, my love, for now, just relax and fix the girls' health once more. She has lost weight and has bags under her eyes. She's taking this extremely hard, losing a family again after feeling she belongs. The poor soul! Rose needs to see us strong for her to be strong on her journey."

"You are wise tonight, my husband, and such a loving and caring man and father. I am happy and blessed to have you in my life; we are blessed with our kids and our life together. You are my moon and stars that shines light upon my path at night, and my sun in the day that shines strength and love upon my soul."

"Oh, my darling, Popi, you gave me a poem. Let me say that my night and day are made easier with you by my side, and without you, nothing will exist or be so beautiful."

"I love you, Var!"

"Oh, my sweet, hush now." He kissed her on the lips before blowing out the candle.

TWENTY-TWO

The four women finished lunch and were having a relaxing day; Astrid, the older sister, joined them for the day. She was gaining weight, and her stomach was huge. She looked healthy and cheerful. Rose wondered whether she would be around for the child's birth. She hoped she would. They were all sitting and eating; Rose and Sigrid, as usual, were discussing what they have learned so far about injuries and herbs, while Popi and Astrid were discussing a new design for a dress.

Astrid left not long afterward, feeling exhausted and wanting to go home to lay down. Popi asked Sigrid to see where Cnut was and how he was coping with the day. She was always worried about him now, with only one leg to get around. He seemed very depressed lately. As a mother, she felt lost and could only do so much for her child. She had to make that decision as a mother first, not wanting to lose her only son, and then the medicine woman kicked in to remove the leg with perfection. However, the rest was up to him.

Standing by the open door, Sigrid asked Rose if she wanted to join her.

Popi answered, "No, I want her to stay. I have a few words to discuss with her alone. Now, move along, child! The quicker you go, the quicker you'll be back."

Looking upset, she left and half mumbled, "Yes, mom!"

Rose looked at her friend, curious about what she wanted to discuss in private, and waited for her to speak.

Popi had said these words to her before, however, felt the need to repeat them, "I want to discuss all your worries, my child. I can see you are still stressed, and I can't imagine what you must be thinking or what will happen to you out there. Keep in mind that I care deeply for you; we all do. You are part of my family, and you must never forget that! Especially when you are leaving us soon, you being all alone out there scares me, and I worry even more.

"I love you as I do my own daughters. I feel it might be good for you to go back and see how or where Jessie is. If you still feel you want to come back, then we will make it happen. However, in the meantime, enjoy your last days with us. We will sort all those things out when the day arrives. Stress never solves anything; just have faith that all will work out at the end."

She could see that Rose was tearing up. It was a sad and upsetting subject for her. This was her home, her family, and now, she had to leave them!

Rose thought it was not fair! Why would the chief order that? She did not want to question him or ask Popi why and just wanted to change the subject. She was going to miss her terribly, including the freedom on this island. Rose wanted to know more about Popi and the life she had lived up to now. Much has happened that she never had the chance to ask her about her relationship with the chief. Now that her tribe was on the way, she had questions.

To change the subject, she asked Popi, "How old were you when you got married, Popi? How long have you been on this island?" She smiled sweetly at her old friend and hoped she was in the mood to discuss her life with her.

Popi had a thoughtful look on her face and knew what she was trying to do.

"Well, it's a little complicated, little one. To start, I was married at a late age, at twenty, and I've been living happily on this island for thirty years."

"Where have you lived before?"

"I came from the Northern Germanic tribe; we were settled in Sweden. However, I heard that they moved closer to Russia. Their lands are more bountiful with rivers flowing through them, with more hunting and fishing activities. My tribe were fierce and rough Vikings back then, and I assume they are still the same. I believe they are having difficulty with the new changes in life. Times do change, don't they? For the best! Perhaps one day they will come around, but only time will tell.

"Well, anyway... Thorarin's parents used to visit often, at least three times a year. They planned trips and raids together while visiting our tribe. More men raiding meant more quantity of treasures they acquired. Joined as one, they were a fierce bunch. Thorarin and Siv had an arranged marriage between our parents' years before the date. It was indeed a perfect match, and they were besotted with each other. Their marriage symbolized peace between the two tribes forever. As far as I remember, his parents paid a huge dowry, which made my parents very happy.

"Sadly, before their vows, Thorarin's parents died. That is when Olaf's parents, Turid and Gudrun, took him under their wing. You must have heard the story before; they were always close friends with his parents. The wise old couple helped Thorarin through it all when he became chief before his time. His whole life changed then, as did ours.

"My sister, Siv, and I were very close; we were best friends. She was two years younger than I was and much prettier. She had a huge heart filled with love for all humans and creatures and a kind personality."

Rose interrupted, "Just like you!"

Popi smiled, "Thank you, love! Well... the wedding was still on between Thorarin and Siv and was held on our island. When the day grew closer for their departure, my heart literally broke! I cared deeply for my younger sister and was always protective of her. I had a long discussion with my parents, and they accepted that I wanted to join the couple on their island. Much later, I found out that my sister had the same discussion with them, long before I had. I was naturally relieved that she still wanted me around in her new life. When she discussed this with Thorarin, he agreed and said that they needed a new medicine woman anyway."

"Who was their medicine woman at the time?" Rose interrupted again.

"Turid was, dear, Olaf's mother. However, her life took on other more meaningful things, and she wanted out. Her daughter never had the gift, so she did not bother to teach her."

"How fascinating!" Rose exclaimed.

"Yes, well... as you may believe, I was exhilarated. I lived with my sister and her new husband in their home; they all accepted and welcomed me as a new member of the tribe. The chief promised my parents to take good care of me, and he did. My sister and Thorarin were extremely happy together. I admired their relationship and the companionship they shared. I never thought I'd ever be so lucky.

"Var and I somehow always ended up in one's company and enjoyed the time spent together," Popi laughed aloud, "I swear that man injured himself on purpose just to be near me — it was sweet! It took him approximately three months before he got the courage to ask Thorarin for my hand. Thorarin gave us this farm to run for him. It was our duty to make sure the crops and animals were well maintained, and that's it!"

Popi poured them each a mug of mead. Her throat was parched with all the talk.

"What was your sister like?"

"What's with all the questions?" She smiled.

Rose blushed, "Sorry Popi, I'm just curious, that's all!"

Popi downed her mead before speaking, "OK, just this once." She was lost in thought for a few seconds before continuing,

"Siv, as I said before, was beautiful. She had long, light ash-blond hair and was the same height as Kiti. She was kind-hearted and loved her people very much. She always spoke with a sweet, soft voice, even when she was angry. She never raised her voice to her husband or children — not a soul! However, you could hear the change in it when she was challenged. Siv was a loving wife and a caring mother. Her favorite god was Thor. When she gave birth to her children, Thorarin named the firstborn after his favorite god Odin, and Siv named the second-born Thord. Kiti, his twin, was last and extremely tiny at birth, and at the time, they both agreed on the name Kiti. It suited her—"

Rose was confused. *There was another child? Who was named after Odin, and what was his name? Did Siv have triplets?* Not knowing if she should interrupt and ask, she was scared that Popi might stop if she realized what she was saying; Rose left her to speak further and decided to ask when she was done.

"—The three of them were such beautiful kids. They were inseparable and real little Vikings. As they got older, only one child seemed to change more than the other two. Thord and Kiti's hair stayed white, where the older one's hair went darker. If those two were the same gender, you would not be able to tell the difference between them — they were identical. Orinn was a kind-hearted child, just like his mother. The other two were more like their father — free-spirited. Growing up, Orinn became more serious and protective over his siblings. Kiti and Thord never changed; those two were always up to no good," Popi laughed, "Everyone knew the eldest would become Chief one day and follow in his father's footsteps."

She stopped speaking. Popi knew she should not talk about this. Nevertheless, it felt good to repeat his name after so long. She missed him so much!

Rose took the opportunity and asked, "Who is Orinn? It sounds as though your sister had triplets. What happened to him?"

"No, child, not triplets; Orinn was four years older than his twin siblings." She stared at Rose, and with seriousness in her voice, said, "Promise me that what I'm telling you now stays in this house! You will not utter a word of this to anybody on the island! I'm not supposed to be speaking of this, never mind telling you!"

"Why?"

"Promise me, Rose!"

"I promise, I won't voice a word!" Rose made a gesture of locking her lips and crossed her heart. "What happened to Siv?"

"Siv," Popi looked sad. She still felt the pain of losing her sister.

Rose filled their mugs with mead once again and looked at the dirty dishes still on the table since lunch.

Popi also looked at the table and said, "We should clean this up. Let us take these dishes outside, and while cleaning, we can talk some more."

They downed their drinks and carried all the dishes to the washbasin outside. Popi was washing, and Rose dried each item while listening further.

Popi continued, "Let's see. Siv, after the loss of Orinn, became depressed. She loved each of her children the same and never favored one more than the other. She could not handle the stress of losing her eldest son. I tried to help her; I made all kinds of potions for her to drink. I'm not sure if she drank them or threw them out. She would not see anyone for a long time and stayed in her room. I think she blamed herself for allowing him to grow up too soon. Thorarin said that he had to go on raids with them to see what Vikings were all about, especially if he was going to be chief."

She stopped for a few seconds before going on, "He was still too young... Siv did mention this; however, Thorarin said he was the right age. I think he wanted to toughen the kid up a little. He was a gentle soul at his age and different from his siblings—"

Rose could see an innocent young boy being killed in a raid – how sad. She couldn't imagine how any mother would feel and then to blame herself for the loss.

"—I can't say what happened or why she left us. Thorarin woke up one morning with her lifeless body next to his. Siv died in her sleep during the night. She went peacefully, I guess, or would like to think so. It was the saddest time in my life and the first time I lost someone so dear to me. However, I had to put my feelings aside and be strong for the little ones. Thorarin took it badly and was absent for long periods. It took a long time before he got over her – if ever he did. He could not think of taking another wife. No one could replace her – he loved her deeply. He always said she was the only one for him."

Popi was done speaking of the past, hoping that her sister found peace in the afterlife. She was angry with her sister for giving up so soon and leaving the other two without a mother. Although recently, she almost went through the same loss. Though she knew she was stronger and would have survived it, it would have been difficult all the same.

"What happened to Orinn?" They were finished cleaning and stacked all the dishes in the kitchen.

"I think that's enough talk of the past for today," Popi pointed a finger at Rose, "You promised — no asking Magdalene or Sigrid any questions!"

"Yes, Popi," she smiled, "I promised, and I always keep my promises." Rose was disappointed that it had to end so soon, just when things were getting interesting.

It was getting late, and Popi wondered where the kids were. Speaking about the past was painful. No wonder Thorarin did not want Orinn's name mentioned or what happened. However painful the memories, even not voiced out loud, still live on in our minds and hearts.

"Will you explain what happened to Orinn later?"

"No, little one, I think it is best to leave it alone. He's gone and will never return."

Rose thought that his death must have been a dreadful tragedy; she would respect Popi's wishes and leave it be. The thought of leaving this island, never to see Popi or her adopted family again, was upsetting. Rose gave her friend an unexpected hug. Popi accepted it and hugged her back until Rose prolonged it and whispered, "I miss you already!"

Popi hugged her tighter. She had no comment to give to the young girl. She loved her as her own and wanted to tell her that everything would be all right, but she had no idea what was waiting for her or what life would be like back at her own home. Popi wished her all the happiness in the world. The words she desperately wanted to say were, 'Bugger the chief and stay as long as you want, I will handle him,' except she would not dare. Before the tears started to flow, she pulled herself out of the hug and held Rose at arm's length.

"Enough of all talk of sadness. Why don't you go see where Sigrid is? She's taking quite long looking for Cnut."

Halfway through the field, Sigrid came running toward her. "Where's Cnut?" Rose called out.

"Has my mother sent you to look for us now?" She was still upset that she had to walk alone. "I could not find him and had to walk all the way to the village in search of him. I found him in Olaf's shop. You will not believe what he made for Cnut!"

Just then, Cnut came walking toward them on a wooden leg, smiling. Rose was extremely happy for him and saw that he no longer needed a crutch to lean on. He could walk on his own, and in no time, maybe run a little.

Cnut could not hide his emotions any longer and slowly started to walk toward Rose and hugged her. Sigrid was in tears and threw her arms around them both.

They finally decided to tell the kids at breakfast the following day. Rose did not expect it this soon. She was not in the mood to explain why she moved back in with them, with the pain still being too real. It hurt to think she would never see them again. Thus, Rose kept to her daily chores and was happy with the distraction.

In a way, she was also a little pleased that it would be out in the open and that they would know what was happening. They could see something was bothering her and that she was not herself. Sigrid was waiting for her mom to explain things to her, as she usually did, but she said nothing and thought to leave it for now. It must have been important to bring Rose to stay with them, and for once, she was not complaining. However, the news was not what they expected.

Sigrid uttered a few words and ran to her room crying. Cnut just stood there, not saying a word, which shocked them more. He turned and walked out of the house, leaving the three of them at the breakfast table flabbergasted.

Var, Popi and Rose were silent for a few seconds; then Rose spoke up, "Well, that went well!" she said with a straight face, which made them laugh.

Var stated that they were just startled by the news and would get over the shock, something they were not expecting to hear. They were more worried about Cnut; he was withdrawn, which was not like him at all.

Popi looked worried and said, "Cnut not responding is weird! I was expecting a full mouth from him with many unpleasant remarks on the subject."

"He'll be OK. I'll go look for him and we'll have a talk," Var offered.

"If it's fine with you both, could I please speak to him? I think I know where he went, and I believe some time alone with me will help. We are close."

"Well, if you feel you can reach out to him and can find him, then I don't see why not," Var answered.

Rose stood up, and before leaving, turned toward Popi and asked, "Popi, are you all right with the dishes?" She was feeling guilty leaving and not helping to clean.

"Good lord, child, this house is turned upside down with distress! Don't worry your head about dishes. I will take care of them," she said, waving the child away.

"I think I'll go to Sigrid first to calm her, and then I'll be off to find my little brother who needs me." Rose looked sad saying those words, which came naturally these days.

She entered the room and hugged her best friend. They both cried a little before they could utter any words. Sigrid had many questions, and Rose had no answers for most of them.

"We can talk all day and later tonight in bed too, but right now, your brother needs me. He said nothing and just left! Your parents are a little worried, and I believe I know where he is."

"Really? I missed the one moment my baby brother was speechless?" They both giggled.

"Should I come with you?"

"No, I'll be OK. I think alone time is best."

"Where are you going to search for him?"

"Well, as I know Cnut, there is only one spot that I believe he could be, but can't tell you. I was sworn to secrecy. I'll see you later, hopefully at lunchtime." Rose kissed and hugged her goodbye, and Sigrid started crying again. Rose let her be, knowing she would be fine after a while.

Var and Popi were still sitting at the table, nibbling on the breakfast in front of them. She could kick herself for not telling the kids after they ate first. *Well, what was done was done,* she thought.

"How is Sigrid, my dear?" she asked, wondering how sad her kids must be feeling.

"She'll be fine," Rose gave a slight smile. "She'll be out of the room in a few minutes." Rose looked at the untouched breakfast and had an idea, "May I take some food with, in case we get hungry later?"

"Yes, yes, wait, I'll get something to pack it in." Popi was up and off to the kitchen, happy that the food was not going to waste.

Rose sat down and waited with Var. They were both quiet for a while, then Var asked, "How are you feeling, my girl? We are all worried about you!"

She could see the concern on his face and was touched.

"I'm OK, I guess. Thank you for asking. I'm happier to be here with you all than at the chief's place. I suppose I have to get used to the idea of leaving and never seeing any of you again."

"Don't say that! No one can foretell the future. This might help a little; we've discussed and decided that I'll be going with you on your journey, all the way to wherever that might be. Olaf insisted on going too. I don't want to discuss this right now; however, maybe the thought will put you at ease."

"Oh, that's so kind and thoughtful. That's fantastic news — thank you!" Rose wanted to cry that Var would do that for her. Just then, Popi came in with a basket and bowls to pack the food.

"You know where you're going, dear?" she asked, passing the basket to Rose.

"Yes, I believe so. Thank you and see you both later." She kissed Popi on the cheek and surprised them both by impulsively hugging Var before half-running out the door.

"That girl knows how to crawl into one's heart!" Var gave Popi a quick explanation of what was discussed before leaving the house. She had to agree; loving that girl was easy.

Rose knew where Cnut was, and because he couldn't walk far, he took his horse, a subject that hurt him terribly. He loved to run around and be free-spirited, but he could no longer do that. Cnut could walk again without crutches, thanks to Olaf making him the wooden-iron leg, but it was still not the same, though. It still hurt when he put too much strain on it. It was still too soon, but one day, it would feel normal to him and in the eyes of everyone else.

Rose trotted toward their private pool on a mare. As far as they knew, they were the only ones who knew of the place. She went there a few times to have a private swim by herself. She loved it as much as Cnut did. When she arrived, he was in the water swimming. Rose noticed his artificial leg was lying next to his belongings. He must feel free in the water than on solid ground. She took her basket and went closer.

"Hello!" Rose shouted out for him to hear, "Hope you don't mind me intruding?" She sat down, placing the basket beside her, "Thought I'd bring food for later when we get hungry."

"No, you're not intruding; the water helps with the pain in my leg." He swam toward her but did not climb out. "What did you bring to eat?"

"Just leftover breakfast, which your mom was happy to give. No one ate this morning."

She could see the change in his expression and decided now was not the time to discuss any of it. She decided to join him in the pool. Rose had a short linen dress on under her clothing, and she swam in that. He was surprised that she climbed in.

"Oh, this is refreshing!" She plunged under and swam toward the little waterfall, which was gently cascading down into the pool.

"You actually swim well; I never knew that."

"Thank you! My mother taught me at a young age. We lived close to a river; she feared that I might fall in, so she taught me how to swim. I was never allowed to swim alone at first; it was only at a later age that it became my haven. I relax more in water. It makes a person feel free, almost like flying."

"Yes, I know what you mean." He felt whole in the water until it was time to climb out.

Rose was floating on her back when she spoke; she wanted the conversation to sound as normal as possible. She wanted him to open up and to be himself again.

"How are you feeling? You left without saying a word this morning, and I must say, you left us all in shock. It's not like you to be quiet and so distant."

"Honestly, I'm not fine, Rose. I am very pissed! How can the chief just send you away after all you've been through? Not knowing if you still have a home or anyone to look after you. It's been almost a year now since you came to live here, and everyone loves and accepts you as one of us. I don't understand why you can't just stay!" They were floating and swimming in circles, talking to each other.

"I thought about what your mom said to me, and she might be right. She said it might perhaps be a good thing that I'm going back home to see everything again and have closure, so to speak. I'll visit my parent's graves and see my old home. I'll go to the castle and stay there, I guess. I know I'd be welcomed there for the time being. As for the future, I'll just see where it takes me. In all aspects, I do feel like I'm home already.

"I guess life has other plans for me. I truly don't want to leave. I've come to love it here, and I feel safe amongst you all. I love you all so much, and you'll always be my family no matter where I go. You will always be part of my life. We never know if we'll see each other again. Perhaps one day, you can visit, or maybe I'll come back and the chief will accept me this time? Let's hope I'm right!" Rose smiled at him with hope in her eyes.

"Yes, it is a nice thought that we might see each other again, rather than never again!"

"However, short my visit now, I want to remember it as happy times and have fun as we used to. It will be good memories to hold on to."

Cnut rubbed his leg at those words. They used to run around chasing each other; those days were gone for him. They were just a memory and a good one too.

He answered, "Perhaps we can make other games that don't include running?" He needed to accept the fact that he had one leg. Not that he had much of an option. It was being happy or staying unhappy.

"That's what I want to hear!" Rose splashed him with water and laughed. He dived under, surprised her by pulling her leg, and half-dragged her under the water, making her scream.

They played for a while until Cnut was tired and climbed out. He had his eyes on the basket.

"So, what did you pack? I'm starving!" He was moving the basket closer to examine the contents. He was busy unpacking everything and eating at the same time while Rose was floating on her back, enjoying the scenery from a different view.

"Are you coming out?" Cnut called out with his mouth full.

"In a minute, this is so relaxing and peaceful."

"Well, you'd better hurry if you want any of it," he was laughing and feeling a little like his old self again. It was a start.

"All right, hold your tongue." They both attacked the food as though they have not eaten in days. When they were full, they laid down to relax their bellies and to dry off.

"This is perfect!" she said while looking up at the clouds. "A perfect day; swimming, relaxing, good food and good company — just perfect!" She noticed that Cnut was still not saying much, but he looked more like himself. They were both quiet and content and dozed off in the shade, feeling comfortable with each other. They slept for about an hour. Rose woke up last, stretched out and yawned. She gave him a huge smile, "Hello, I hope you slept too?"

He laughed, "Yes, we did. I think it's time to leave, though. We overstayed a little." They packed up and rode back home.

When they returned home, Var went in for an early tea. The discussion was not over yet. They all sat at the table once again.

When everyone was settled, and halfway through their tea, Popi spoke up, "We haven't discussed everything that we wanted to say this morning. It all ended so abruptly, but we want you to know what your father and I decided. We are all very sorry for Rose leaving, and your dad and I have concluded." She paused and winked at Rose, then looked at her kids, "Your father has offered to see Rose safely to her destination, which means he will also be leaving."

Sigrid and Cnut spoke at the same time. As they knew, Cnut also wanted to go, and Sigrid was all for her father seeing Rose safely home. They discussed the matter and explained what their duties would be while he was away.

When that was settled, they told them about the other tribes that were visiting soon and warned them not to roam around the way they usually do when they arrive. They finished their tea and went on about their day.

TWENTY-THREE

It was almost time for the '*Jola Blot*'— the mid-winter celebrations to begin, and no one had arrived yet. There was also no news regarding which date Rose would be leaving. She was becoming more anxious as the days went by. She was taking in as much as she could and was always busy helping around. Everyone was busy preparing for the feast. Rose decided to party hard this time, as it would be her last celebration with them all. In her mind, she took it as a send-off party. It made her smile just thinking about it.

Rose and Sigrid woke early with great enthusiasm. Today was the start of the celebrations, and everyone was getting ready to be on time for the sacrifice. As quick as they could, the girls washed, dressed, and were out the bedroom door. Popi was waiting for them to emerge as she had a surprise for Rose. They were all going to walk together, so they sat at the table waiting for the last person to finish.

"Rose, dear, I made you a new dress for the festival," Popi was beaming with excitement and knew she would love it.

Rose thought the dress was gorgeous and went straight to the room to change.

"Wait, I'm coming too!" called Sigrid.

"Wait for me too," called Cnut, teasing the girls.

"No!" they screamed mutually and ran to the room laughing. Popi and Var laughed as well. The house was back to normal again. They were also relieved that Cnut was starting to be himself.

"Wow!" Sigrid said. The dress was made from satin, and it was long and flowy — it fitted like a glove. The sleeves were long, and at the wrist, it was wide and loose. A long V-line reached almost to her belly and was enlaced with red strings to tie on top. Rose thought it was a little too revealing and felt shy.

"I can't walk out looking like this!" She protested.

"Why not? You look gorgeous!"

"Everyone will be staring at me! You know me, Sigrid; I don't like too much attention. I like to fit in and be one with the others."

"Well, Rose, you can't upset my mother, can you?" she said, smiling, "Trust me; there's nothing wrong with it. Everyone wears their best outfits for these occasions, so come, I can hear mom calling. It's time to leave and no time to change. Don't forget your cloak; it looks like it going to rain." She was out the door.

When Rose eventually had the guts to step out of the room, everyone was in awe.

Var said, "You look lovely, Rose."

"Thank you, Var." She blushed.

"Ah, my Rose, you look stunning."

"Thank you, Popi. I do love the dress."

"OK, come, everyone, let's go!" called Var.

While walking to the village, Cnut walked beside her.

"Wow! That's all I'm saying — wow!"

"OK, Cnut, thank you."

"Wow!"

Rose hit him on the arm. "Enough!" They were all laughing when they arrived at the altar.

It was the same as the last, except one person was missing. Everyone could see that it affected the chief not to have his son with him. Thord's presence was missed. Rose felt sorry for the chief. She felt a chill and pulled the cloak tighter around her body.

Olaf was in his place. He was the one bringing the lamb to be slaughtered, and his face was gloomy as well. The festival was starting to be depressing; no one seemed to be in a festive mood. Everyone cheered when the sacrifice ended, and Var went over to speak to Olaf. Helga came over to greet them, and they all walked over to where the feast was held. Strange that no one ate first as they usually did. Most of them had a few drinks to get in the mood. It took a while before the atmosphere changed, and everyone started to be joyful.

At first, there was plenty of food, but it would not be such a bountiful because of the winter season approaching. The main menu consisted mostly of fish and bread, and they all ate their fill. Rose felt relaxed and content.

A week had passed during the celebrations, and Rose woke up with a massive headache every morning. She wanted to climb back into bed and sleep for a week. However, she did not want to miss a single thing at this festival — not if it might be her last one. This time, she was a sport and joined in most of the games. She improved immensely with archery. Olaf and Helga were the loudest to cheer when she won.

Each morning, Sigrid and Rose took medication for their headaches. They had to take enough with them to the village because people kept asking for cures, and they had to ride back every time to pick up something. Therefore, before leaving every morning, they packed what they thought would be needed for cuts, headaches, stomachaches, etc.

Today, they woke up a little later than usual — it was almost noon. While they were packing the medicine bag, Popi walked in and said, "I need wild mushrooms from one of you and the other I need help with a deep cut in the village. I will need to give stitches. So, who will be doing what?"

Sigrid loved hands-on jobs and did not shudder as Rose did when she had to stick something into somebody.

"I'll fetch the mushrooms, and Sigrid can go with you," Rose volunteered, "I'll pick enough to leave here and bring to the village too. I'll meet you both there."

Taken – Part 1

Rose walked into the woods where the mushrooms grew. It was raining for days, and it was muddy everywhere. She had to tread carefully in case of slipping. It took longer to get there on foot, and she kicked herself for not taking a horse.

She eventually reached her destination, took the bag from her shoulders, kneeled, and started to fill the bag with mushrooms. She was about done when she heard something and froze. Popi told her to always leave her weapon on her person, and Sigrid showed her where to hide it. Right now, her little knife was tugged securely under her dress on her upper thigh. Var and Cnut taught her how to stand and stab a wild animal when being attacked and how quick she needed to be. Rose was nervous; however, she was ready for the test. Optimistic, she thought whatever the outcome, Popi and Sigrid were there to heal her.

Rose heard twigs breaking and turned toward the noise. Her knife was still in place. She was not sure who or what would come out around the trees. She waited a while, and nothing came jumping out, except silence. She turned and bent down to pick up her bag and threw it over her shoulders.

Before walking back to the house, she turned one last time to make sure she was alone and safe and wouldn't be attacked from behind. Rose got a fright when a strange man appeared from nowhere and stood smiling at her. She had never seen his face in the village before. Just then, it dawned on her that the visitors might have arrived, but which one? If this was Popi's tribe, she'd better tread carefully.

"Good day to you, young lass," he said, sauntering toward her. "Who do you work for?"

He thought Rose was a slave; she'd better answer as one just to be safe.

"Good day Sir, Miss Popi. I work for Miss Popi. Just picking some mushrooms for her. I have to get back; she's waiting for me," she said, hoping he would leave her be and get on his way. She was unsure what his intentions were, so she took small steps back as he walked toward her.

"You're a pretty little slave. How long have you been working for my cousin?" He was very close to her and made her nervous.

Oh, thank God. He was related to Popi. He must be OK; she thought and smiled back. "Just over a year, Sir," Rose answered.

He was close enough to touch her. He had a smirk on his face. Just then, he grabbed her and said, "Why don't we go and get better acquainted!" He was trying to pull her further into the woods.

"Unhand me this instant! Let go of me!" Rose pulled herself free. "Please, let me be on my way, Sir!" She was not sure what to do in this kind of situation.

"No! You will please me before you go on your way." The stranger laughed out loud at his own stupid joke.

Rose turned to run and got a few feet from him when she slipped and fell, with her hands and knees deep in the mud! She turned around and faced him from the ground.

"Just where I want you to be, on the ground, ready and waiting." He was on top of her in an instant. Kissing her neck and forcing his lips on hers. She kept her lips tightly locked and kept moving her head away from his intolerable advances.

"Stop fighting me, lass. It will be over in no time — just let it be and enjoy it."

"No! Let me go!" Rose was fighting to get him off, but he was much stronger.

"It will be more fun for me if you fight back, remember that. More pain for you." He pulled her dress up, and his hands were going for her privates." She realized there was no pleading with this man. She reached for her knife and stabbed him in the arm.

"You little bitch!" He hit her with a fist across the face. She fell back, and his smile grew wider.

"Stay down, you wench. I'm going to have my fun."

With all her might and breath she could muster, she shouted at the top of her lungs,

"HELP—HELP!"

"Shut up!" he shouted and hit her twice in the face and then in the stomach. He knew no sound would come out of her now. He put all his weight on her and started to kiss her once again while he untied his pants.

Her knife lay helpless in her hands.

Popi sent Cnut to see why Rose was taking so long. He first went to the house before strolling toward the woods, where he knew she would be picking the mushrooms. Just then, his father called out, "Cnut, where are you off to?"

They were all surprised to find Popi's tribe there in the village that morning. The visitors were all drunk when they arrived. They must have had drinks on their voyage long before arriving. The village was in a state, and Var was not in the mood to be around such people. He came home to have a breather and to warn Rose to stay indoors. Popi was still busy with cuts and all.

"Looking for Rose, dad. Mom is worried about her."

"All right, when you find her bring her straight home! I want to have a word with her."

Cnut stood close to the woods' entrance, and Var stood outside the front door, looking at his fields. Out of nowhere, they heard a loud scream, "HELP—HELP!" Not sure what was happening, they both ran in that direction. Cnut was first on the scene.

What he saw shocked him to his bones. Without thinking, he ran and tackled the man off Rose. He saw what state she was in and hit the man with all his might.

The stranger stood up, attacked Cnut with full force, and said, "You can have her after I'm done with her!"

"I will kill you before you touch her again, you insufferable oaf!" Cnut continued to hit him.

Rose stood up slowly; she was slightly off balance as her knees were weak, and her entire body was shaking. Her knife was in her hand, and this time, her grip was tighter. The man hit Cnut down and told him to stay down while he finished what he started with the girl. The stranger walked toward Rose and grabbed one of her breasts while his other hand flew under her dress. Just then, her hand flew up on impulse; she stabbed him in the neck once and pulled the knife out. The man reached for his wound and took a step back before falling, bleeding out to death.

Var arrived just when the man was advancing toward Rose and groped her. He ran ahead to stop him — then Var stopped dead in his tracks. Rose fell to the ground and started crying. He went over to inspect the man that was bleeding out. He gave him one look, was satisfied, and turned to give Rose his full attention. Var slowly walked toward her, not sure how far this man went with her. He showed Cnut to be careful not to move too fast.

He knelt slowly next to her and said, "Rose, I'm so sorry this happened to you! We must get you inside, my girl. You need to be cleaned." She was covered with mud from head to toe and shaking badly from shock.

"We will call Popi immediately to come to your aid. Rose, are you all right?"

She turned and saw the fear in Var's eyes and how ill he looked. Rose threw her arms around his neck and cried, not wanting to speak. While she was holding onto him and crying, Var slowly picked her up in his arms. He sent Cnut ahead to call his mother while he carried the girl home. Cnut was on his horse in no time and was gone. His father warned him not to mention any of this to anyone — only Popi. He took Rose to the room and laid her down. Rose was shivering — irrespective of the mud, he covered her with a blanket.

When he turned to leave, she pleaded with him, "Please, don't leave me alone. I don't want to be alone right now," She could barely speak; her jaw was throbbing and paining from the beating.

"It's fine, lass, you are safe! I'm not going far; just getting the bathtub in so that when Popi arrives, they can clean you up. I'll be right back, and then I will need to fill it with water. So, I'll be in and out the whole time. Just relax — you're safe at home."

Var wanted to go straight out there, revive that man and kill him, himself — that's how angry he was! He wanted to shout and hit something with force! He kept it all inside for her sake, for now. He couldn't promise what would happen later. He knew this was not over. Rose killed a member of their tribe; big trouble was on the way. He was looking forward to it too.

Popi and Sigrid arrived with Cnut. They found Var sitting next to her on the bed and the tub full of water. Rose was sleeping.

"My word, husband, what happened?" Popi was shocked at the sight and state Rose was in — there was mud everywhere.

"Did Cnut not tell you?"

"No, he just said to hurry and that Rose needed me immediately!"

"Cnut, stay with her and don't touch her; she's jumpy. She doesn't want to be left alone. I will have a word with your mom and sister outside." Var took them out of the room and told them what happened and a dead man laid in the woods. Popi was shaken and in tears. Sigrid started crying too.

Var went on to explain, "My love, I'm not sure how far he went or what happened before we arrived, but Cnut was brave and fought well to stop him. When he fell, he struggled to get up with his injured leg, with the ground being muddy and slippery. That's when it all ended."

"Oh, my poor child!" Popi whispered, then said, "OK, Sigrid, I will need your help. We will first clean her and see where she is hurt and how badly and go from there. Var, we will need clean sheets and bedding. I will let you know as soon as I know what's wrong with her." Popi saw the anger in his eyes, "Be patient; this will take time, and thank you for being there for her." She kissed him on the cheek and walked back into the room with Sigrid following behind.

Sigrid ran in and out of the room to get things. They had to wake Rose gently. When she saw the two of them, she cried and threw her arms around Popi. It took a while for her to calm down. The mud was dry by now, so they had to cut her clothing from her body. They placed Rose in the tub, while Popi washed her, Sigrid made a fresh bed. Popi carefully inspected her body before dressing her.

Rose had one big bruise on her ribs and a few scrape marks on her legs and arms from the ground attack with the small twigs and stones lying around. Her face was the worst; one eye was closing and her jaw was swelling badly. All Popi could do right now was rub some soothing ointment on her face. She made some warm tea and mixed a sleeping concoction in it. She decided to wait for the tea mixture to work before asking any questions — questions they needed to know. Rose might need to drink a sour mixture to prevent any unwanted pregnancy. While waiting for the tea to take some effect, they rubbed ointment on all her cuts and bruises.

When done, Popi asked, "Rose, dear, do you want to talk about what happened?"

"Not really, no, not now," Rose answered in a whisper.

Popi thought it would be more difficult for her to speak tomorrow with her face looking the way it did. So, she tried once more, "Why, I ask, is that I don't know what happened, and I don't want to alarm you. I want to know if I should give you something else to drink. If that man dishonored you, there might be an unexpected pregnancy."

Rose looked at Popi, "Sorry, Popi!" she started crying again.

"Why are you sorry, love? You must never blame yourself for what happened. That man was wrong, not you!"

"No, it's not that. He was your cousin and I killed him!"

She was shocked to hear this. Her cousin? That made her angrier. *Well, good riddance*, she thought.

"It's fine, my child. *I* am sorry, especially if he was related to me! Answer me if I should make that tonic or not?" Both women were holding their breath for her answer.

"No, Cnut got there in time to save my honor. If it wasn't for him... I don't know what would have happened." Rose cried some more. The women cried too with relief that Rose was still innocent.

"Sigrid, please stay here with her until she sleeps. I'm going to get a drink."

"Of course, mom — whatever Rose needs!"

When Popi emerged from the room, her husband and son stared at her with worried expressions. She still had tears in her eyes. Just then, Olaf also walked in with Helga. His voice was too loud and cheerful after all that had happened.

"Good! I found you all; why are you here at home and not cele..." Olaf stopped dead in his sentence when he saw Popi's fatigue. "What on earth is going on?" He saw Var's anger, and Cnut had a shiner and dried blood on his nose.

Helga, also worried, asked the same question, "Popi, what's wrong?"

Var asked them to sit, and Popi asked Cnut to bring them all some mead. She downed hers and poured another while Var and Cnut explained what happened.

Popi went on to explain, "The worst of all is that he was related to me. Rose told me he was my cousin." Popi looked exhausted, and before she went on, the tears came again, and she said, looking at Var, "And no, she still has her innocence, thank the gods." She looked at her son, "Thanks to you, you arrived just in time to stop him. She's very grateful to you, my boy. She told me you were brave."

Cnut was in tears with relief. He had thought that he let her down and felt hopeless. He was relieved that she was unharmed. Olaf started pacing; Helga went straight to the room to see how Rose was doing and found her asleep; what she saw shocked her to her core.

"The poor thing!"

Looking at Var, Olaf said, "You know what's going to happen now, don't you?"

"I welcome it and anything that comes my way." He was in the mood to break some bones.

"OK, so now we have to retrieve the body, take it out to show the chief, and tell him what happened. Helga, you stay here in case any other unwelcome visitors stop by when they find out." Helga was capable of handling anyone.

Olaf went in to see Rose before leaving, which triggered a fit of new anger in him. He was jubilant with anticipation of what was about to happen.

"I want to come with!" said Cnut.

"Fine, bring a blanket so that we can cover him before revealing him to the others," answered his father.

The chief was outside socializing with the villagers and newcomers, and Kiti was always by his side. Var and Olaf took the horse as far as possible to the main house's front door and carried the dead man in. While they took the dead man to the meeting room, Cnut went to call on the chief and told him that Var and Olaf urgently needed to see him. Chief Thorarin had no idea what was so urgent.

Kiti thought it might be to ask for Rose to stay. She would not want to miss her father declining their proposal. She loved her uncle Var and respected Olaf, but it infuriated her how they all wanted her to stay! Why doesn't she want to leave? What was wrong with her? Kiti would love to take her place and leave this closed-up island. She so wanted to see the world and to be part of something greater. She thought she was close to leaving, but her father needed her by his side more now with everything that had happened. All that they loved was gone and buried. She was all he had left. Kiti felt forlorn.

They did not expect to find a dead man on the floor covered in a blanket. Their chief first sat down before asking what happened. Then Var and Cnut explained the whole story from when they first arrived at the scene. Thorarin went white in the face, and Kiti's hands flew to her mouth in shock. Var put their mind at ease and said she still had her honor, thanks to Cnut.

"And you, Olaf, how do you fit in all this?" the chief wondered.

"When Helga and I noticed they were missing, we went looking for them. We found them all at home in a state, so we decided to bring the matter to you and discuss how we are going to handle this, chief."

"Yes, I see. Where is Helga now?"

"She's at Popi's place waiting for me."

"This is a dilemma. How is Rose doing now?"

"She's sleeping, chief. I must admit that when she wakes up, she will be in much pain. Her face is distorted."

"OK, I'm not having this in my house. Bring that body and I'll address everyone outside. Be prepared; this will not end pretty." He saw his daughter was missing. He didn't even notice that she had left. It was probably better that she was not with him right now. He was going to tell her to stay indoors.

He stood tall and proud and shouted, "Silence!" Everyone looked at him with interest.

"I would like to welcome my wife's home people on my island. My food is your food, and my mead is your mead. On another matter, we have a problem that just came to light, and I would like to announce..." He looked at the other chief – his brother in marriage – and continued speaking, "One of your men attacked and violated one of my people. I welcome you on my land, and your people disrespect me by hurting my own."

Bui called out, "Who was attacked, Chief?"

Thorarin looked at Olaf and Var, told them to remove the blanket, then went on to say, "He was killed in self-defense. It was a normal reaction, and I'm sorry for your loss. However, I must admit that if he survived, my men would have killed him themselves."

There was anger among the newcomers. Two men ran to retrieve the dead body. Thorarin's people kept asking who was attacked; Var eventually shouted, "Rose was attacked!"

There was anger everywhere from both tribes. The two chiefs looked at each other, and the other one said, "What's to be, so it shall be...!" That was a sign for his men to take their anger and loss out on Thorarin's tribe. His dead cousin was always a handful – he wasn't that surprised to hear he was killed, though he did not expect it to happen so soon and with one of Thorarin's people.

As Vikings were, they loved to take revenge and fight as only they knew how. Thorarin's people were more than willing and welcomed the challenge. Var and Olaf jumped in with eagerness while the two chiefs watched the brawl from the side. The fight went on for a long time until everyone got tired and thirsty. When it was over, the two chiefs came together to speak.

"I asked around about Thord; I wondered where he was? I apologize; his presence will be sorely missed; he was a good and honorable man. I am sorry for your loss, my brother. It's an awful tragedy!"

"Thank you, my brother! We are still coming to terms with our loss." Thorarin was not in the mood to discuss his dead son at this very moment. He was also not expecting the following words to come out of the other chiefs' mouth.

"What do you have planned for your daughter, Kiti?"

"What do you mean?"

"Marriage, my wise chief. What else?"

"What are you implying?" He was a little irritated with his visitor by now.

"Well, my sole purpose for visiting was to bring a marriage proposal, perhaps to come to some arrangement — your daughter Kiti with one of my cousins?"

Thorarin laughed, "My daughter will never agree to that, and anyway, she'll be too much for any of your men."

"Well, we do have our ways of taming our women." The visitor laughed, thinking his joke was funny. Thorarin gave him a deadly look. Those words infuriated him!

"I know what your men are capable of!" Thorarin answered in a loud voice.

"No, my brother. I never meant it like that! It was supposed to be a joke!" The visitor lifted his hands in surrender. "I guess those were the wrong words at the wrong time. I'm sorry! I must tell you I chose a good man for her; he's well respected by my people. He'll be able to make her happy."

Thorarin wanted to bash the man's face in, right there and then. He could picture himself doing it and enjoying it! His hands were tightly closed in a fist. To control his rage, he half-sat on his hands in case they had a mind of their own. He gave one look at the man, which spoke volumes.

"Enough of this talk! There will be no arrangement of a marriage of any kind. I do not accept your offer!"

The man knew when he lost; he would never admit to anyone that he was scared of Thorarin, so he changed the subject, "So, who is this girl that was attacked? Is she all right?"

"Popi is looking after her, so she'll be fine."

"Yeah, but who is she?"

"One of Popi's."

"Are you telling me that the bastard was killed by one of my niece's thralls?"

"No! A member they take as family as everyone else does on my land."

"She's a slave girl? Are you telling me that a slave girl killed one of my own? She should be hanged!"

"She's not a slave girl!" Thorarin's voice got loud with authority. "It's a long story, which I'm not in the mood to explain right now!"

"Fine, maybe one day. We will be leaving on the morrow once my men have recuperated. They are all dog-eared at the moment."

"I'm not chasing you, my brother. All I ask is that when you visit, you keep your men in line. To respect my people as we would yours. That goes for all and everyone on my island, no matter who they may be."

"I agree, but we will need to leave to send my deceased cousin to his family so they can make the necessary arrangements for his afterlife. On the other hand, the tension is not good for us to stay longer either."

"Very well, whatever you wish." He was happy that they would be leaving soon.

Olaf and Var were sitting and discussing the fight with a small group of their own clan. They were having a drink and laughing. After a good brawl, they felt alive and relaxed and knew this was not over until their visitors left. For now, everyone was exhausted.

Olaf slapped Cnut on the back, "Saw you fighting. I'm very proud of you, my boy, and Thord would have been impressed as well."

That meant a lot to Cnut. "Thanks, it was fun though, now I understand." He smiled.

Olaf laughed aloud, "You're now a true Viking – a man today!"

Var was also proud of his son and voiced his approval. He was brave and fierce today. He hadn't seen that side of him before.

Cnut was smug and joined the men in a drink.

Not long after, Helga came into the village, carrying two men on either side of her. They were knocked out. The villagers were silent once again. It was the same two who retrieved the body. They must have followed Kiti, knowing she would see 'the girl,' but they did not expect Helga to walk out!

She dropped them on the ground and announced to all, "They are not dead, but if they ever threaten me or threaten the life of Rose, I will kill them or anyone who challenges me!"

Everyone burst out laughing, and Olaf shouted, "That's my girl!"

Chief Thorarin looked at his visitor with a smirk on his face, "I think it's best if your men recuperate on your ship before any more unwanted deaths happen, which we both don't want." Thorarin could not help smiling.

𝕿he next day the visitors' ship was gone. The celebration continued. Now, there was more excitement and life in the village. The chief went over to Popi's place to see how Rose was doing. She brought him and Kiti mead and something to eat while Rose was asleep. Not long afterward, Sigrid came out of the room, saying that Rose was hungry.

"Good, she's awake. Bring me a bowl of soup while we go in to see her."

Kiti and Thorarin followed Popi to the room. They were shocked to see what state her face was in. Kiti and her father stood by the door.

He did not want to go in and said, "Good heavens, Popi, she looks dreadful!" He felt awful. "Rose, I'm so sorry this happened to you! Are you all right? Are you in pain? What am I saying? Of course, you must be in pain!"

Her face was distorted; Rose's jaw was poorly swollen, and her one eye was entirely closed. Popi gave her several pain medications. All Rose could do was give a nod. Her jaw was too sore to speak. Thanks to Popi, the pain was bearable. Rose tried her best to smile but could not, so she shook her head and gave him a thumbs-up, saying she was OK.

Popi answered for her, "She is heavily sedated with pain medication. She feels a little pain when using her jaw. In all, she will be all right."

Rose gave her a thumbs-up as well. Kiti was not saying a word; you could see it bothered her that this happened.

Popi said, "People have been coming all morning to show their respect. Olaf and Helga said that they couldn't stand to see her this way."

"Yes, I understand. It must have been a huge ordeal for her!"

Sigrid came in with the watery soup and passed it to her mother. She started to spoon-feed Rose — it was difficult for her to swallow, and the soup was trickling off the side of her mouth. Soon, she had tears of pain and frustration in her eyes.

"It's fine, my *Lillé*. You'll be able to talk and eat properly again soon."

Kiti could not stand it any longer and stepped out. Sigrid was always there to help and give support; she sat next to her to console her. Rose turned her head away from the chief so he couldn't see her break down. He left the women alone and joined his daughter in the other room.

Kiti eventually spoke when Popi came out of the bedroom, "That was dreadful to watch. Sorry, father and Aunt Popi, but I need to leave. I can't see her like this!"

"Yes, I agree. I truly feel for Rose and wish her well. Please send my regards and good health. Keep me informed with how the healing is coming along."

It took a week before some of the swellings went down before she could speak properly, but that did not slow her down or keep her indoors. Popi was thankful that she was still herself and that the ordeal she went through had not changed her in any way. If Var and Cnut did not look for her or find her at that precise moment, she feared the child would have lost her spirit in those woods. Their Rose that they loved so much would have been gone! Thank the gods; she was still the happy and cheerful girl they came to love and adore.

No one knew how to treat her at first, but she showed them that she was fine and still herself, making jokes and laughing and putting them all at ease.

Var could not be prouder of her inner strength. She was a true Viking by heart.

Two weeks after the incident, a week after the festival ended, the eastern tribe arrived. Chief Thorarin made sure to put down some rules. He explained a few details of what happened, how Rose came to stay with them, and they were allowed to meet her. Rose was still healing, and she was not shy; the swelling went down; however, her face was still badly bruised. They were shocked and were sympathetic, but everything went smoothly. Well, almost, there would always be rivalry between tribes.

A man named Orig kept teasing Olaf, saying that he was going to steal his wife away on their ship when departing. It was not a pretty fight when Olaf attacked him — calling him a stinkfart and the devil take you! He kept his eye on the man throughout their stay. Helga knew the man was teasing and found it amusing.

Kiti got friendly with the chief's son, Tehran; he was a handsome man. Rose and Sigrid thought he was gorgeous and that he suited Kiti well. He was friendly and spoke to everyone as equals; he never excluded anyone. Rose and Sigrid were always flushed after having a conversation with him.

Thorarin noticed his daughter's constant companion and wondered whether she would ever agree to marry the future chief of the eastern tribe? He approved of the man. They were good people and heard they were evolving in their region. They stayed not far from a village where they often traded. Perhaps

Kiti would like that? They were there for a week and were due to leave the next day. Thorarin had to know if he should offer a marriage proposal and discuss a dowry before they departed.

Kiti and the chief were invited for a meal at Popi's, which they accepted. After relaxing after the huge dinner and feeling satisfied, he asked his daughter what she thought of marrying Tehran.

"What! No! Just because I like a man or have spoken to him does not mean I want to marry him. Is this going to happen every time I talk to a man? Please, father, let me choose whom I want to spend the rest of my life with!" Kiti was upset with her father and pleaded with him to understand her feelings.

"Kiti, I just want to see you happy and not to be stuck forever on this island by my side. You need a life of your own! Tehran is a good man. Did you not like him?"

"Yes, father, I do enjoy his company, but I don't feel anything for him!"

"Maybe you could come to feel something in the future; love does grow, you know."

"No, I will know when it happens, and I will let you know. Tehran is not for me; we won't be happy," she said, begging her father to drop it.

"OK, I give up! Come, it's time to go home. This day has exhausted me, and I'm feeling my age at this hour. Popi, my dear sister, the meal was superb — thank you!" They said their goodbyes to everyone and left.

TWENTY-FOUR

Rose was still bound for her travels. At last, she heard when that day would be. They were waiting for her to be fully healed before sending her off. The ship was packed with merchandise and was anchored at sea. The last time Rose was on a ship was when she was ill and couldn't remember anything. She had to admit to herself that she was a little excited about the new adventure. However, the thought of leaving her new family and friends stabbed her in the heart.

Popi was fussing over her the whole time since early that morning. Sigrid could not stop crying.

"Do you have everything, my *Lillé*? Make sure all your belongings are packed and set. I can't believe this day has arrived!" She walked away feeling the tears coming on. Popi's heart was literally breaking.

Cnut could not sit still. No words were said at home — the house was gloomy. Astrid was there early to greet her father and Rose and wished them both a safe trip. She left again, not feeling up for the day. Her stomach was huge.

They all ambled toward the village. They had to walk through the village to get to the dock where the longboat was waiting. The kids were walking in front of Popi and Var, each holding one of Rose's hands and her belongings in their other hands. Var had all that he needed in his bag that was thrown over his shoulder, holding his wife's hand as well. It was a sad day for this family.

All work had stopped when they entered the village; the villagers greeted Rose and bid her farewell. The chief was waiting with Kiti to say goodbye. He knew he made a mistake – one he couldn't take back and wouldn't for her sake. It had to be done. Rose had to go home; it would be good for her to see her island again.

Kiti was friendlier toward her after the incident. She gave her a warm greeting and bid her a safe trip. One after the other, they kissed her on the cheek and said, "May Aegir be with you on your journey."

Magdalene was there too and in tears. She hugged her mistress. "Goodbye, Miss Rose; I'm truly going to miss you!"

"Thank you for all you have done for me, Magdalene. I'll miss you too. Let me ask you one more thing before I leave."

"Anything, miss."

Rose half-whispered so that only she could hear, "Who is Aegir, and why must he be with me on my journey?"

Magdalene laughed at this. She was too glad to explain one last thing to her favorite mistress.

"Aegir is the god of the sea, miss. It's to wish you a smooth sail home with no danger of being swallowed up in a storm. All sailors fear him; they believe that Aegir could occasionally appear on the surface to take ships, men, and cargo alike to his hallway at the bottom of the ocean. A long time ago, I heard they sacrificed a slave before sailing to appease him. His wife is called Ran, and they have nine daughters. There's much more to tell, miss, but that's about it!"

"And enough, I may add." she laughed, "Thank you, Magdalene." Rose hugged her one last time.

She was stopped by many. Even old Gudrun, Olaf's father, came out to say goodbye. She felt blessed to have so many close friends in her life and truly wished she would see them all someday in the future.

They were all on the deck with the ship floating on the water. Var first said his goodbyes to his kids and then his wife, knowing that Rose would have all their attention soon. Olaf and Helga climbed on as well and waited for them. Cnut hugged her first and held her tight with tears in his eyes, which made her cry too.

"I'll miss you, Rose, take care and look after yourself."

"I'll miss you more. I love you, Cnut!"

"I love you too!' He turned around and walked away. It was too much for him to see her leave.

Sigrid was crying so much that she could hardly speak. Rose hugged her. "Farewell, my sister. Until we meet again, I pray that day is soon. I'm going to miss you so much!"

"I love you, Rose!" was all she could muster through her sobbing.

Rose and Popi stood facing each other, staring and smiling sadly.

"Come to me, my *Lillé*" She opened her arms, and Rose walked into them, crying and hugging her tight, never wanting to let go.

Popi spoke softly in her ear, "You are not my blood, but you will always be my daughter. My home is always open to you when you feel the need to come home." There was a pause, "Rose, my sweet, sweet Rose, how you changed all our lives. Don't ever forget us. I love you so much, my dear child. I'll always be praying for your safety and happiness."

This time, Rose could not speak, and she cried like a baby in Popi's arms. Everyone that witnessed their exchange was affected and cried too.

"I love you, Popi! It feels like I'm losing a mother all over again. Thank you for saving my life, on many occasions, for freely and openly bestowing love upon me, accepting me in your home and life. You will always be my family, no matter where I am. You will forever be in my heart!" Rose did not want to let go of their embrace.

Popi eventually broke the hold and kissed her on the lips.

"Be safe, my child. If anything happened to you, my heart would break. Look after yourself and be strong and brave as I know you can be."

Rose gave her one last hug. "I love you, Popi. I'll miss you every day that we are apart." Rose climbed onto the longboat, still crying.

Popi looked at Var and spoke through tears, "Var, my love, look after our little one, deliver her safe, then come home to me."

"I will, my sweet. Miss me until my return."

Olaf was too scared to speak — his throat was choked up. Helga could not help to shed a tear.

The ship was off. Rose was waving to everyone who stood on the shore. Popi and Sigrid were holding each other, crying and waving until they could not see them anymore.

Strange how the island felt empty without her.

Everyone felt her absence . . .

Part two of the series will be coming soon
A short preview in the next chapter of her life . . .

Rosaline Labella Dumont

1

After being taken and cared for by the Vikings for over a year, Rosaline Labella Dumont was back in her homeland and living at the king's castle. When she first arrived, everyone was shocked and surprised to see her, especially King Louis, after hearing from his son, Philippe, that the Vikings took her. At first, they had no idea where to begin the search – then they were restricted with limited resources due to the measles epidemic when Rosaline disappeared. All they could do was hope and pray that she would persevere and somehow return to them. Nonetheless, now that she was back, Rosaline looked healthy and unscathed – much to the king's relief. Everyone greeted her with open arms and treated her with respect and concern, not knowing what she had been through.

In their uncertainty and curiosity to know the truth and facts about her disappearance and captors, they began to ask many questions, and she answered as best she could. Rose assured them that she was treated well and as a guest. The king was observing her while the small group asked their many questions. He was listening intently too, even though he was feeling optimistic with her return, yet, he could not help wonder, and noticed that even though she always smiled, Rosaline's smile never reached her eyes. *Why did she look so sad and not relieved or animated to be home amongst her own people?*

Not so long ago, Rose said her farewells to Olaf and Var – a family she came to trust with her life. Every waking moment she felt the pain of their loss; even though it was not a loss of death, it was much the same. She was separated from the only family she had come to love dearly – it still stabbed her at her heart – she needed her privacy to break down in tears.

Rose quickly explained the Viking's tragedy at sea while on a trading voyage, a voyage during which a few lives were lost, with most of the remaining crew severely injured. It was a tragedy that still haunts them, including her! Rose felt so lost that she could not yet explain her true feelings to anyone – she missed them terribly.

While caring for her during her amnesia recovery caused by her illness when she first woke up on their island, their care and humanity resulted in her adopting them spiritually and becoming a family. A family that welcomed and loved her for who she was; she grew close to the Viking clan. If it were up to her, she would have never left. After all, it was not her choice to leave; the Viking chief decided on her behalf that it was time that Rose returned to her own people.

Rose was exhausted and was growing weary of all the questions and opinions related to what she felt was more a private matter and all too soon to discuss in full detail.

After Rose explained enough to appease their basic curiosity about her life with the Vikings, she wished to be excused; she felt exhausted from the trip and wanted to retire before they queried her any further.

This was her first destination, and she saw no point in returning to her own home – a place that felt so far removed, especially with her parents no longer there, the people who made it her home – her home would never be the same without her parents around. The pain going there first was too much to bear; thus, Rose decided the castle was a better choice for now. However, right now, though, that peace and quiet would have been welcoming.

They listened to her last statement of the voyage incident and tried to understand; thus, they gave her time to mourn out of modesty.

In the beginning, Rose was constantly in her quarters. No one bothered her much, and was grateful for the solitude. She mentally felt all her loss and loneliness in her seclusion and began to lose her appetite for food and life, and started losing weight. Rose could not see a future for herself, either here at the castle or her childhood home.

Prince Philippe, however, became worried and thought it was unhealthy to be cooped up all the time; Rosaline needed to get out and socialize. After giving her over a week's solitude and respecting her privacy, Philippe thought it best to visit Rosaline every day and personally invite her to join him for breakfast or the evening meal with walks in the garden. He said it might help her cope if she got out and mingled. On their outings and dinners, which he half forced her to participate in, he noticed she was despondent and did not socialize with anyone.

One evening, at the main dinner table, an event King Louis invited her to attend, Rosaline was lost in thought. As part of her nature with living with the Vikings for so long, out of habit, she picked up her duck meat with her hands and started biting into it, oblivious to the shocked stares she received. Upon taking her third bite, Rose looked up, noticed all eyes were on her and realized what she had done.

Half embarrassed, she just smiled politely, placed her duck back on her plate, picked up her knife and fork, and continued to eat the rest of the meal as was generally expected. While Rose started eating appropriately with her utensils, everyone went back to their normal conversation at the dinner table.

Part 2

Rose's thoughts wandered once again to how she grew too accustomed to the Viking's eating habits. She felt awkward and uncomfortable at first, seeing how they consumed certain food with their hands. Eventually, she too started eating with her hands, mainly meat and bread. To her amazement, it was more satisfying that way – who would have guessed...

Life once again had changed; she was not sure if this was what she wanted, yet, she knew, for now, there was no other alternative.

Rose had to start all over with the old ways, an act she needed to uphold for her namesake and that of her parents. On the other hand, she could also not be bothered by what people might be thinking.

During her spell of extensive memory loss and being with the Vikings at that time, Rose forgot her most general memories and what her mother had taught her, lessons regarding life on how to be a proper lady in society. She learned new ways, experienced new things, and picked up other habits that no one would approve of when it came to a 'lady of the aristocracy.' Rose no longer had the freedom to roam around and have fun – to feel free-spirited. As per their standards, she was expected to act as society expected, to be rooted in one spot, always acting polite and decent.

Not that she was not well-mannered with the Vikings; it came more naturally while being with them. And after remembering her parents were no longer alive, Rose always felt that she belonged with that Viking clan, especially when she had nothing to return home to. She felt more at home with the Vikings and her new family – a family she was separated from by circumstances beyond her control, forced to return to 'her own kind.' Now, many tears later, Rose felt cast out, as if she was being punished for something she could not comprehend.

Rose felt weird being at the castle without her parents around, occasionally having feelings of deja-vu, recalling snippets of her past. Lately, her mother and father were more frequently occupying her thoughts; she remembered and missed them more than ever before.

She wondered if news still got around and if Jessie would arrive soon and hoped that the reason for her delay was not ailing. Jessie was her guardian and was part of her family long before Rose was born and their town's healer. She desperately needed to see Jessie and wanted her company more than anyone else's. There was much she wanted to share with her.

Rose was so absorbed in her own world that the noise of chairs moving and loud speaking signified the meal ending, snapped her back to the present to her unwanted circumstances.

Life at the castle became more intense; the castle filled daily with new visitors, most curious about her return, and stories about her captives intrigued them. Daily guests wanted to ensure they were on the invitation list for the ball the king was organizing in Rosaline's honor to celebrate her safe return home.

Part 2

Rose did not expect such a thing and was certainly not looking forward to it. At first, she informed the king that it was unnecessary for such a lavish event, especially in her honor – just to have returned home! He responded by explaining that her father was his most trusted and reliable friend, and he would have wanted this for her. Rose had the urge to argue the fact with the king, but she knew its futility; instead, she simply smiled and thanked him politely.

The days were almost all the same, starting with breakfast, followed by some fruitless activities in which Rose was forced to partake, then dinner with the king and his guests, after which she would always excuse herself and retire to her chambers for some solitude.

More than a month had passed since her arrival and only a week left before the ball, which she had much dread for. While with the Vikings, Rose would rise early for her daily chores; this morning, she became restless and bored with barely a reason to get up. Most of her days were spent in her chambers, seldom invited by someone or another to include her in their events, which was uneventful and not productive as the duties she was used to having with Popi – her adopted mother figure with the Vikings.

Not that she did not have fun there; their duties fitted in their lives, and she immersed herself into tasks and activities that had a purpose or a goal – and when it was time to relax or have their ritual celebrations, they went all out! She missed the continuous busy life.

Rose was in dire need of some fresh air and *alone!* She knew if she mentioned an outing, it would only result in more fussing over her, with the ever-so courteous Prince Philippe planning a picnic or some other outdoor activity to accommodate her.

She was not in the mood for the constant staring from the company that attended these outings, eyes watching her every move. Philippe was a dear, doing his utmost to make her feel welcome and at home, but it was becoming too much. His constant presence and wanting to please her was overwhelming; Rose needed to feel a little of the freedom she had lost and wondered if she'd ever feel better and accept her destiny, which was not so clear nowadays.

She needed space outside this room where she could feel comfortable to be herself; with this in mind, she needed a disguise. Rose still had her Viking clothes, made by Popi and her two daughters, which included two woolen cloaks with hoodies attached. The red one would be too noticeable, making the white one the obvious choice. Urged into action by her new adventure, she quickly dressed in her most common Viking outfit and put the white cloak on.

The sun was still rising when she covertly left her room and quietly sneaked out the servants' stairwell. When she entered the kitchen, the only way with a back door as far as she knew, a few servants noticed but let her be on her way. Rose was grateful that it wasn't so busy at this hour yet. When stepping outside, she covered her head with the hoody – feeling relieved that her escape plan went unnoticed with unwanted attention. She felt a little excited being so sly.

As Rose walked with no destination in mind, she thought of the whispers she overheard. Not everyone knew where she was or what happened to her, and she was not in the mood to explain to strangers about her 'abductors' – as they called them. The king and Philippe knew a little, and that should surely suffice, for now. They were also not sharing any information as she was told.

She understood that they were simply concerned, thinking the worst of the Vikings as they were regarded as common barbarians by society. Therefore, everyone felt sorry for her and assumed the worst. Rose knew she would have to explain the full extent of her story at some point, but not now; her heart was still aching to be with them.

Rose walked far out to the meadows where the cows were roaming – what she wouldn't give for a horse right now to fly across the field, not a person in sight. Every day on the Viking Island, she rode around freely, exploring the beauty and wonders the island offered.

She took a deep breath and relaxed for the first time since arriving. Rose was lost in thought and wondered what the Vikings were doing right now and tried to picture them all in her mind going about their odd jobs. It made her homesick. She realized that those days, that life on the island was over, and as far as she could see, unlikely to return. Popi gave selflessly, a loving and caring mother figure, the one who gave her so much to live for. Perhaps she should start accepting her life here and attempt to go on, accepting what each day had to offer, whatever came her way. For Popi's sake anyway, she had saved her life, and now it was time to live it.

Rose needed something to distract her mind from her sorrows, maybe start a hobby of some sort to keep her mind busy while she figured out the next step and perhaps also the next phase in her life.

While clarifying her troubled mind and thoughts and trying to come up with something worthwhile to keep her busy, Rose heard a yelling sound. It sounded like an animal was distraught. At first, she could not identify the direction of the noise but followed it as best she could. She walked between the cattle, who also started to moan with her invasion. There were cows everywhere making a noise, so she stood still and tried to hear the odd moan of a stress call. It was quiet for a few seconds, then it came again to her right, and she turned in that direction.

The ground was uneven due to digging and covering it up again to find a water flow, almost like finding a waterhole for a well. Not far was a small hole in the ground dug up long ago for drinking water for the animals. When Rose closed in towards the main waterhole, it was surrounded by a few cattle; disturbed by her presence, they all departed immediately, except one.

Rose then noticed the problem. It was a medium-sized circle and was big enough to climb in, but no one knew its depth, only the person who dug here who might be long dead.

Inside this drinking-hole was a calf trying to get out! Hanging on for dear life – calling for help to his helpless mother, who stood by watching and moaning as well. She was anxious for her child – not being able to help it. It was a sad scene.

Without thinking or hesitating, Rose threw off her cloak and shoes, grabbed the grass on the side, and climbed into the cold water. With this stranger in the water as well, the calf, seemingly with new hope, started splashing and fighting for its life. Rose used her legs and pushed the calf closer to the edge. When it had a grip, she used all her strength to heave the calf back on dry land. All exhausted, Rose gained her breath before climbing out herself.

The calf was shattered, trying and fighting for who knows how long to get out; it just sat there motionless. With satisfaction and wonder, Rose witnessed as the mother examined her child and gave a loud moo sound. Rose saw the interaction between them and was touched by their affection. She had never seen this among animals before and thought of how hopeless the mother must have felt by not being able to help her baby.

With such a simple task, Rose felt good inside and not so useless. She sat fixed on the same spot when climbing out, tears running down her cheeks with emotion. The calf started to stand with shaky legs, and after walking around a little, it came closer to Rose and sniffed. She did not move in case she scared the animal. It was almost as if it was saying thank you. She slowly lifted her hand, touched it on the side of the face, and said through teary eyes and smiles, "It's a pleasure!" The mother was curious as well, strolled over to join them, and was sniffing her head. Without knowing what to expect, the cow licked Rose full in the face. She burst out laughing and said, "Don't mention it – it was the least I could do to help!"

Rose shook her head, thinking she must be going insane speaking to cows. The animals walked off away from the water to feed further afield. She started shivering and stood up to ring her dress dry as best she could and put her shoes back on. She grabbed the cloak from the ground and wrapped it tight around her. Freezing, she slowly walked back to the castle. Rose was still on the castle grounds; hence, there was no danger of her being out alone, or so she thought.

Not far from the scene was a man enjoying the fresh air of the early morning. He, too, came out to the fields to be alone. He arrived just in time to witness the whole rescue ordeal and could not help but be amazed at this young woman for her bravery. She was wise to use her legs and not her arms. The calf would have pushed her down, trying to survive, not knowing any better. He would have intervened if that should have happened and so stayed rooted to his spot. He had never witnessed a scene like he had today, the emotion and affection she expressed – he was intrigued by this beautiful woman and had to meet her before she disappeared.

Rose was deep in thought – wondering whom to approach regarding the waterhole problem and unsure how it could be fixed. The king was no good; he would not bother himself with such petty things. Perhaps Philippe would help, but then again, no, not him. To share her concerns would highlight that she went out alone, unescorted, which might bother or worry him further. He was always kind toward her and constantly made light conversation at the dinner table. Rose was fond of him; he would make a good King one day.

The best alternative was to approach Prince Antoine, Philippe's younger brother, with the matter; as she recalled, he was easy to speak to. She felt more comfortable discussing this with him, especially with them being around the same age. After deciding that, she thought of a way to fix the hole – lost in thought...

"Excuse me, miss!" came a male voice behind her.

Rose jumped with fright and was startled nearly to death; she thought she was alone! Although it was too late to hide her face, she lifted the hood over her head and turned to face the stranger.

Part 2

The man was tall, well-built, and not dressed as a commoner. She was astonished at how good-looking he was – and those eyes! They made her feel uneasy. It reminded her of someone.

"Do I know you?" Rose asked.

His smile made her more curious, stunning her; he was really dashing.

"No, my lass, I would have remembered if I ever met a damsel like you. I want to add that what I saw you perform in the waterhole was brave, and not many would have helped the poor creature."

She felt uncomfortable. He was staring with too much interest and walked closer toward her. It reminded Rose of her attacker on the Viking Island – fear took over. She took a step back and looked around to see if anyone was about, fearful that something should happen. He addressed her as if she were a common laborer and not a lady. Rose could not blame him for thinking that because she was dressed as one.

Suddenly realizing what he just said, if he saw the whole scene, why was he not the first to take action to help the creature? Rose reacted in anger, allowing rage to overcome her fear, and responded, not knowing he only came on the scene once she climbed in the shallow well.

"Instead of helping the creature, you simply looked on. I'm sure someone else would have helped, though not you, for you stood hiding and not caring for the cries of distress. And if I, a woman, did not take action, you would have allowed it to

347

drown!" Rose tried to act brave, yet he still came closer. "I beg you, whoever you are, not to harm me, or you'll be sorry!"

He was amazed at her approach toward him. He had this overwhelming urge, an impulse that even surprised him, to enfold her in his arms and kiss her - for the life of him, he knew not why. It was never his intent to harm her, though he noticed the fear in those beautiful eyes. She must belong to someone important in the castle. He would find out who she works for, even if it was the last thing he did. He put his hands up and took a step back.

"No need to call the cavalry. And to enlighten you, I arrived just when you entered into the water, I would have helped, but it seemed you had everything under control! I just thought of introducing myself. My name is Ollie Waters, and what may yours be?"

"I'm no concern of yours. Good day to you, sir," after which Rose turned around and hastily walked back to the castle.

While watching her half running away, he shouted, "Will be seeing you around then!"

Rose was upset by the whole incident, captivated by her own thoughts, 'the audacity of it all!' When he shouted his last words, she almost tripped and went ice cold. She pulled the cloak tighter around her. His words brought back painful memories; those were nearly the same last words Thord told her before departing on his voyage - and her last kiss - Rose will never forget! - 'Look after yourself! I'll be seeing you soon.' - before he turned and walked out of her life forever!

Part 2

Tears were streaming down Rose's face as she ran through the kitchen again, up the servants' staircase to her room. The sun was long up; undoubtedly, many of the guests were wandering around, yet thankfully, she reached her quarters without anyone noticing. Her handmaiden, Clara, was busy tidying the room and jumped with fright at the lady's sudden entrance. Rose wiped her eyes dry and asked Clara to prepare a bath and bring something to eat. For some reason, she was starving . . .

www.ingramcontent.com/pod-product-compliance
Lightning Source LLC
Chambersburg PA
CBHW021440240626
47153CB00001B/231